She couldn

Anna wanted him to kiss her more than she could remember wanting anything in a long time.

His head bent slowly, either because he was giving her time to retreat or because he himself was hesitant. She quit blinking, only stared into his eyes. And then his lips touched hers. They were cold, but his puff of breath warmed her face.

A sound seemed to vibrate in his chest, and he tilted his head to fit their mouths more closely together. Anna reached out and gripped the sleek fabric of his jacket, her knuckles bumping something hard. Was he carrying a *pistol* under there? But right this second, she couldn't bring herself to care. Her eyes closed and she reveled in the astonishing feel of him nipping at her lips, his tongue stroking the seam until she opened her mouth and let him in.

And then it only got better.

Dear Reader,

I've created many troubled heroes—heck, they're my specialty!—but Reid Sawyer is one of my all-time favorites. He was more of a challenge than some to write, too, because he's not an angry man, he doesn't lash out and he rarely if ever raises his voice. Most people see him as cool, strong, unemotional. He feels driven by duty and, yes, vicarious revenge on a brutal father. In fact, he sees himself as damaged, incapable of real emotion, especially the softer kinds. This is a man who is utterly self-contained, capable of suppressing any powerful emotion almost before it appears.

Maybe that's what made it so satisfying to challenge his beliefs. First he discovers he has a younger brother who needs him, and then he falls in love with a woman despite himself—and the poor man doesn't recognize what's happening to him! Hmm. Come to think of it, he may be the perfect man: calm, competent, protective, quiet and tidy. Well, okay, a guy who says "I love you" once in a while is nice, too!

I never plan my books by thinking, "this one is about the hero," or "this one is about the heroine." But most often they come out that way, with the focus most intensely on one character or the other. Sometimes I'm really taken by surprise. I've got to admit, though, with only a couple of exceptions, my favorites among my books are hero-centric ones. So maybe I should plan better....

Here's hoping you, too, fall in love with Reid while you're saying goodbye to Angel Butte, Oregon, the setting for what was originally intended to be a trilogy but grew to five books. And you never know—I may decide to revisit Angel Butte one of these days!

Janice Kay Johnson

JANICE KAY
JOHNSON

—

This Good Man

HARLEQUIN®SUPER ROMANCE®

Recycling programs
for this product may
not exist in your area.

ISBN-13: 978-0-373-60868-3

THIS GOOD MAN

Printed in U.S.A.

ABOUT THE AUTHOR

An author of more than eighty books for children and adults, *USA TODAY* bestselling author Janice Kay Johnson is especially well-known for her Harlequin Superromance novels about love and family—about the way generations connect and the power our earliest experiences have on us throughout life. Her 2007 novel *Snowbound* won a RITA® Award from Romance Writers of America for Best Contemporary Series Romance. A former librarian, Janice raised two daughters in a small rural town north of Seattle, Washington. She loves to read and is an active volunteer and board member for Purrfect Pals, a no-kill cat shelter. Visit her online at www.janicekayjohnson.com.

Books by Janice Kay Johnson

HARLEQUIN SUPERROMANCE

SIGNATURE SELECT SAGA

*The Russell Twins
**A Brother's Word
+The Mysteries of Angel Butte

Other titles by this author available in ebook format.

PROLOGUE

THE SHOPPING MALL in a suburb of Spokane was new since Reid Sawyer had grown up in this northeastern corner of Washington State. Reid glanced around, approving the choice of this end of the mall. The boy didn't know him. He'd been smart to pick someplace busy enough to be safe and yet deserted enough that they wouldn't draw attention. The kid had good instincts.

The thought was followed by a soundless grunt. The boy's instincts had been honed in the same hard school his own had been. Of course his wariness had been sharpened to a razor edge.

It was the same instinct that had Reid choosing a hard plastic seat with its back to a wall. The seats were situated at the corner of an L where, by barely turning his head, he could watch both the little-used mall entrance in one direction and, in the other direction, a wing that eventually dead-ended at a Macy's. The small stores closest to him didn't depend much on browsers, which meant that, down at this end, traffic was light and teenagers few and far between. Pearle Vision, Regis Salon, Sleep Country USA, a vitamin and food supplements store—all destination businesses. Reid could almost relax. He settled down to wait.

He watched idly as a mother ushered two kids into Pearle Vision. A middle-aged man and wife entered Sleep Country. None of them so much as glanced Reid's way.

Reid saw the boy outside well before he reached the mall's glass doors. For all his obvious youth, he moved like a cop—long, athletic stride, acute awareness of his surroundings. His head kept turning. He looked casual but didn't miss anything. Before entering, he assessed the two women with a baby stroller opening one of the other doors, and dismissed them as a threat.

Once inside, his gaze locked almost immediately on Reid. The momentary hesitation in his step wouldn't have been noticeable to anyone not watching as closely as Reid was.

Reid saw something else, too: a limp that was almost, but not quite, disguised.

The boy walked like a wounded cop who didn't want anyone else to spot his injury and therefore vulnerability.

A tide of rage rose in a man who, until a week ago when he discovered the existence of this kid, hadn't felt anything like that in many years.

He slowly rose to his feet, his own gaze never wavering from the boy.

My brother, he thought with an incredulity he couldn't seem to shake.

Until now, he hadn't been 100 percent sure the boy *was* his half brother versus a stepbrother. He'd have been here either way, but—damn. He could be looking at his own fifteen-year-old self.

Lean to the point of being skinny, muscles not yet having developed. Spiky hair the same shade of nut-brown as his, with an unruliness that hinted at the waves that had always irritated him. A bony face with cheekbones cut so sharp, they gave the kid a hungry look Reid saw replicated in the mirror every morning when he shaved.

The eyes he couldn't be sure about until the boy got close. Then he felt another jolt. This Caleb Sawyer had Reid's eyes, too, a hazel so dark as to look brown in dim lighting, but in the sun could appear as green as thick bottle glass.

He had his father's eyes. Reid's father's eyes.

Caleb came to a stop a few feet from him, his shock apparent. "You're really him," he blurted.

"Your brother," Reid agreed.

"He always said you were dead. That you had to be."

"I might have been if I hadn't gotten away."

That too-familiar face clouded. "Where have you been all my life?"

"I didn't know about you." The defense was inadequate, Reid was well aware; he should have made sure he found out if his father ever had another child. "Once I was eighteen, I checked on him. Kept checking for a few years, but he hadn't remarried." His shoulders moved. "He was in his mid-forties by then. I thought he was unlikely—" He stopped, then said the most inadequate words of all. "I'm sorry."

Caleb didn't acknowledge that by so much as a nod. Instead, his stare challenged Reid. "Why now?"

"Because I did run a search out of curiosity and came up with court proceedings. An abuse allegation."

"Dismissed." No kid that age should be capable of such searing bitterness.

"Yeah. The few times we made it as far as court, it was always dismissed, too."

Dean Sawyer was a cop. He was also a violent drunk who had beaten the shit out of his first wife and son. Reid's mother died when she slipped in a spill on the kitchen floor and hit her head on a sharp corner of the cabinet top—or so the police report said. Nobody remarked on the fact that her skin displayed a road map of old and new bruises. Without an autopsy performed, nobody but her son and grieving husband knew how many bones in her body had been broken in the years of her marriage.

Several times one of Reid's teachers or a school counselor called Child Protective Services. The final report always concluded that Reid Sawyer was clumsy—and it had been true that, like many boys destined to be tall men, he'd tended to trip over his too-large feet—or that father and son had scuffled, but the incident was understandable because Deputy Sawyer's son was rebellious and prone to acting out. Counseling had sometimes been recommended for Reid. Once, his father—a sergeant by then—had been court mandated to take a class in anger management. He had known whom to blame for the inconvenience and humiliation, and he had vented his fury appropriately.

"You're hurt," Reid said now. He had shoved his hands into the kangaroo pocket of his hooded sweatshirt to keep the boy from seeing his fists.

A flick of one shoulder said, *Yeah, so?*

"What about your mother?" Reid asked reluctantly. The mother would be more of a problem.

"She took off. Like three years ago."

"And didn't take you."

"He wasn't bothered enough to go after her."

"But he would have gone after you."

"I'm his son," Caleb said simply, with that same blistering anger. "He hates you, you know."

Reid made a sound in his throat. Yes, he knew. No, he didn't give a damn. Then he nodded toward the row of hard seats. "Let's sit and talk for a minute."

When he settled in one, stretching his legs out and crossing them at the ankles in an appearance of relaxation, Caleb chose a seat one removed from Reid's. His boneless slouch didn't hide his tension.

"Why did you want to meet me?" he asked, eyes

dark with turbulence. "You planning to start send-ing me birthday cards?"

"I came to see how bad off you are. Whether you're ready to ditch Dad."

The kid's head came up. He struggled against it, but didn't hide his hope any better than he had his misery. "You mean, like, go home with you?"

"No." Reid's voice came out gravelly. He hadn't expected to feel so much. To want to say, *Damn right you're going home with me.* "He could find me with no trouble, which means he'd find you."

"If you contested—"

"The chances are good he'd win. He has so far, hasn't he?"

The boy ducked his head. His shoulders hunched. He didn't say anything.

"You need more than I can give you anyway," Reid said slowly. "Hugs. Affection." Something al-ways softened inside him when he thought of the Hales and how much they'd given him. "Discipline, school, healing."

"Like a foster home?"

As an officer of the law, Reid didn't like know-ing he'd be breaking the law. But, within hours of learning all he could about Caleb online, Reid had made peace with his conscience. Not often, but oc-casionally, the letter of the law contradicted what was just and right. He was living proof of that. The law had failed Caleb, too.

"A shelter. One that's...different." Reid held his

brother's eyes, determined that he listen to and understand every word. "It would mean you going off the grid. You'd have to be homeschooled, you wouldn't be able to get your driver's license until you're eighteen and Dad couldn't come after you anymore. It would mean obeying the rules and not doing something dumb that would bring the authorities down on you and the other kids in the shelter."

His brother eyed him sidelong. "The way you say 'authorities.' Are you into illegal shit? Do you deal or something?"

"Drugs?" Reid gave a short laugh. "No. I'm in law enforcement." He was very aware of the irony.

Caleb lifted his head to stare at him in disbelief. "Just like Daddy."

"No. Not just like Daddy. I'm currently a sergeant in charge of the Family Violence Unit. I put men like Daddy in jail." He sounded hard and didn't care.

"Do *you* have kids?"

Reid shook his head.

Caleb nodded as if he understood. "I guess you're, like, too busy for me," he said after a minute, no longer looking at Reid.

"Yeah, I probably am, but…that's not the main reason I think you'd be better off with these people I know. People who took me in when I ran away from home." Even though he was looking down, he was aware the kid was listening. He couldn't think of any way to say this but to come right out with the truth. "What you need isn't anything I have in me. I'm what our father made of me. Damaged."

The boy shook his head and laughed, the sound corrosive. Then he shot to his feet and looked down at Reid. "What a crock of shit. What you are is a coward. Daddy made you a coward," he taunted.

The stab slid home. Reid's jaw flexed, but he didn't let his expression change. This wasn't about him. "The place I want to take you…it's good. These people saved my life."

Caleb kept shaking his head.

Reid took a business card from his pocket and held it out. "This has my phone number on it. Call me when you decide."

"I've decided." His gaze was flat and emotionless. "Mr. Damaged Goods. You're no use to me."

"Take the card."

The boy wasn't proof against the voice of command. He hesitated only a moment, then grabbed it and shoved it into his jeans pocket without even looking at it.

"When you need me, I'll come."

Eyes so much like his own swept over him in one last scathing look. Then Caleb shook his head again. "Sure," he said. "See you around." He turned and sauntered away, back toward the mall entrance. Over his shoulder, he added, "Not," and kept going.

Reid didn't move for a long time. Whatever he felt wasn't anything he recognized. All he knew was that he didn't like it.

Closing his eyes, he let his head fall back until it bumped the wall. He'd blown it, but if there was another way, he couldn't see it.

Usually he was patience personified. *Im*patience implied an emotional component he lacked.

Something new.

A month. If he didn't hear from Caleb within a month, he'd try again.

And then again. And again.

This was his brother, who had no one else.

SEVENTEEN DAYS LATER—and Reid had been counting—his mobile phone rang. Sitting at his desk, he'd been concentrating on the long history of allegations against a husband and father one of his detectives had just arrested. Tearing his gaze from the computer monitor, Reid picked up the phone. He didn't recognize the number, but he knew the area code. His pulse quickened. "Sawyer here," he said.

"Uh, this is Caleb." The voice was slurred. Drunk? No. Coming from a mouth that was swollen. Maybe missing a tooth or two. "You know. Your brother."

"I know who you are," Reid said gently, even as sickening rage filled him. "You ready to go?" His hand was on the computer mouse already; he went online and straight to Kayak. He could buy an airline ticket within the next minute or two.

"So ready, I've packed my duffel and I'm gone."

"Then you can count on me." Reid chose a flight, and they set up their meet.

Fifteen minutes later, he'd arranged to take two days of vacation and was walking out of the police station. To hell with any lingering qualms he felt about his course of action. He was doing what he had to do to save his brother.

CHAPTER ONE

"DON'T TELL ME to wait twenty-four hours." Anna Grant gazed unflinchingly at the desk sergeant who was trying to make her go away. He should know he was wasting his time; he and she had butted heads before. "I'm not suggesting Yancey was abducted. He took off on his own. Twenty-four hours would give him time to disappear." She leaned forward over the counter to emphasize her words. "Right this minute, he's probably out on the highway waving his thumb. In case you hadn't noticed, it's cold out there." March was the dead of winter on this side of the Cascade Mountains. "He needs to be picked up *now*."

"Ms. Grant." Middle-aged and graying, Sergeant Shroutt looked exasperated and frazzled. "We've been through this before. You know there's nothing we can do yet. No crime has been committed. You have no reason to think this kid is in danger—"

"No reason?" She hoped her eyes were shooting sparks. "This *kid* is thirteen years old. He's so small for his age, he looks about ten. What if your own son that age was out on that highway, Sergeant?"

"Of course I wouldn't like—"

"Wouldn't you think the police should be concerned?"

"What seems to be the problem, ma'am?" asked a deep, calm voice from unnervingly close to her left.

Even as she swung around to face the newcomer, she took an involuntary step back. She hated the fear instinct that surfaced when someone startled or sneaked up on her. Anna prayed it didn't show on her face.

"Captain." The sergeant's relief was obvious. "I was just explaining to Ms. Grant—"

"—why no one in the Angel Butte Police Department can be bothered to help me find a thirteen-year-old boy who has run away from his foster home and has no place to go that any sane adult would consider safe," Anna concluded, even as she evaluated the tall man who stood on her side of the counter, but who was evidently a member of the department, and a senior one at that.

He was also an extraordinarily handsome man, his face all angles and planes, nothing soft about it except possibly his mouth, which she was annoyed at herself for noticing. His eyes were… She couldn't tell. A dark hazel or unusual shade of brown, maybe. A gray suit fit as if it had been tailored for his big body. The knot of the conservative tie he wore was just a little loose, as if he'd given it a tug recently. Only when her gaze lowered did she notice the badge clipped to a narrow black belt and a glimpse of what she assumed was a weapon. At the moment, his expression was mildly curious.

Wait. Captain. Could he possibly be the new hire she'd read about, the one who'd accepted the position vacated by Colin McAllister, who had defeated the incumbent county sheriff in the November election? That would make this man captain of Investigative and Support Services, not patrol.

Still...he was right here in front of her. And if he'd paused only to help the desk sergeant get rid of her, well, screw him. At least she wasn't likely to encounter him again.

"I'm Anna Grant." Inexplicably reluctant to touch him, she nonetheless held out her hand. "I supervise foster homes for Angel's Haven Youth Services."

His eyebrows flickered as if she'd surprised him, but that was the only change of expression she detected. "Ms. Grant." He engulfed her hand in his much larger one and squeezed before releasing her. "Captain Reid Sawyer."

"Unfortunately, I don't need an investigation. I was *hoping*—" she darted a look at the sergeant as she emphasized the word "—that I could get the city's patrol officers to watch for a missing child."

Captain Sawyer raised those surprisingly expressive eyebrows only a little, but it was enough. "Sergeant Shroutt?"

"He's been missing three hours!" the sergeant burst out. "He might be smoking weed out back of the high school—"

"Except that he's an eighth grader, not a high school student," Anna pointed out. She almost felt sorry for him.

"Or panhandling in the Walmart parking lot. Playing *Gears of War 3* at some buddy's house!"

"Then why did he leave a note saying he was taking off?" she asked.

He glowered at her. "What note? You didn't say anything about a note."

"You didn't give me a chance."

"What did the note say?" interjected a too-reasonable voice with a velvet undertone.

Pretending the sight and sound of Reid Sawyer didn't make her quiver, Anna held herself stiff. "That we shouldn't worry. He knew a good place to go." Guilt and a shimmer of fear erased her momentary sexual awareness. "His stuff is all gone."

Captain Sawyer had been reading every expression as it crossed her face. She couldn't seem to look away from his eyes, which she concluded were an unusual shade of deep green.

"The boy's name?" he asked.

"Yancey Launders. And no, his name doesn't help. Kids make fun of it. He was born in Alabama. I'm told Yancey is a more common name in the Deep South."

"He likely to be heading for Alabama?"

"I'm afraid so," she said wearily. "He has a grandfather down there. That would be the one who kicked his mother out because she was pregnant and he didn't want anything to do with her kind of trash. After she died, the grandfather was contacted. In his own words, he refused to have anything to do with some bastard kid whose father could be an ex-con or even racially mixed for all he knew."

The captain made a sound in the back of his throat. "The boy know this?"

"His mother apparently believed heart and soul that her daddy would relent eventually and let her and Yancey back into Eden. Yancey said she talked all the time about the farm."

"We're a long way from Alabama."

She knew what he was saying. "She drifted. Yancey has been in a dozen schools or more already. I guess there was always a man, and wherever the current one went, she went, too, and dragged her son along. Whoever the last man was, he didn't want a twelve-year-old boy once she died."

"So this Yancey became a ward of the court."

"Yes. This is his second foster home. He has struggled," she admitted. "The other boys in the home make fun of him."

The police captain merely looked at her.

"I was trying to find something more suitable," she said defensively, even as guilt dug in its claws. She'd *known* that poor, sad boy was ready to crack. She'd just believed she had longer.

The unnervingly emotionless gaze switched to the desk sergeant. "Do I need to involve Captain Cooper?"

Sergeant Shroutt sighed. "No, sir."

Reid's pleasant and yet disquietingly inscrutable eyes met Anna's once again. "You can give a description, I assume."

"Yes."

"Good." He nodded. "Now if you'll excuse me, I'm afraid I have a meeting."

The words almost stuck in her throat, but she got them out. "Thank you."

His mouth curved into a smile that was oddly sweet, even if it didn't reach his eyes. "You're very welcome."

She watched as he strolled away, seemingly in no hurry but, with those long legs, crossing the lobby quickly and disappearing into an elevator that seemed to sense his approach and open for his convenience without him so much as pushing the button.

Anna turned back to the desk sergeant and realized he had been watching the new captain, too.

She could feel his resentment when he produced a form from behind the counter and said, "Please repeat the boy's name, ma'am."

At least he was apparently planning to be polite, probably because he was afraid of Captain Reid Sawyer. Who could blame him? She'd been intimidated, and she was willing to take on anyone to protect the children who were her responsibility. Thus her unpopularity in too many quarters.

"Yancey Launders," she repeated and began to give a description.

Fortunately, she was unlikely to have anything to do with Captain Reid Sawyer in the future. Even if one of her kids was murdered—or murdered someone—she'd be dealing with one of Captain Sawyer's detectives, not the great man himself. She hoped. Anna didn't like anyone who made her feel vulnerable, however fleetingly.

INTERESTING WOMAN, REID thought as the elevator doors closed, shutting off his last view of Ms. Anna Grant, social worker. It was her voice as much as what she had been saying that had caught his attention as he'd passed by the front counter. It had been an intriguing combination of martinet and seductress, both crisp and throaty. On hearing it, he'd had a fleeting fantasy of a school principal who ruled her fiefdom with an iron will, but went home to shed the gray suit and reveal black lace. He had been compelled to find out what the owner of that voice looked like.

Now he knew, although he kind of doubted she wore black lace, or whether it would suit her if she did. She looked about seventeen, although she must be in her late twenties to early thirties to have the kind of job she did. He wondered if she ever used her apparent youth to disarm opponents. His mouth curved at the thought. No, he thought it was safe to say Anna Grant was a woman who would despise the idea of employing subterfuge to get her way.

The elevator doors glided open and he strolled down the hall toward his office, nodding at a couple of people as he passed, but still thinking about the social worker.

Ghost-gray eyes were her greatest beauty. She'd probably been blonde as a kid, but her hair had darkened to a shade between honey and brown, straight and worn shoulder length and tucked behind her ears, nothing unusual except that it was thick and shiny. His fingers had tingled for a moment as he imagined the texture, a reaction he'd tamped down quickly. Ms. Grant was medium height or taller, but with a slight build. Almost...delicate, which contradicted a personality he judged to be bossy, even abrasive. Maybe caring, too, or maybe she was just the rigid kind who wanted everyone and everything in their place, and who didn't accept no as an answer. She had definitely terrorized Sergeant Shroutt. Amusement awakened again; Reid doubted she'd needed his intervention, but as he'd walked toward her, he'd heard enough to ensure he gave it. Whatever her motivation, she was worried enough about that boy to raise hell and keep raising it until he had the help he needed.

Satisfied by his conclusion, Reid greeted the temp serving as his personal assistant until he hired a permanent one. He entered his office, stripping off his suit coat, and was surprised to realize he hadn't succeeded in dismissing Ms. Grant from his thoughts. Instead, he wondered what she *did* wear under her businesslike slacks and blazer. Serviceable white? Scarlet satin? Sweetly feminine petal-pink with tiny lace flowers?

He grinned as he sank into his desk chair. Probably not sweetly feminine anything. That'd be like dressing a Doberman in a tutu.

But, damn it, he'd gotten himself half-aroused imagining her slender, pale body next thing to naked.

He booted up his computer and frowned at the lit monitor. He knew what his trouble was; he hadn't hooked up with a woman in… He couldn't remember, a bad sign. Six months? Eight months? He cast his mind back. Good God, longer than that. This was the middle of March. It was last spring when he'd been seeing that assistant prosecutor. Courtney something. Coulson. That was it. Unlike Ms. Grant, Courtney had had generous curves. Like most women, though, she wanted more than an occasional dinner followed by sex. She'd hinted, he had pretended to be oblivious, and eventually she'd told him she was seeing someone else. He hadn't much minded. He never did, except for the inconvenience of no longer having someone he could call when he wanted sex.

He should check email. He got as far as reaching for the mouse but didn't move it. Instead he kept frowning and thinking about the woman he'd just met downstairs. No ring; he'd noticed that. Was she the type to be interested in something casual, assuming she wasn't already involved with a man? Once Yancey Launders was picked up, Reid could call her and ask how the boy was doing. Suggest a cup of coffee.

He remembered those eyes, though, and felt uneasy. He hadn't thought ghost-gray because of the color, he realized belatedly. It was more as if, in looking into those eyes, he'd seen her ghosts. He tended to stick with uncomplicated women. The scrape of his own scars against someone else's would be…uncomfortable.

Reid shifted in his chair, unhappily aware that he'd remained aroused because he was thinking about her. He hadn't reacted this strongly to a woman in a long time, and couldn't understand why he had now. Anna Grant didn't advertise her sex appeal, that was for sure. And, truth was, she might not have much, as skinny as she was.

Delicate.

He mumbled a profanity, relieved when his internal phone line rang. What he needed was a distraction.

Once the caller identified herself, Reid said, "I'm free now, Lieutenant. If you are, too, why don't we get an early start?"

She agreed, and he was finally able to turn his mind from Anna, thinking instead about Lieutenant

Jane Renner, who supervised detectives and whose rank placed her immediately beneath him. They'd planned this time to talk. She was bringing personnel files to help him familiarize himself with the investigative division. He'd already met with several key people in the support division he also headed—crime-scene technicians, clerical and records staff, fleet maintenance and more. That was the part of this new job most unfamiliar to him, where his learning curve would be steepest.

He was curious about the young woman with a bouncy ponytail who'd risen to lieutenant over an entirely male group of detectives. So far, he was reserving judgment, although she'd seemed sharp when she participated in his initial interviews. Police Chief Alec Raynor had spoken highly of her. Reid knew she'd recently married a sergeant with the Butte County Sheriff's Department. Passing some of his female clerical staff in the hall yesterday, he'd overheard whispered gossip that made him wonder if Lieutenant Renner might be pregnant. Of course, he couldn't ask her; HR would have his hide if he did. Assuming it was true, he had to trust she wouldn't wait until it was painfully apparent, especially if she intended to quit. He hoped there was someone under her who was competent to step in while she took maternity leave, at the very least.

At the knock on his door, he called, "Come in,"

and rose to his feet with automatic courtesy. When he was done with this meeting, he decided, he'd drive out to the Hales' place and spend a little time with Caleb, however awkward that time would feel for both of them.

On the way out, he might stop at the front desk and ask Sergeant Shroutt to let him know when Anna Grant's wandering lamb was safely back in her care.

AFTER LEAVING THE downtown public safety building, Anna drove a route that led from Yancey's foster home and eventually all the way out to Highway 97, the main north-south corridor through central Oregon. Turning her head constantly in search of one undersize boy, she kept her speed down enough to annoy drivers behind her, one of whom decided to crowd her bumper. She was oh-so-tempted to slam on her brakes, but she didn't want the hassle of having to leave her car in an auto-body shop. *And* she'd have to deal with the police, who might not be feeling very fond of her right now.

Too bad. Somebody had to make them do their jobs.

Tension rising as the miles passed with no sight of Yancey, Anna went south on 97 and continued through La Pine. She'd reached Little River when her phone rang. As she pulled into a gas-station parking lot, she answered crisply, "Anna Grant."

"Ms. Grant, this is Sergeant Shroutt. We've picked up the boy. He's currently at Juvenile Hall."

She sagged with the rush of relief. "Oh, thank goodness."

"No, thank Officer Cherney," the sergeant said drily. "Can we assume you'll be picking up young Yancey and taking responsibility for him?"

"You may," she told him. "And please do thank Officer Cherney." She hesitated only briefly. "And thank you. He's…a sad boy. I was worried about him."

"I do understand. It's our preference to help, you know."

"I'll keep that in mind."

They left it at that. She put on her signal and waited while a semi lumbered onto the highway, wondering if Sergeant Shroutt would be any more cooperative the next time she came to him. In one way, it was a pity that Captain Sawyer *wasn't* in charge of the patrol officers, as he might conceivably have turned out to be a useful ally. She'd be more convinced of that, though, if he had displayed even a tiny hint of real emotion. Plus, she'd been hit by sexual attraction, which he'd shown no sign of reciprocating. No, it was just as well that she wouldn't have to deal with him often.

Making up her mind, she made a call rather than starting back toward Angel Butte.

"Carol? Anna Grant. Listen, I know you wanted a longer break before you took another kid, but is there any chance you'd house a boy for a day or two until I can find another place for him?"

Carol Vogt was, hands down, Anna's favorite among the foster parents associated with AHYS. A widow whose own two boys were in their thirties, she worked magic on troubled teenagers.

"A day or two." Carol snorted. "What you mean is, 'Will you take him just long enough so you decide you didn't really want that break anyway?'"

Anna grinned. "Guilty as charged. But I promise, I'll move him if you ask me to. Yancey is only thirteen, and he's being tormented by the older boys in the home I had him living in. Which was his second since he came into the system. He ran away today and the police just picked him up. I've got receiving homes, but…"

She didn't have to finish. This was a kid who needed stability, not another way station.

A sigh gusted into her ear. "Fine," Carol said. "But you owe me one."

"I already owe you a few thousand," Anna admitted. "Bless you. We'll be an hour or two."

"I'll have his bedroom ready."

Anna was smiling when she finally made the turn out onto the highway.

CALEB HOVERED AT the head of the stairs where he knew he couldn't be seen. Voices drifted up from the kitchen.

"I'm not sure where he is." That was Paula Hale,

who with her husband ran this place. "Caleb's been spending a lot of time with Diego. They're probably over in the cabin Diego shares with another boy."

"I'll take that coffee, then. Thanks." This time, Reid's voice came to Caleb clearly. He must be facing the stairs. "Sugar?"

"You always did have a sweet tooth. And you can't tell me you've forgotten where I keep the sugar bowl."

Caleb's brother gave a low chuckle. "I was being polite."

"You weren't polite when you lived here. Why start now?"

This time they both laughed.

Caleb felt weird, an unseen third presence. He knew Roger, Paula's husband, was outside working on Cabin Five. This place was an old resort that must have been shut down, like, a century ago. Most of the boys were paired up in the small cabins. The Hales' room was on the main floor in the lodge, and Caleb and another guy were in bedrooms upstairs. If there were any girls in residence, Caleb had been told, they always had the rooms upstairs in the lodge so they were near the Hales. Otherwise, those bedrooms were used for new boys, until they had "settled in." That was how Paula put it. Caleb wasn't sure how he would ever prove he had, or even if he wanted to. He didn't like it here—but nothing on earth would make him go back to his father's.

"You know he doesn't have to be here." Paula's voice came especially clearly.

What did *that* mean?

Stiffening, Caleb strained to hear Reid's answer. It was brief, an indistinguishable rumble.

What you need isn't anything I have in me. Remembering the expressionless way his brother had said that, Caleb sneered. Was that what Reid was telling Paula?

He couldn't catch the beginning of what Paula said in response, but the tail end made his heart thud. "…you could prove abuse if you wanted to."

"You refusing to keep him here?" Reid asked more clearly.

"You know that's not what I'm saying."

"Then what are you saying?"

"He needs to know you want him."

Caleb quit breathing through the long silence that followed. And then his brother's voice was so soft, he came close to missing it.

"I do." Pause. "And I don't."

A skim of ice hardened in Caleb's chest. The *I do* part was a joke. The only honest part of that was *I don't.*

Paula said something, and then Reid did, but their voices were fading. They must have left the kitchen for what Paula called the great room.

He needs to know you want him.

I don't.

His brother had found him, rescued him, but

then palmed him off on someone else because he couldn't be bothered.

Caleb eased down the stairs, then out the kitchen door without even pausing to grab a parka.

"YOU DON'T?" PAULA SAID. "What's that supposed to mean?"

Reid made an impatient gesture. "Come on. You know what I mean. I'm not father material. I told Caleb I'm damaged, and it's true."

Paula didn't take her gaze from his as she sat on one of the benches at the long tables where meals were served in the main room of the lodge.

Despite having stayed in touch and contributed financially, he hadn't actually seen either of the Hales in something like ten years until the day he'd brought Caleb here. He had been shocked to see Paula's long braid was turning gray. She'd always looked like an aging hippie to him, but that had been from the perspective of a boy. Now she really *was* aging. Roger's dark hair and beard were shot with gray, too. That wasn't supposed to happen. He'd imagined them, and this refuge they guarded, as eternally the same. Reid hated to think about the time when they couldn't take in kids anymore.

"Damage heals," Paula said calmly.

Straddling a bench across the table from her, he had the uneasy feeling she was seeing further below the surface than he wanted her to. He'd forgotten the way she could always do that.

"I think you're underestimating yourself, Reid. You've changed your life for the sake of a boy you didn't know a couple of months ago. What's that but love?"

Love? He snorted. "I feel responsible." So responsible, he'd started job hunting in central Oregon the minute he'd brought Caleb here. Left a job that satisfied him for one he wasn't so sure he was going to like. Yeah, he'd gone out on a limb for this brother, but he'd rather call it guilt than love.

"Responsible? Why?"

He eyed her smile warily. "He's my brother."

"You'd never met him. It's not as if you grew up with him."

"I swore I'd know if that son of a bitch ever had another kid. Instead, I let it go. Caleb has gone through hell because I shut my eyes."

"No," she said, correcting him, "he's gone through hell because your father is abusive. You have no responsibility for your father's sins."

He stared at her, baffled and frustrated by her refusal to understand what he was saying. "So I should have shrugged and gone on with my life?"

"Neither of us could have done that."

"Then your point is?"

"Is this about Caleb at all, or are you trying to save yourself?"

Not reacting took an effort of will. "What kind of psychobabble is that?" he scoffed.

"Same kind I've always thrown at you."

Reid gave a reluctant chuckle.

"Do you see yourself in Caleb?"

"Save the crap, Paula. I'm not a kid anymore."

"You'll always be one of my kids." Her voice had descended a register, letting him hear the tenderness, tying and untying a knot in his chest.

Reid cleared his throat. It didn't do anything for the lump centered beneath his breastbone. "I'm sorry I haven't been back to visit in so long."

"Caleb made you revisit your past."

Oh, crap. Here we go again. "I'm giving him the same chance I had, that's all."

"You're doing more than that, or you wouldn't have moved to Angel Butte," she pointed out. "You're trying to be family, Reid." She reached across the table and laid her hand over his. "He needs you and you need him."

He bent his head and looked at her hand, which was getting knobby with the beginnings of arthritis. So much smaller than his hand. Still so unfailingly...loving.

Shit. Did that mean he knew what the word meant after all? He'd have told anyone who asked that all he felt for Paula and Roger was gratitude and admiration, but...now he wasn't sure that was true. He'd just as soon the possibility hadn't occurred to him. Love had never been a safe emotion for him.

"Maybe so," he said, hearing his own gruffness. "And I'd better go hunt him down before he decides I'm not here to see him at all."

"Yes, you should." She let him come around the table to her and lean over to kiss her cheek, but she grabbed his hand before he could turn away and looked at him with those penetrating eyes. "You're a good man, Reid Sawyer. Trust yourself."

He felt about seventeen again, as if his feet were still too big, and his cheeks turned red at any compliment. "I may be a decent man," he said finally. "But good? No. You're a good woman, Paula Hale. I don't measure up."

He tore himself away then. Her voice followed him. "You will, Reid. I have enough faith for both of us."

Faith. Out of her hearing, he grunted. There was a word more foreign to him than *love.*

So, okay, she could be right that on some subconscious level he was seeing himself in this younger brother, who looked so much like him. Why else the cauldron of emotions he'd been feeling, the ingredients of which he didn't even want to identify? That kind of transference was probably inevitable. He'd needed to be saved; now it was his turn to do the saving. Paying it forward was what people called it these days. *That's all I'm doing.*

He didn't think about why he was looking forward to seeing Caleb. Or why he was so disappointed when, twenty minutes later, he conceded defeat.

The disappearing act was so good, it was clear his brother didn't want to see him. Reid told himself that was okay. The two of them hardly knew each other. When Reid had first come here, he'd been like a feral animal in a trap, suspicious of anything that looked like affection. He didn't know why he'd expected different of Caleb.

The Hales had a gift for healing wounded, fearful young men. Paula was wrong; Caleb didn't need his brother, the stranger.

Which raised the question, why *had* he turned his own life upside down to be nearby when he'd already fulfilled his responsibility? He could have stayed in touch long-distance well enough.

He laughed, short and harsh, as he climbed into his Ford Expedition. Taking a last look at the ramshackle lodge that anchored a line of even more rundown cabins strung along the bank of Bear Creek, he breathed in the distinctive odor of ponderosa-pine forest, sharp despite the near-freezing temperature. Trust Paula to get him analyzing his choices. One of her more irritating characteristics.

But he was a big boy now, capable of resisting. A big boy who, for whatever idiotic reason, had taken on a new job with more scope than he'd anticipated. What he needed to do was concentrate on that job, not hanker for some elusive connection he'd lived his whole damn life without.

CHAPTER TWO

"IT'S ARSON," REID said flatly. He crouched and stared closely at the distinctive pattern of charring that climbed the interior wood-paneled wall of the cabin. He'd been lucky to find it, given the extent of the damage. "I'm no fire marshal," he said, rising to his feet, "but I don't have to be."

Beside him, Roger Hale grunted. "I thought I smelled gasoline."

"Hard to miss," Reid agreed.

He hadn't expected to hear from either of the Hales so soon after his Wednesday visit. On this fine Sunday morning, he'd been sprawled in bed trying to decide whether he could roll over and get some more sleep or was already too wide-awake when his phone had rung. Given his job, he kept the damn thing close, despite how often he cursed its existence. Hearing what Roger had to say had driven away any desire on his part to be lazy.

When he arrived half an hour ago, a cluster of boys had hovered on the front porch of the lodge. Caleb wasn't among them.

Walking to greet Reid, Roger had seen where he was looking. "Probably his turn in the shower.

We were all pretty filthy by the time we got the fire out."

Paula had been the one to spot it, according to Roger. She'd gotten up to use the john and seen a strange orange glow out the small window. Roger had yanked on clothes and run outside to find the fire climbing the back wall of the last cabin in the row. Even as he'd hooked up hoses, he had yelled to awaken the boys.

"This wasn't one of the occupied cabins," Reid said, turning slowly to examine the interior. Frigid blue sky showed through a gaping hole in the roof. There hadn't been much furniture in the cabin. No mattress—or at least no springs—but the wooden bed frame was so much half-burned firewood now. On instinct, he started picking through the debris.

"No, we haven't put anyone in here in…oh, five or six years," Roger replied. "I'd been thinking I either needed to raze it or do some serious work. But you know we never fill all the cabins." His expression was troubled. "You're saying our firebug didn't want to hurt anyone."

Yet. Reid didn't like thinking that, but had to.

"No, this was done either for fun or to get some attention."

He debated whether to say more, but suspected he didn't have to. Roger was a smart, well-read man. He'd already been thinking hard, or he wouldn't have summoned Reid to take a look.

Arson wasn't like shoplifting or half a dozen

other crimes Reid could think of, tried by a kid once out of curiosity or on a dare, then forgotten in a generally well-lived life. Famously, arson was one of the classic precursors of a serial killer. A budding pyromaniac, who set fires for the thrill, was bound to escalate in a different way.

This fire had been relatively harmless. The cabin hadn't been close to any of the others, and given that the last snowfall had melted only a few days ago, sparks had been unlikely to find dry fuel in the surrounding woods.

Reid found what he'd sought and wordlessly held out what was left of the side rail of a bed for Roger to see. One end was seared; the other was freshly splintered. As he'd suspected, the bed had been broken up to serve as firewood that would give the blaze what it needed to grow until it had the size and heat to bite into the solid log walls.

Roger shook his head. "We've had our share of troubles, but never a kid who wanted to burn up the world."

"There's a first for everything."

"We can't be sure it's one of the boys."

Reid kept his mouth shut.

"Goddamn." Roger vented by kicking at a still-steaming pile of half-burned wood. One piece fell away, revealing an orange spark beneath. Part of the headboard, Reid diagnosed, as he stamped out the ember beneath his booted foot. "Shit," Roger growled, "we'd better rake through this and be sure there's nothing that can start it up again."

"Yeah, you got lucky none of the neighbors spotted the glow and called the fire department."

Everybody around here had acreage, so there were no close neighbors. This fire must have leaped pretty high into the sky before they began fighting it, though. The last thing the Hales needed was a fire marshal out here asking questions. He or she wouldn't be able to help but notice that the Hales had too many kids. Even if Paula and Roger succeeded in hiding some of them, it would take barely a casual glance to see that a number of the cabins were occupied. With the addition of Caleb, there were currently ten boys in residence in the old resort, which was actually fewer than Reid knew they sometimes had.

Roger paused in the act of kicking through the charred debris. "Could that have been the point?"

"To rat you out?" Nice thought. "Only if you've got a kid who doesn't want to be here."

"Who says it has to be one of the boys? The middle of the night, anyone could have brought a can of gasoline and a matchbook. With this cabin down at the end, he'd have been unlikely to be heard."

"It's a possibility." Reid wasn't sure it was one he liked any better than the idea that one of the boys here was a newbie arsonist.

Roger gusted out a sigh. "We'll talk to all of them.

Along with Caleb, we've got two other relatively recent arrivals."

Something in Roger's tone caught Reid's attention. He turned slowly to meet his shrewd gaze. Damn. Of course that question had to be asked.

"Caleb has no history of anything like this." His jaw set. He made the reluctant addition, "That I know of."

Roger waved his hand in what Reid knew was a conciliating gesture. "Didn't think so, but he's the newest."

"And you've never had a fire before."

"No. We've never had a fire before," Roger echoed. "Guess it had to happen sooner or later."

The resigned, even philosophical conclusion wrung a reluctant laugh from Reid.

They both heard the sound of approaching voices. End of discussion. Damn, he didn't like to think what was to come. Once the Hales started separating boys and probing, the atmosphere would be poisoned by suspicion. How could it help but be?

He wouldn't be the only one looking at every one of these boys differently from here on out—including the brother he didn't know all that well.

Frowning at that blackened wall, he shook his head. He almost hoped the fire had been set for fun. Because if it actually had been intended to draw attention to the existence of this illicit shelter, it had failed in its purpose. Whoever he was, the arsonist would not be happy the fire had been put out quietly, causing only the slightest stir and some un-directed finger-pointing.

The back of Reid's neck prickled. *Fun* was a misleading word to start with. Fire suggested rage. Would the next blaze be bigger, causing more damage? Or would whoever set it try something completely different?

PUSHING HER CART down the aisle at Safeway, Anna caught a troubling whiff of smoke. Not tobacco—burning wood. Although there might be a hint of something else. Frowning, she came to a stop in front of the displays of boxed pastas and turned to look around her.

A man, also pushing a half-full cart, was directly behind her. Captain Reid Sawyer, no less, who had been featured on the front page of this morning's *Angel Butte Reporter.* In well-worn jeans, boots, a heavy flannel shirt and down vest, he was dressed a whole lot more casually than he had been the last time she saw him.

He gave her a slightly crooked smile. "I thought I recognized that hair."

"Hair?" Her hand rose to touch her head. *Yes, it was still there.* Feeling foolish, she snatched her hand back and wrapped it safely around the handle of the cart. "It's brown," she said repressively. "How could you recognize my hair?"

"It's not brown." He sounded amused. "It's dozens of colors. I'll bet you were a towhead when you were a kid, weren't you?"

She and her sister both had been. She shied away from a memory that was borrowed from a snapshot rather than real, of two girls standing stiffly, side by side, staring at the camera. She thought it was one of the times when they'd been delivered to a new home.

"Once upon a time." The smell was stronger, if anything. "Do you smell smoke?"

Strangely, he bent his head to sniff at himself. "Ah, that would be me. I'm sorry. I should have gone home to shower. I didn't realize I'd soaked it up."

She finally identified that illusory *other* component of the smell. "Gasoline."

His eyes sharp on her face, he said, "Yeah. You've got a good nose."

"What were you doing, cheating when you lit the briquettes?"

His chuckle was the first she'd seen echoed in his eyes. "That sounds suicidal."

"I had a—" She stopped, said more stiffly, "I knew someone once who used so much lighter fluid that there'd be a huge burst of flame when he tossed on a match."

"Also suicidal." His gaze was thoughtful now, as though he wondered what she hadn't wanted to say. "In my case, I was checking on a fire a friend had to put out on his property. He wanted to know what I thought."

"You mean, whether it had been set on purpose?"

He dipped his head.

"And it was."

"Thus the gasoline," he agreed.

"Did you call the fire department?"

"No, it wasn't that significant. More of an annoyance. But since I had to go right by the store on my way home, I decided to stock up for the week."

"Oh. Me, too." *Duh.* "Well, um, I'd better—"

"I hear Yancey was found alive and well."

"Yes." Anna was impressed that he'd remembered the name. The help he'd offered her had to have been a trivial part of his week. "He hadn't gotten as far as the highway yet."

"So Sergeant Shroutt told me. You return him to his foster home?"

"I found him a new one," she corrected. "For the time being, he'll be the only child in the home, which I think he needs. If I have to put anyone else in it, I'll send, I don't know, a ten-year-old girl."

"A child who might look up to him." He sounded approving.

"Yes." Anna didn't like feeling as if she had to defend herself, but she hadn't liked his expression Wednesday when she'd told him she had been trying to find Yancey a better placement. Or, more accurate, she hadn't liked her own sense of having failed one of the children for whom she was responsible. "This particular foster parent is one of my best. The brother and sister she had were returned to their parents, and she'd asked for a break. I was hoping Yancey could hold out until she was ready for another child. My mistake was not telling him what I planned."

Something had changed on his face. "Returned to their parents," he repeated in an unreadable tone. "That must be hard on a foster parent."

"It depends. Sometimes we all have doubts about whether the family can be stable, but in this case, Carol had developed a close relationship with the mother in particular. She thought it was time. I know she plans to stay in touch. And of course the kids' caseworker will keep an eye on the situation."

He nodded. "Does this Carol keep kids long-term?"

"Usually not." She hesitated. "Yancey has been freed by the court for adoption, but given his age it's unlikely there'll be any takers. I hate to have her tied up for that many years, but…" She sighed. "I think she'll love Yancey, and he'll love her. So…I hope she's able to keep him."

Something clanged into her cart and she turned quickly.

"I'm so sorry!" The woman had clearly been try-ing to squeeze her own, heavily laden cart past. "I'm a lousy driver."

Anna smiled. "And I'm blocking the road." She pushed hers out of the way, then glanced back at Reid Sawyer. "I'd better get on with my shopping now that I know the store isn't going to burn down."

"I should, too, before I scare anyone else." His gaze rested on her face with a weight she'd never felt before. "Any chance you'd like to have a cup of coffee when you're done?"

A curl of warmth low in her abdomen battled with the bump of alarm in her chest. She didn't like the way he seemed to hear more than she meant to say, but... Oh, lord, if he was attracted to her, too...

Could he be? He was law enforcement calendar-cover-model material, while she knew perfectly well she was ordinary personified.

One eyebrow rose. "I'll accept a polite no. You don't have to agonize."

"No." Oh, for heaven's sake—now her cheeks were heating. "I mean, yes. I was, um, just juggling my schedule in my head. Coffee would be nice. If you don't mind waiting until I finish," she added hastily.

His eyes had warmed. "I have a ways to go myself. In fact, I was going to grab some rotini as soon as you moved."

The rotini she was blocking. No wonder he'd lingered to make conversation.

"I'm sorry," she blurted and pushed her cart forward. Then remembering she needed pasta, too, she turned back to grab lasagna noodles at the same time he was reaching past her. They bumped. He dropped the box he'd been taking from the shelf, and she apologized several more times and felt like a klutz and a social disaster by the time she wheeled around the end of the aisle and out of sight of the single sexiest man she'd ever met.

ANNA WAS JUST getting into line when Reid accepted his receipt and decided to put his groceries in the back of his Expedition so he'd be free to help her stow hers.

The store was a busy place today, and he intercepted several interested glances in the parking lot. He managed civil nods in response. Much as he hated the idea, he'd had to cooperate when the newspaper decided they wanted to run a piece on him. He wasn't just a cop anymore; he was a public official, symbolizing this small city's police department. Unfortunately, there'd been more interest in him than there likely would have been if his predecessor had accepted a job somewhere else and faded away. No such luck for Reid. Colin McAllister had run a very public, highly scrutinized campaign right here in this county and unseated an incumbent sheriff that the Hales, at least, had described as lazy and self-satisfied. The reforms McAllister was instigating in the sheriff's department were drawing a lot of press, too. It wasn't surprising that people were curious about the man who had replaced him in his old job.

Reid hoped he'd hid how very uncomfortable he was about that kind of scrutiny. He'd done his damnedest to deflect personal questions and talk instead about what he saw as his professional role.

One thing he couldn't do was admit he'd ever lived in Angel Butte. Instead he'd implied he had vacationed here in the past, liked the area, jumped when he saw the job opening. No, he wasn't a fisherman or hunter and he'd never alpine skiied, but he did cross-country ski, hike and kayak. Yes, he was looking forward to the recreational opportunities.

"Clean air is good, too," he'd said, and the quote appeared in the paper. As had a photo of him that he'd scrutinized for several minutes this morning, the newspaper spread open on his table. Even though he saw that face in the mirror every morning when he shaved, he hardly recognized himself in print. It was a peculiar experience.

He had very few pictures of himself. When he had run away from home, it hadn't occurred to him to take anything like baby pictures along. He'd brought a couple pictures of his mother, that was all—ones he'd secreted away from his father. As for the rest of the family photos, he had no idea whether his father would have kept them in a box in the closet or burned them. Maybe he'd ask Caleb sometime. Reid knew the Hales had taken pictures, but not a lot. He'd never had reason to go to a professional photographer. The few times he'd appeared in the newspaper, he'd been caught as part of a scene, or, a couple of times, when he was giving a statement or was arriving at or leaving court. The focus hadn't been so intensely on *him*.

Now he put the last grocery bag in the rear cargo

area and slammed the door. He was glad to see Anna leaving the store just then and strode to meet her.

"Oh!" She looked shy. "I wondered how to find you."

"I got done first."

She stopped in front of a bright blue Toyota RAV4, one he thought was several years old but still in good condition, and unlocked the rear hatch. His hands were large enough to grab the handles of several bags at once, and he made short work of unloading.

"Why don't you come with me?" he suggested. "I can bring you back to your car later."

"There's a Starbucks inside the store."

He'd noticed it. The tiny tables in the middle of traffic weren't what he had in mind.

"There has to be someplace we won't be on display."

She eyed him curiously. "I saw you in the paper this morning."

"You and every other person shopping today." He knew he sounded grumpy. He had an odd moment of wondering whether her interest in that article had been more than casual and whether her eyes had lingered on the photo.

With a smirk, she inclined her head to draw his attention to two women passing, both of whom were staring.

He was getting good at those polite nods.

"Like I said, I'd enjoy a cup of coffee a lot more if people weren't gaping at me."

She opened her mouth, then closed it. Intrigued, he said, "What?"

"I just…" Her cheeks were a little pink. She made a face. "I was going to say, what's to stop *me* gaping at you?"

He grinned. "Gape to your heart's content."

Yeah, he liked this lighthearted exchange. No ghosts here. He wasn't sure if she was flirting with him or not, but she had said yes to coffee, and that meant something. He was getting more interested by the minute in finding out what she wore beneath today's close-fitting jeans, knee-high boots and thigh-length sweater over a turtleneck. Slightly more revealing than her utilitarian work getup—he could at least tell she had fabulous legs—but not much. Of course, given the temperature outside, everyone was dressed in bulky layers.

Seeing her looking more stylish today, though, he was close to ruling out the serviceable white undergarments. The field was now open. Her personality had enough contradictions, he had no idea. Fortunately, he liked mysteries.

Besides, he could strip off panties of any color or material just as quickly.

"Why don't I drive?" she suggested. "I gather you haven't been in town very long. Do you know where to go?"

"I'd stop at the first place that said *coffee*," he

admitted, not telling her he'd spent his first day in town doing nothing but driving around. He was like a cat, needing to know his territory and where the outermost edges of it were.

Angel Butte had changed one hell of a lot since he had left after turning eighteen, and nearly as much since his last visit when he was twenty-four or -five. Then, it had still been a small town. The mall, Walmart, Staples and the rest weren't here. An annexation had extended the city limits to take in a whole lot of new development, as well as empty country he had no doubt would be developed in the next ten years. Many of the new homes weren't for full-time residents, which made Angel Butte different from anyplace else he'd ever lived. He imagined it as something of a ghost town during the in-between seasons: after the ski lifts shut down, but before hiking trails were open and fishing licenses issued, and then again in the fall when the reverse happened.

Reid suspected Anna was challenging him by offering to drive. Cops were notorious control freaks who didn't like being driven by someone else. The generalization applied to him, all right. Still, he figured he was safe with her behind the wheel given what a short distance they had to travel.

"Sure," he said, hiding his smile at her surprise.

Turned out she wasn't a bad driver at all. He only compressed the floorboards with his right foot a couple of times and grabbed for the armrest once. She laughed at him that time.

They ended up at a place called The Butte, only a couple blocks from the public safety building that housed the police station, but on a side street. He'd seen it, but not yet been in. From the length of the line inside, business was bustling.

"Best coffee in town," she told him as they waited. He listened to conversations around them and decided most of the people were locals rather than tourists.

She looked at him askance when he ordered an Americano and then narrowed her eyes and said, "Not a word," before asking for a gingerbread latte.

"A froufrou drink," he murmured in her ear.

She accepted it from the teenager behind the counter and breathed in happily. "Dessert and caffeine all in one. I *love* gingerbread."

"I'm not sure I've ever had any," he remarked as they wended between tables to an open booth on the side.

"Never eaten gingerbread? Not even a gingerbread man?"

Her outrage made him smile. "I don't think so."

Even though he would have remained more anonymous if he had sat with his back to the door, he maneuvered her so he could sit facing the room. He liked knowing what was behind him.

At first they chatted about Angel Butte, edging gradually to the kind of questions people asked when they wanted to know each other: What do you enjoy doing in your spare time? Where did you grow up? How'd you end up here?

They both admitted to being readers, enjoying some movies. Both were runners, although she was taking a step-aerobics class right now instead. He worked out at a gym, too, and played basketball and racquetball.

"I've already played in a few pickup games at the Y," he said, smiling slyly. "Beat the mayor himself at racquetball."

"Noah Chandler?" She looked intrigued before grinning at him. "Well, you ought to be able to. He's got to be too muscle-bound to be fast."

"I wouldn't say that. It was a hard-fought game."

He admitted to having grown up in Spokane, then repeated the lies he'd told the reporter about having vacationed in central Oregon.

"I've lived all over Oregon," she said, her lashes veiling her eyes and making him wonder what she didn't want him to see. "I finally graduated from high school in Bend."

Reid nodded; Bend was the largest city in central Oregon and only about a forty-five-minute drive from Angel Butte.

"Parents still in the area?" he asked casually.

He'd have sworn the gray of her eyes darkened, as if a cloud had passed over the sun. *Oh, damn,* he thought—he'd been right about the ghosts.

"I grew up in foster homes," she said after a minute, so casually he realized she must say this often.

Which made sense. Telling her story would be a good way to connect with the kids on the job. "My parents split up when I was three or four, I think. I never saw my father again, and I barely remember my mother. She couldn't cope on her own."

"Was she abusive?" A familiar ball of anger and something else formed in his chest. He was disturbed at how clearly he could see that little girl, skin and bones, pale hair and the eyes that were still huge and haunting.

But she shook her head. "No, nothing like that. Just…negligent."

He curled his hand around his coffee to keep from reaching for her. "Did you miss her?"

Tiny crinkles formed on her forehead as she seemed to ponder. "I suppose I might have. I don't remember."

"You've never looked for her? Or your father?"

"No." That lusciously sexy voice had gone hard. "I have no interest in them."

"I suppose this answers the question of how you chose your profession," he said thoughtfully.

"I consider it a vocation."

No nine-to-five for her. Apparently the two of them had something in common. Unlike most cops, he'd hungered for the domestic-abuse calls. He'd never dreamed about working Homicide; he wanted to bring down the assholes like his father.

Of course, he'd found himself arresting not only men but women, too. Not quite as many, but plenty

of them. Mostly for child abuse, but occasionally
they were the aggressors against the men in their
lives, too.

"I've…always felt the same about my own job,"
he said slowly, zinged by the sense of shock and,
yeah, panic that came when he let himself wonder
what in hell he had thought he was doing here in
Angel Butte. The Family Violence Unit had been his
goal from the minute he joined the Orange County
P.D. in Southern California. It had been the next
thing to a religious vocation for him, although he'd
never used that word before. Now he was an admin-
istrator who would rarely deal directly with people
in crisis. Supervising major investigations, sure, but
also juggling the demands of different departments
for paper clips, printer ink cartridges, air filters for
the police cars and more clerical help.

God help him.

"What about your parents?" Anna asked softly,
dragging him back to the present.

He sat very still, doing his best to give away nothing. "My mother died when I was ten. My father…
is also a cop. Spokane P.D."

"You took after him."

"No." There was more bite in the one word than
he'd meant to put there. Her eyes widened. "I consider myself his antithesis," Reid said calmly. "He's
a son of a bitch."

"I…see."

He was afraid she did. Those extraordinary eyes

gazed at him as if he were a crystal ball and the mist within was clearing to reveal what she wanted to know. The sensation made his skin crawl.

Why had he started this, against his original instinct? It wasn't only her eyes that were spooky; it was *her*. A casual sexual relationship wasn't going to be possible with this woman.

He made a production out of draining the last of his coffee and then glanced at his watch. "We probably shouldn't linger too long. Our frozen food will melt."

She didn't call him on the absurdity of that, when the outside temp might conceivably have reached a not-so-balmy forty degrees Fahrenheit. Instead, she took a long drink of her latte and said politely, "You're right. I'm ready if you are."

On the drive back to the Safeway parking lot, he asked how long she'd lived in Angel Butte. Seven years. Although she enjoyed cross-country skiing, she'd never taken up alpine. She hadn't learned as a child and couldn't afford the sport now even if she'd wanted to try it. He felt guilty for asking, when she had already told him she'd grown up in foster homes. Of course she hadn't had the opportunity.

When she came to a stop right behind his SUV and said "Thank you for the coffee" in a tone that told him she knew his interest had cooled, Reid felt…regret. He didn't like knowing he'd probably hurt her feelings.

Be smart.

"My pleasure," he said, opening his door. "Glad I ran into you."

She said something as meaningless. He nodded, shut the door and dug his keys out of his pocket as he walked around the driver side of the Expedition. By the time he got in and glanced in the rearview mirror, she was gone.

Out of sight, out of mind, he told himself, but his chest constricted uncomfortably.

All the more reason to stay clear of her. Thinking hard these past nights since his Wednesday visit to the shelter, he'd recognized that Paula might be right. A part of him did want to love this newfound brother and be loved in return. If so, it was a major step for him. The kind of intimacy it took to really love a woman… No. He did know his own boundaries. Anna Grant was outside them.

CHAPTER THREE

CALEB LEAPED UP from the bench and stared at Paula in outrage. "You think I set the fire."

"No." Her gaze was kind, but when she said, "Sit down," he didn't mistake her firmness. He'd already figured out that, despite first impressions, Paula was the hard-ass, Roger the easy touch of the two.

"Then why are you asking me—"

"All we're trying to do is determine whether any of you saw anything. If possible, we'd like to be sure none of you boys set the fire."

"Why would we?"

She gave him a little lecture about how arson was a form of acting out and how some of the boys who came here were troubled. Good word—*troubled*. He hadn't yet asked anyone else why they were here, but he knew it had to be shit as bad as he'd experienced. And, like had happened with him, the police and courts had screwed them over, too. That was what this place was—a last resort.

Hey, pun.

Caleb repeated that he'd been asleep until he heard Roger bellowing for help. He'd looked out his window but hadn't seen anything—his window faced the wrong way—but then he'd stuck his head out into the hall to find out what was going on.

"I heard you yelling there was a fire, to hurry and get dressed, so I hammered on TJ's door." TJ was the other guy who had a room upstairs at the lodge. Caleb didn't really like TJ, who had a major chip on his shoulder and an explosive temper. "He yelled, 'What?' You know, like he was pissed I'd woken him up."

Paula nodded. TJ was always pissed. It was March now, and Caleb had been here since right after Christmas. TJ had already been here a couple of months then. He was probably stuck living in the lodge because no one wanted to share a cabin with him. Caleb had a really bad feeling they'd end up paired whether he liked it or not.

"Was he dressed when he came out?" she asked.

Caleb cast his mind back. "No, he was buck naked. His hair was flat on one side and sticking up on the other. I told him there was a fire and Roger needed help putting it out. He sort of shrugged and went back into his room." TJ had eventually showed up to help haul buckets of water from the creek.

"You were a big help fighting the fire," Paula said. "Thank you."

"You weren't using that cabin anyway, right?"

She gave him sort of a funny look. "No, but the flames could have spread. And what if the same somebody decides to set another fire?"

"How do you know it wasn't, like, bad wiring

or something?" he asked, feeling awkward but not liking what she was suggesting. What if whoever it was set the lodge on fire next time?

"Didn't you smell the gasoline?"

He frowned, remembering. "I guess. I thought it was propane. I mean, there's a tank outside the lodge."

"But not the cabins."

He nodded after a minute.

"And you know your brother was here this morning to take a look. He showed Roger where the fire started. It wasn't near an electrical outlet or in the kitchen area where there were any appliances."

Your brother. He hadn't gotten used to those words. They made him feel…twitchy. As if he couldn't sit still.

"I know you boys are talking about it." Paula sounded weary. "I wouldn't normally encourage any of you to rat on each other, but this is serious. Even scary. Please come to Roger or me—or Reid," she added, "if you hear anything that makes you uneasy."

That was one of the reasons he wasn't settling in here. It was knowing the only reason they'd taken him was Reid. That Reid was like their *real* son, and Caleb was only a favor they were doing for him.

He nodded, even though he didn't know if he was really agreeing to anything, and asked, "Can I go?"

"Yes. Thank you, Caleb. If you see Isaac, will you send him in?"

"Um…sure."

He went outside to look for Diego, who'd been grilled right before Caleb. Fun Sunday—taking turns facing an inquisition. And after they'd all busted their asses helping to put out the fire last night.

He found Diego splitting wood, watched by two of the other guys, Damon and Isaac. They must have been talking, because they all turned and looked at him.

"Paula wants you," Caleb said to Isaac, a lanky, beak-nosed seventeen-year-old. He was some kind of math genius who'd helped Caleb with his geometry the other day.

Isaac nodded and left. He never had much to say. He'd probably been doing nothing but listening to what the other two were saying.

Diego lifted the ax and swung. *Thud.* A chunk of wood split and fell from the big round of fir they used as a base.

Damon glanced over his shoulder, as if to make sure Isaac was really out of earshot. "Palmer doesn't think Isaac was in his cabin when Roger woke everyone up," he said.

"What?" Diego stared at him, the ax dangling from his hand. "How would Palmer know? He's, like, two cabins away."

"That's what he says. Only Apollo came out."

"Did anyone ask Apollo?"

Damon sneered. "Like he'd say. They're tight."

"Tight enough to lie about something like that?" Caleb asked, almost reluctantly.

"Shit, yeah!"

"I don't know." Diego sounded doubtful.

"What?" Damon stepped forward, his stance aggressive. "You're saying Palmer's lying?"

"I'm saying maybe Isaac was sound asleep and slower to get up. He's been here, like, three years. If he wanted to set fires, why wouldn't he have done it before?"

"Who says he hasn't? None of the rest of us have been here that long."

Caleb shook his head. "This is stupid. We don't know anything. We shouldn't be making accusations because somebody said somebody else said."

Damon swung an angry stare at Caleb. "Who are you calling stupid?"

Caleb balanced on his feet in case this asshole decided to make it physical. "Nobody. I'm saying we should stick together, not whisper about each other."

"You would say that."

Caleb was getting pissed. "What's that supposed to mean?"

"It means *you're* new here. You could have gone out easy. Come back in just as easy."

"I don't set fires," he said flatly, when what he wanted to do was plant his fist in the guy's mouth.

"Yeah? We don't know you."

"You mean, *you* don't know shit," Caleb shot back.

Damon launched himself. A moment later, they

were rolling on the ground and Caleb had the satisfaction of feeling his knuckles connecting with Damon's nose.

CALEB'S SPLIT LIP had crusted over. The black eye had faded to mauve and puce, but was still visible. Reid assessed the range of colors. The fight must have taken place in the neighborhood of three days ago. Today was Wednesday, so the injury had likely happened Sunday after the fire. When suspicion had begun to gather.

"What?" Caleb snarled. "I suppose you're here to give me some big lecture about being a good boy and not fighting while your best buds the Hales are being generous enough to give me a home."

They were in the front room of the lodge, temporarily alone. Determined to hide the tension his brother had awakened with his obvious hostility, Reid leaned back where he sat on the sagging sofa and clasped his hands behind his head. "I didn't know you'd been in a fight until I saw your face," he said mildly. "I came to see you."

"Oh, right. Like they didn't call you the minute it happened."

Reid shook his head, his experienced eye dating the progression of the bruises. "Has to have been a few days."

Caleb stared stubbornly at him.

Reid sighed. "This is not a school. They don't call me every time you get in trouble."

"I don't believe you."

"Your privilege." He raised his eyebrows. "Do you want to tell me?"

It was disconcerting seeing the sullenness gathered on a face that looked so much like his own. Caleb must be giving the Hales flashbacks. "What if I say no?" his brother challenged him.

"That's your privilege, too."

They sat in silence for what had to be a minute. Clattering came from the kitchen, but nobody appeared. It wasn't Paula; Reid knew she'd driven up to Bend to load up on basics at Costco.

Caleb glanced toward the kitchen, but the two of them were far enough away to go unheard.

"There's been a lot of shit talked since the fire," he mumbled. "This one guy said I'm the newest, so it must be me who set it." He shrugged. "I told him I didn't, and to shut up."

Reid's mouth quirked. "He didn't like that, I gather."

"He'll know better than to go for me next time. I broke his nose."

God. How was he supposed to handle this? A fatherly lecture wouldn't go over well, assuming he knew how to give one. All *their* father would have wanted to know was why Caleb had let a fist get through his defenses.

I'm not his father. I'm his brother.

Yeah, no on-the-job experience there, either. The feeling of helplessness didn't sit well with Reid.

"So you know how to fight" was the best he could come up with.

Caleb bent his head so Reid couldn't see his face. "I guess."

"You miss being on sports teams?"

Caleb shrugged.

This was going nowhere. Reid decided to let it drop and get to what he'd come out here for. Besides visiting his brother, making sure he was okay.

"Dad called."

"What?" The boy's head snapped up. "You mean, that stuff about him thinking you were dead was bullshit?"

"He never thought that," Reid said flatly. "He just didn't want to give you any ideas."

Caleb shook his head as if dazed. "Wait. He knows where you *are?*"

"After I turned eighteen and started college, my guess is he's always tracked me. I thought about changing my name, but I never did. I figured, what could he do to me?" Reid's turn to shrug. He didn't like saying this, but had to. "He asked if I had you."

Fear darkened Caleb's eyes. "What did you say?"

"No, of course." That wasn't all he'd said. He'd also said mockingly, *So you lost another son. Guess you didn't learn anything the first time around.*

It might have been smarter to ask who the hell Caleb was. He doubted his father would have bought the pretense, though. If he'd kept checking on Reid over the years, Dean Sawyer would know his oldest son was a cop. They were a paranoid bunch, and his father was more paranoid than most, as well as arrogant. He was bound to assume Reid had remained wary enough to keep checking up on *him*.

Caleb jumped to his feet, his face pinched with fear. "What if he comes here looking for me?"

Reid let his hands fall to his sides. "What if he does? Not many people know what the Hales' place is. It's way out of town. How could he possibly find you here?"

"I don't know, but— Jesus."

Reid straightened. "It does mean you need to stick close to home. Don't go into town for now. If a car pulls into the driveway, stay out of sight. If Dad comes down to Oregon to look around, he'll find out I live alone. The job was a promotion for me. There's no reason for him to question why I moved here. I haven't told anyone about you or my connection to the shelter."

"You don't know what you're talking about! He won't let me go."

Reid added steel to his voice. "You're already gone. You told me that yourself. Remember?"

"If he shows up, some of the guys would tell him in a second I'm here!" Caleb's panic was unreasoning. He backed away and almost stumbled over a side table.

"And why is that?" Reid asked.

His brother's face twisted into an ugly expression and he let loose an expletive. "Has to be my fault, right?"

Reid rose to his feet. "I didn't say—"

"Yeah, well, you've warned me." His gaze raked Reid. "Nothing like having a brother who'll nobly risk everything for my sake."

The churning inside felt like heartburn or something worse. Reid held Caleb's gaze. "You want to come home with me right now? Take Daddy on? Is that it?"

"No!" the boy shouted. "I don't need you, okay? Thank you for coming. Goodbye."

The front door of the lodge slammed behind him. Reid was left standing alone, baffled, frustrated, angry…and hurt.

ANNA DIDN'T REMEMBER ever setting eyes on Reid Sawyer's predecessor in real life. On television when he was campaigning, but that was different.

So she couldn't believe it when Reid appeared at the back of the room when she was giving a talk at the library Wednesday night. "The Joys and Frustrations of Providing Foster Care: An Honest Q & A," the flyer had said. She'd been pleasantly surprised to have an audience of twelve people. Who knew, she might get a new foster home out of this group.

She'd been rolling along, being truthful but upbeat, even eliciting some laughs, when a flicker of movement drew her gaze to the man who'd paused in the open doorway leading to the lobby. It had been only a few days since he'd stung her by making it plain he wouldn't be calling. What were the odds they'd happen to run into each other three times in one week?

Hair tousled and wearing jeans and an unzipped parka with gloves sticking out of one pocket, he might have gone unrecognized by her audience if she hadn't felt such a flare of…something. Anger, she told herself, and knew better.

With malice aforethought, she said in a ringing voice, "Captain Sawyer. How good of you to stop in." Her entire audience swiveled to stare at the newcomer. "Folks, this is our new Angel Butte Police Department captain of Investigative and Support Services. Say hi."

A chorus of voices greeted him.

His eyes met hers very briefly, expressing an astonishing amount given that she doubted anyone else in the room would so much as notice.

"Glad to see such a turnout," he said, inclining his head.

"Would you like to join us?" she asked.

"No, I, uh…" He backed up. "Just thought I'd look in."

His retreat duly noted, the audience turned back to her. Trying to put him out of her mind, Anna struggled to remember where she'd been in her familiar script. She sneaked a glance at the clock. Oh, well. With only fifteen minutes left to go, she could fill the time with questions.

When she asked if anyone had any, a gratifying number of hands shot up.

By the time she finished, she felt really good about the evening. Several people talked to her afterward and took the brochures and initial applications she'd brought. The last of them left, and she gathered up her material and notes, then started for the door. She still had ten minutes before the library closed to take a quick look at the new books. Anna was chagrined to catch herself wondering whether Reid might still be in the library.

She was reaching for the light switch when he once again filled the doorway.

"Anna."

"Captain Sawyer."

"Surely we're to the first-name stage."

She pretended to look surprised. "Are we?"

His jaw tightened.

"Did you need something?" she asked, keeping her voice pleasant. "You know that I'm more involved in supervising foster homes than in working directly with the kids. But if you have a question, I might be able to refer you to someone who can help—"

"I don't have a question." His irritation was obvious.

"Then?"

His jaw muscles spasmed again. "Never mind. Have a good evening, *Ms.* Grant."

He was shrugging on the parka and walking

toward the exit when she hurriedly followed him out into the lobby. She'd been a bitch, and all because he'd made it obvious he wasn't interested in her. Politely.

"Captain... Reid," she said more softly.

For a moment she thought he wasn't going to stop. He was almost to the exterior doors when he hesitated and turned. "Anna."

Now she felt awkward. "You must have had something you wanted to talk to me about."

He looked at her for a long moment, his face unreadable, as it so often was. "Call it an impulse," he said finally.

"I'm really not in any hurry." She didn't move closer to him, but kept her voice down for reasons she didn't understand. The moment seemed...significant. The two of them were very alone, though there was activity behind her in the brightly lit library proper, while headlights were coming on out in the parking lot. They were bound to be interrupted any minute; with the library closing, patrons would be streaming out, or someone would emerge from one of the restrooms. She suddenly, desperately, wanted to know why he'd hung around to talk to her.

"I have a problem with a teenager," he said slowly. "I thought you might be an expert available for consultation."

Her disappointment was acute. So he'd wanted her only in her professional capacity. Of course.

Trying for brisk, she said, "I don't know that I'd call myself an expert on teenagers in particular, but I'm happy to help if I can." She did owe him one. She shifted the weight of the heavy bag slung over her shoulder and started toward him and the exit. "You're welcome to call me, or—"

"It's my brother." Lines had deepened on his forehead. He looked disconcerted, as if he hadn't meant to say that.

"A teenager?" she blurted in surprise.

That very speaking eyebrow of his twitched. "Think I'm too old to have a brother that young?"

"Well, um, yes?"

He grimaced. "You're right. I am. I should have said *half brother*. Who I didn't know existed until a few months ago."

"That sounds like a story." He wasn't moving, so she came to a stop.

"It is." He shook his head. "You probably just want to get home."

"Actually, now you have me interested," she admitted. She didn't know what had happened the last time they had seen each other. She would have sworn he'd been checking out her body, if smoothly. He wouldn't have suggested coffee if he hadn't been attracted to her, would he? It was more as if she'd said something wrong. The annoying part was having no idea what that could have been. It might be that he'd happened to be at the library tonight, saw that she was speaking and thought, *Aha! There's someone I can talk to.* He did say it was an impulse. But...she didn't believe that. He hadn't been carrying any books earlier, and he didn't have one in his hands now, either. She had a feeling he had come looking for her.

"I suppose you've had dinner." He sounded almost tentative.

"Actually, no. But you don't need to feed me."

"I wouldn't mind having something to eat myself. How about Chandler's Brewpub?"

"They often have live music," she pointed out. "Not so great if you want to talk." She hesitated. "Will you be shocked if I confess I was planning to go to A&W? I really wanted a root-beer float."

He flashed a grin that made her knees wobble. "A root-beer float and French fries sound damn good to me." He pushed open the door, letting in a blast of cold air, and waited for her to go through.

She gave an involuntary shiver. "You know where it is?"

"I do."

"My car's that way." She gestured vaguely. "See you there."

He raised a hand and strode away.

ANNA INSISTED ON paying for her own meal, a clear message. She carried her tray toward a far booth even though the place was empty but for one other couple, leaving him to place his own order and follow a minute later.

He slid onto the hard plastic bench across from her. "Think we'll hear our numbers from here?"

"I thought you might not want to be overheard," she said coolly.

"You're right."

He still didn't know what he was doing here. Not an unusual state for him these days. Confusion seemed to *be* his new usual. Still—he'd made the decision to stay away from Anna, and yet here he was, three whole days later, having sought her out.

Weirdly, when he had driven away from the shelter this afternoon, he'd immediately thought of her. By serendipity, he'd spotted a notice in the morning paper for her talk at the library, so he guessed that was why she'd been at the back of his mind. He could talk to her about Caleb's issues, he'd thought, without saying anything about his relationship to the boy. Then what was the first thing out of his mouth? *He's my brother.*

"There's mine," she said abruptly, sliding out of the booth.

Her number. He'd been so busy brooding, he hadn't even heard.

She was still up there when his was called, but when he turned, Anna waved him back to his seat. She returned with his food, as well as her own.

"Damn, that smells good," he said, hungrily reaching for his French fries. "This was a good idea."

"Yes, it was." She took a slurp from her root-beer float then unwrapped her cheeseburger.

"How'd your talk go?" he asked between bites, aiming to put off a conversation he still wasn't sure he wanted to have.

"Hmm? Oh, good. We're always short of homes, which means I put in a lot of time recruiting new foster parents."

"Is Angel's Haven local only?"

"You mean Butte County? Mostly, but we do have some scattered foster homes in Deschutes and Klamath Counties. If someone good prefers to work with us rather than an agency closer to them, we don't turn them away. The home has to be near enough for us to visit easily, though."

He nodded. She talked about some of the questions people had asked tonight, and about the fears she thought kept people from being willing to take in children who might—and often did—have problems.

She switched gears when she finished her burger. "Are you going to tell me how you didn't know you had a brother?"

Reid grunted, no closer to having made a decision about how much to tell her. "I haven't stayed in touch with my father. Didn't know he'd remarried. A few months ago, I ran a check on him. Turns out he's divorced, but they had another kid who stayed

with him rather than going with the mother. Caleb.
He's…a mess."

Anna's big gray eyes were compassionate. "In
what way?"

"Our father was abusive." He paused, frowning. "Is."

"I…see."

Damn it, there she went again. Wasn't that exactly what she'd said over coffee that scared the shit
out of him? The trouble was, she meant it. She saw
more than he'd said. And this time he'd set himself
up for it.

He reached for a French fry, attempting to look
more casual than he felt. "I'm…trying to build a relationship with Caleb. He doesn't want to trust me."

"Maybe he can't."

"Can't?" He stared at her, inexplicably angry.
"What are you suggesting? That he's broken and
unfixable?"

Like me? The quick thought was unwelcome. If
he believed himself to be permanently damaged…
maybe Caleb was, too. Maybe he'd found him too
late. It was disconcerting to realize how pissed he
was at the very idea.

But Anna was frowning repressively at him. "Of
course not. I'd never suggest anything of the kind.
I've seen too many children from horrific homes
blossom when they feel safe and loved."

Damn. She sounded like Paula.

"I hardly know him," he said. "Love… That's asking a lot."

"Can you bring him to live with you?"

"I don't see that as an option."

"Why not?" she asked.

He should have known she wouldn't let it go that easily.

"Aside from the fact I have a job that demands a whole hell of a lot more than forty hours a week?"

"How old is Caleb?"

"Fifteen," he said reluctantly.

"Unless you live way out of town, he could get himself home from after-school activities, to friends' houses. He could take on responsibility for putting dinner on the table some nights. He doesn't need the same time commitment from you that a younger child would."

His appetite had deserted him. "His father won't let him go without an ugly court battle."

"So you're just going to leave him?" Her spine had straightened and her eyes held the light of battle. Despite the topic and the fact she was judging him, Reid was disconcerted to find his body responding to the fire in her. Apparently, he was turned on by a woman who could take to task not only a crusty desk sergeant, but also a stone-faced police captain.

At least she hadn't commented on what he'd said—*his* father. No one he wanted to claim.

"That's not entirely my decision," he pointed out.

"What I'd like to understand is why Caleb is trying to reject me, too."

He basked in the way her face softened.

"When you were his age, would trust have come easily to you?" she asked.

He gave a short, harsh laugh. "No." He'd been with the Hales for a year or more before he felt anything close to that for them. "You're saying I need to prove myself to Caleb."

"I'm saying that he's testing you. He's pushing you away to see if you'll go." She leaned forward a little, as if to underline the urgency of what she was saying. She exuded such intensity, he couldn't have looked away from her if someone wearing a ski mask had walked in with a gun and told the cashier to stick 'em up. "What you have to do is refuse to go," she said. "He needs to see you digging in for him. By fighting for custody of him, if necessary, or only by giving him an ear and a refuge."

An ear and a refuge. Wasn't that what he'd been trying to offer? He couldn't be Caleb's home, although he thought he'd provided an even better one. He was giving everything he could. Pushing himself into places he'd never gone.

"He's testing me," he said slowly.

"Without having met him, I can't say for sure, but that's my guess."

"It fits," he admitted. "I hadn't thought of it that way."

There was more, of course; Caleb had wanted his big brother to wade in with fists flying to rescue him. Eventually, he'd see that this way was better. Safer.

A thought crept into Reid's head, a follow-up to things he'd been brooding about anyway. Okay, it was possible he had, without realizing it, come to love Paula and Roger, but…would they actually love Caleb? Did they love all the kids they took in? Some of them? None? Certainly, back then Reid hadn't thought of the word in association with them. His mother was the only person he'd ever been sure loved him—or known he loved, despite the limitations on *her* love.

Whatever Paula and Roger gave was enough for me.

He was stunned by the voice that whispered, *Was it?*

No, that was ridiculous. Sure, what kid wouldn't rather have a normal family? Mom, Dad, sister, brother, cat and dog. The cynic in him thought, *Fresh-baked cookies when I came in the door from school, gentle lectures when my grades dropped, a parent in the stands at every football and basketball game. A father who talked openly to me and laid a comforting hand on my shoulder while he listened when I told him my worries.* A warm-hearted TV-sitcom childhood. If they existed, he hadn't seen one up close and personal. Some of his friends seemed to have it good, but who knew what went on behind closed doors? Shame had kept him from telling any of those friends his father beat the shit out of him on a regular basis. He'd never said, *My father killed my mother and got away with it.* So they might have been keeping quiet for the same reason. Once he became a cop, stable, loving families weren't the ones he saw.

But that's what I wanted.

That's what Caleb wants.

A sound escaped him, one even he didn't know how to label. Glimpsing Anna's startled expression, he snapped his guard back into place. She'd seen too much already. He knew better than to lay himself out naked like this.

"That helps," he said, sounding easy, but for a residual roughness in his voice. "Thank you."

She studied him long enough to make him sweat, but he playfully snitched a French fry from her tray, since his were gone, and then stirred the last of his float before peeling off the lid and drinking it.

"You're welcome," she said and swatted at his hand when he reached for another French fry. "Hey!"

"You're not eating them."

She wrinkled her nose at him. "My eyes were bigger than my stomach."

She'd hardly made a dent in the fries and half her root-beer float was left. No wonder she stayed skinny.

Delicate.

They chatted for a few more minutes. He made a concerted effort, though he needed desperately to be moving, to be alone. He didn't want her to know how he felt, especially since, as usual, he didn't know what he *did* feel.

"I was kidding. Here, you can have the rest of these." She offered the fries, but he shook his head.

"I've had enough."

"I should get home," she said, her expression completely unrevealing.

They bused their table, then walked out together. The other diners had long since left. The parking lot was dark and empty; the only remaining vehicles besides their own were parked toward the back of the building and probably belonged to employees. He wanted to kiss her good-night—and yet he didn't want to. Or didn't dare.

More to be confused about. He felt some of the same panic he had when he'd admitted to Paula that he both wanted and didn't want to take Caleb home.

Even if he'd formed the impulse, Anna unlocked her Toyota and hopped in too quickly to have given him the chance to act on it. "Good night, Reid," she said, slammed her door and started the engine immediately. She was backing out before he'd circled around to the driver's side of his own vehicle.

Because she didn't want to start anything with him? Or because he'd had his chance and blown it?

Or—most unwelcome possibility of all—because

she'd read him all too accurately and knew a man running scared when she saw one?

He swore under his breath and told himself it really would be better to keep his distance.

CHAPTER FOUR

"ANOTHER FIRE?" REID stopped midstride, only peripherally aware of other people parting to go around him, barely sparing him a glance. The snowy sidewalk meant everyone needed to watch their footing. Having become accustomed to Southern California winters, he had almost forgotten that mid- and even late March did not qualify as spring in this part of Oregon.

It was Monday morning, and he had been striding from the parking lot toward the public safety building, wishing he'd worn boots for better traction, when his phone rang and he saw that Roger was the caller.

"Not as major," Roger assured him. "Might've been the snow that made it fizzle."

Reid stepped off the sidewalk into deeper snow on the lawn, separating himself from the stream of people heading into work. A late-winter storm had left three or four inches of snow the past couple of days. Gazing at the ice-rimmed Deschutes River, he asked, "What was lit this time?"

"Woodshed. One of the boys got up to take a leak and spotted it."

Not Caleb, then. No, wait. Reid visualized where the woodshed was in relation to the cabins and lodge, and realized that Caleb could have seen this fire from his bedroom window. God damn it. Had this been a direct attack on Caleb?

Not a very effective one, he reassured himself. Caleb would have seen the flames in time to escape downstairs and out.

"Which boy?" he asked.

"Trevor."

Reid grunted; he recognized all the boys by now, but couldn't say he knew them.

"You think to do a bed count?"

"Yeah, I did. Felt like a shit, but I went cabin to cabin. Everyone was where they were supposed to be except Trev, who'd come running to get me, and his cabinmate, Diego, who'd dragged the hose over by the time I got out there."

Both men were silent for a moment, Reid thinking. Video cameras were out. They'd need too many to cover grounds that extensive.

"Damn," he concluded. "What you need are regular patrols."

"Yeah, I think Paula and I are going to start taking turns making the rounds." He gave a rough, unhappy chuckle. "Give us a couple nights, we'll be feeling like new parents constantly having to get up with a screaming baby."

"Yeah, you can't keep doing that. I might sneak out and set up surveillance some night."

"In this weather?"

"You've got some empty cabins."

"Let me know so I don't shoot you if our paths cross."

"Good enough. Hell." Reid rubbed the back of his neck and discovered his hand felt like a block of ice. "I don't like this," he said unnecessarily.

"You and me both."

"I wish you were inside the city limits."

"What would you do, send patrols by?"

Of course he couldn't do that. "All right," he said. "Let me know if anything develops."

"Glad you're here," Roger said unexpectedly and then was gone.

The foot traffic had thinned somewhat while Reid had stood out in the cold talking. Snow crunched underfoot until he was back on the sidewalk, where the smooth sole of his dress shoes skidded. To hell with this, he thought. Nobody would notice or care if he wore dark boots with a decent tread. And... this *was* March. With April to follow. How many more times was it likely to snow before the seasons turned?

He wasn't looking forward to his day. The morning plan was for him to interview a couple of applicants for the personal-assistant position. He'd been just as glad his temp apparently hadn't wanted the job; she didn't seem to be all that well-informed and he had the impression he'd scared her. He was hoping to hire internally; he felt so damn ignorant, it would be good to have a PA who knew the ropes. About once an hour, he cursed Colin McAllister for having taken his PA with him when he changed jobs.

This afternoon, he intended to take a tour of every department in the building, starting with Records in the basement. He was beginning to realize that he'd misinterpreted his "territory" when he arrived in Angel Butte. He'd felt satisfied after driving damn near every road inside the city limits, memorizing the way house numbers ran, which neighborhoods looked run-down, where the bars and taverns were, the location of parking lots that would be dark enough at night to put women walking alone to their cars in peril.

Truth was, he should have been mapping this building and the maintenance garage, where most of his responsibilities lay, so he had the slightest idea how to respond the next time someone came to him with a request.

Once the first applicant showed up, Reid blocked everything else from his mind, including both his afternoon agenda and the threat to Caleb and the shelter. His skill at compartmentalizing was useful.

This applicant currently worked in Technical Services and might be a whiz at computers and social media, but the way her eyes shied from his and her cheeks stayed rosy the whole time they talked, he could tell she was intimidated by him, too.

Irritated after he saw her out, Reid wondered—

not for the first time—why he had that effect on so many people, not only women. He was a big man, sure, but lean, not mountainous. He didn't have an alarmingly ugly face. He rarely raised his voice. So what the hell was the problem? Why couldn't he find someone like—

There she was, in his head again. Anna Grant, of course. *She* hadn't been afraid of him.

So, okay, he needed a woman like her, someone brisk, businesslike, organized and determined. And, please God, someone who knew the police department from the lowliest of supply closets to the most obscure of requisition forms.

Applicant number two turned out to be a maybe. This one was a man who at least didn't jump every time Reid shifted in his chair. He was internal only in the sense he was already a city employee, however; his current position was second assistant in the mayor's office.

Maybe, Reid thought, hiding his grin, that was why the guy wasn't scared. After all, he'd presumably gotten used to Mayor Noah Chandler, who was an ugly bastard and, rumor had it, tended to be brutally direct.

Reid thanked the man for coming, said he'd let him know and glanced at the clock. He was embarrassed at how much he looked forward to lunch.

Last week, Lieutenant Renner had told him the best place to eat lunch in Angel Butte was the Kingfisher Café, only a couple of blocks from the police station. Reid had given it a try on Friday, walking down there late enough to miss the lunch rush. The door had opened before he reached for the handle, and he'd found himself face-to-face with Anna. She had appeared as startled as he'd felt. After their dinner at the A&W, he sure as hell hadn't intended to seek her out again.

But courtesy demanded they exchange a few polite words, during which he'd asked whether she was a regular at the café.

"I come at least two or three days a week," she had admitted, then wrinkled her nose. "I know I shouldn't eat out so often, but I'm not a morning person. Half the time, I forget to pack a lunch."

"Ah. Well, maybe I'll see you here another day," he'd remarked and was unable to interpret a look that might have been wary, shy or hopeful.

Damn it, after that accidental meeting, she'd been in his head all weekend, with the result that here he was Monday morning, panting to sit down to lunch with her. Stupid thing to do or not, he wanted to talk to her.

Since finding his brother and moving to Angel Butte, Reid had never felt lonelier. He didn't understand it and sure as hell didn't like it. No matter who he was with, he felt an uncrossable distance.

The one exception was Anna. He refused to analyze why. Did it matter? She was someone he could talk out some of his confusion with, that was all.

He was going to be very disappointed if this happened to be one of the days she'd remembered to pack herself a lunch. It wasn't quite time to leave yet, though, which gave him a few minutes to brood.

He envied Mayor Chandler his view of Angel Butte, the volcanic cinder cone that rose right in the middle of town and was topped with the huge marble angel that gave the town its name. *His* office looked out on the brick wall of the jail. Not bothering to swivel his chair to look out the window, instead, he frowned, unseeing, at the closed door while he let his thoughts rebound to the shelter and the fact that a second fire had been set only a week after the first.

He briefly pondered the timing. The first fire had been set on Saturday night, the second on Sunday night. Chance? Or was there a reason their arsonist had chosen weekends?

This fire wasn't an escalation. That was a positive. The lodge or one of the occupied cabins, now, that would have been scary. This fire, too, could have been set for entertainment value. It could have been a warning…although of what, Reid couldn't figure. What worried him most was the possibility it was part of a campaign of terror. Everyone at the resort must be edgy now. No one would be sleeping well. The boys would all be watching each other. The fight Caleb had been in wouldn't be the last.

Nobody out there would feel safe.

This was where, reluctantly, he had to ask himself

whether it was a coincidence that Caleb had been the most recent arrival.

What if Caleb *was* angry enough to light the world on fire? Or what if this was a campaign not to terrorize, but to make Reid believe he should take his brother home to live with him?

To keep him safe.

Or—and this was the most unwelcome speculation of all—was there any possibility that their father *had* found his runaway youngest son? Had Reid screwed up big-time by moving to Angel Butte? Could he absolutely swear that when driving out to the old resort a couple times a week, he hadn't been followed?

"Damn," he murmured.

He hadn't let Caleb know how much that phone call from their father had shaken him. In the nearly twenty years since he had seen Dean Sawyer, Reid had tried to think about him as little as possible. He didn't like knowing how much he resembled his father physically. Sometimes he'd stare at himself in a mirror with an incredulity he had to shake off. But he couldn't have so much as described his father's voice.

But the minute he heard it on the phone, the hairs on his arms had stood on end as if he'd come in contact with a bare electrical wire. The feeling that rushed over him had been bad. He'd been thrown back, as if all the years since had never happened. Dad had just walked in the door, and Reid could see that he was mad about something. Could have been anything—some imagined slight at work, a detective junior to him getting a headline for a press-worthy arrest, an asshole who'd cut him off on the drive home. Didn't matter what, unless the "anything" had to do with Reid directly. Say, the school counselor had called and said, "We're concerned about the number of bruises your son has had recently." Those days were the worst.

By fifteen, Reid had been as tall as his father; he thought he must be a couple of inches taller now that he'd reached his full height. But then he'd been skinny, like Caleb was now. Unable to stand up to a muscular, angry man.

He shook off the recollection, if not the shadow of the memory, of blows falling.

The day he'd called, the first words out of his father's mouth had been "So you're a cop like your old man."

"Not like you," he'd said flatly, just as he had to Caleb. "I'm the kind of cop who should have investigated Mom's death."

"I didn't have anything to do with it," Dean had snarled.

"Sure you did. I was young, not deaf and blind."

"You ever make an allegation like that, you'll find yourself in court and I'll take you for every cent you make in the next fifty years."

He had managed to sound bored. "Is there a point to this call?"

And that was when he'd demanded to know whether Reid had snatched Caleb.

It wasn't even a lie to say no. Helping the boy get away was a whole other story.

But mocking his father…that wasn't a good idea. It was bound to have made him suspicious.

Shit, Reid thought again. *I need to find out whether he could be in Angel Butte.*

His gaze strayed to the time at the bottom of his computer monitor.

Yeah, he'd have to make a few calls…but not now. Right now, he was going to wander down to the Kingfisher Café and hope to feed his unexpected craving for another person's company.

ANNA TOLD HERSELF she'd chosen to sit where she did because the light was better if she ended up pulling out her book to read while she ate. *Not* so she could keep an eye on the door. If Reid happened to eat here again today, what were the chances he'd be alone? He'd consider the lunch hour to be a good time to conduct business.

But she remembered the way he'd asked *You come often?* And every time the door opened, she glanced that way.

The waitress was taking her order when he came in. Alone. He scanned the entire restaurant in one lightning sweep, analyzing and dismissing everyone he saw, until his gaze reached her and stopped.

She felt as if a heat-seeking missile had just locked on target.

He lifted an eyebrow, the slightest of quirks, but it was enough to ask a question. Throat closing, Anna inclined her head toward the chair opposite her. He smiled, ignored the hostess as if she wasn't there and crossed the room to Anna's table.

"May I join you?" he asked in that deep, velvety voice.

The waitress turned, startled. "Oh!"

"Of course you may," Anna said, then, to the waitress, "Why don't you hold off on my order until Captain Sawyer decides what he wants?"

"Yes. Um, of course." Plump and tattooed, the young waitress retreated in disarray.

He pulled out the chair across from Anna, immediately making her feel crowded. This table beneath the window was tiny, sized for two who knew each other really well. His knees bumped hers, and he murmured, "Sorry."

She shifted to give him room. He made no move to open the menu she handed him. Instead, they looked at each other.

Deeper than usual lines creased his forehead and carved crevasses between his dark slash of eyebrows.

"Something's wrong," she said slowly.

"What?" He sounded startled.

"You look… I don't know. Disturbed."

He stared at her. "Hasn't been the best of days,"

he said finally. Now he did pick up the menu, but she sensed he was doing it as much for camouflage as anything else.

She waited until he'd apparently made a decision. Then she said, "Is it Caleb?"

The lines on his face became deeper. "Partly," he said gruffly.

"What's the other part?"

Now both eyebrows rose. "Anybody ever tell you you're a nosy woman?"

She grinned. "I consider that a compliment. I wouldn't be any good at my job if I wasn't."

"Speaking of..."

She raised her eyebrows, but he'd broken off at the waitress's approach. Once he'd given his order, he said abruptly, "It's the job."

"Isn't it...well, similar to what you were doing? I gathered from the article in the newspaper that you were supervising quite a few people at your last job."

He grimaced, more expression than he usually allowed himself. "Supervising, I'm comfortable with. On the investigations side, I'm not used to always being one step removed. I get the feeling I'll rarely be going out to a crime scene, for example. I'll be sitting behind the desk nodding while my underlings report to me."

"You mean, you won't be doing real police work."

"Right." The trace of discomfiture lingered on his face. "That'll take an adjustment, but I can make it.

When it comes to the support-services part of my job, though, I feel like a fish out of water. What do I know about fleet and facility maintenance, for God's sake? Did you know we have communication technicians? I've got to tell you, they talk right over my head." He tugged his hair as if he wanted to tear it out. "Thank God Personnel and Human Resources are handled by the city."

"You must have known you'd be heading those departments when you took the job," she said tentatively.

His grunt was half laugh. "Sure I did. I just thought I'd be accountable for their budgets, hiring or firing heads of departments." He shrugged. "I didn't know they'd expect me to understand what they actually *do*."

Anna wondered if he knew how plaintive he sounded, but suspected he did and hated it.

"So, how are you handling it? Dodging phone calls?"

This rough laugh was closer to the real thing. "Something like that."

Their orders arrived, but neither reached immediately for their forks. "Is there any reason you can't admit ignorance and say, 'Educate me?'"

"Sure, if it was just one area. But across the board? I don't even work on my own car. Who am I to decide whether we ought to be performing the regular maintenance on the vehicles in our fleet every three thousand miles versus four thousand, or, hey, five…? And I'm competent on a computer, but do you know how fast technology is changing?"

She frowned at him. "Yes, but that's why you employ experts in every department. You *can't* know everything. Anyway…" She hesitated. This probably sounded stupidly elementary, but she decided to say it anyway. "I'll bet you're good at research. Why not look at each problem the way you would some aspect of a crime you're investigating? Haven't you become an expert, however fleetingly, on some esoteric field because it was entwined in a crime?"

She couldn't read his stare at all until he nodded slightly. "Yeah. I have. I know more about health regulations on tattoo parlors than you'd want to hear, and the handling of bodies in funeral homes. Not to mention midwifery—that one turned out to be a murder—and appropriate practices in pest control." His eyes crinkled with a real smile. "Thank you."

"Surely you've been going at it already with that attitude," she said, wondering if he was humoring her.

But he shook his head. "I've been discovering how much I dislike feeling out of my comfort zone."

"You look so—" She tried to stop herself, but that eyebrow of his insisted she finish. "I don't know. Untouchable. Invincible." Not a word she could ever remember using before, but it seemed to fit.

"Invincible," Reid echoed in a strange tone. "We can try, but is achieving that possible?"

"I…don't know." Was he saying he wanted to

make himself impervious to all human failings? Or the tumult of human emotions? "It wouldn't have occurred to me to go for it."

"No," he said. "Not you."

"What's that supposed to mean?" she demanded.

His mouth curved. "Nothing that deserves your indignation. Only that…I'm beginning to think you're always willing to care."

"*Beginning* to think?" Now she was indignant.

He held up a hand. "Pax. I've met plenty of social workers who are just going through the motions, not throwing themselves in heart and soul."

"Well, I'm not sure I do that."

Reid only smiled and began to eat. After a moment, Anna did the same.

He started talking, telling her a few anecdotes that had led to his awareness of how deep and wide his ignorance was, and when he asked about her week, she told a few stories in return.

She liked listening to him, and the way his attention never wavered from her when she talked. What she didn't do was make the mistake of thinking this happenstance lunch meant their relationship was going anywhere. He'd made it clear enough he had no intention of letting that happen.

She *was* nosy, though, so she asked over coffee how things were going with his brother.

"No better." A muscle in his jaw twitched. "I'm following your advice and hanging in there."

"Good." She smiled at him. "At least he's taking your calls. If he really wanted to reject you, he wouldn't."

Something fleeting crossed his face. As usual, she was unable to interpret it.

"He...dodges me when he can," he said. "Speaking of dodging."

Had they been? Oh—departmental queries.

"You said you don't have any kind of relationship with your father," she said, remembering, and then discovered how completely he could close down.

"No."

She'd never heard a word uttered so impassively, while conveying emotions so bleak. All she could do was nod.

"How's Yancey doing in the new foster home?" Reid asked in an obvious change of subject. He hadn't so much as moved a muscle, but she somehow knew he was itching to be gone.

"Really well." She finished her coffee and reached for her wallet from the messenger bag sitting at her feet. "Carol insists he's musically gifted and has put him in piano lessons. Apparently, he played the trombone back in fifth and sixth grades, and now he may join the middle school jazz band."

"Ah. Clever woman." He barely glanced at the waitress, but she veered toward the cash register.

"Carol has a gift for, well..."

"Finding out what other people's gifts are?"

"Exactly."

The waitress presented their bills. Reid tried to

take both. Anna said, "No," and handed hers with a twenty-dollar bill back to the waitress. "I don't need change," she said pleasantly and tucked her wallet back into her bag. When she stood, he did, too, and walked out with her. Fortunately, she'd been lucky enough to find a parking spot right in front. She used her remote to unlock before looking at him. "Thanks for your company over lunch."

"I'm the one who owes you the thanks." This time his voice was a little huskier than usual. "You give good advice."

"My gift."

"Maybe," he said. She passed him to step off the curb, and he stopped her with a hand on her arm. "Any chance you'd like to meet about the same time here on Wednesday?"

Anna went utterly still. "So I can give you more advice?"

"Because...I like you." He frowned a little, his hand dropping from her arm. He stepped back. "If you're not here—" and now he sounded completely indifferent "—I'll get the message. Have a good day, Anna." And he walked away, leaving her stunned, even though *I like you* wasn't exactly the stuff of soaring romance.

After a moment, she circled her Toyota and got in.

REID DECIDED TO make the call to the Spokane P.D. right after lunch, before he began wandering the departments under his authority.

"Sergeant Sawyer has today off," the voice on the phone told Reid woodenly. "I can switch you to his voice mail if you want to leave a message."

Sitting at his desk staring at a blinking red light indicating an incoming call waiting, Reid thought, *Sure. I want to leave a message on the voice mail that Dad can access from anywhere. Say, Angel Butte.* That would answer all his questions.

"No. Uh, what about Mike Reardon? Is he in?"

"He retired last year."

Retired? Well, damn. Reid adjusted his thinking. Yeah, some of Dad's cronies had been graying even back then. Stood to reason they were getting up to retirement age now.

"What about Bob Sarringer?"

There was a little silence. The guy was polite enough not to ask whether this was old-home week. "Let me check." He came back in a moment. "Lieutenant Sarringer is in."

A familiar voice came on. "This really Reid? Dean's kid?"

"That's me."

"You've got a nerve calling. You know what you did to him?"

A hot flash of temper seared Reid's usual composure. "I know what he did to me."

"What's that supposed to mean?" his father's old friend blustered.

"You were around. You heard the rumors. The

allegations. And you're surprised I lit out? And, what a shocker, his younger son did the same?"

"He was hard on you. That's all. He wanted you to be half as tough as him."

"You have any idea how many broken bones I had? How many implants and bridges I have in my mouth to replace teeth he knocked out? For Lee's sake, I sure as hell hope your idea of raising 'em tough wasn't the same."

The silence felt stricken. Reid had been friends with Lee Sarringer. He'd never had the guts to ask whether Lee's dad knocked him around, too.

"You being straight with me?" the lieutenant asked.

"Yes." Suddenly impatient, Reid said, "I'm trying to find out if Dad's in town. I'm told he's off today."

"He's taken some time. I think he's looking for Caleb— Wait, do you know where he is?" Suspicion had crept into Sarringer's voice.

Reid managed a natural-sounding snort. "I don't care where Caleb is, as long as he found a good bolt hole. I didn't even know I *had* a brother until recently. Dad called and threatened me. I'd just like to know if he's completely gone off his rocker and is hunting me, or whether he's actually showing up for work mornings and acting more sane than he sounded."

"He's taken a couple of long weekends," his father's crony finally admitted. He sounded shaken. "Like I said, he's looking for his boy. He didn't say anything about you. I didn't even know if you were still alive."

"Oh, it turns out Dad's known where I was for years. I took a new job a couple of weeks ago, and he knew all about it. I admit, recently I've had a few moments of wondering if Daddy isn't watching me. Don't much care for that feeling of having the hair rising on my neck, if you know what I mean."

Sarringer was a cop; he knew. But he had his loyalties, too, even if Reid had just damaged their underpinnings. He asked what Reid did for a living, and they had a reasonably civil chat.

When Reid ended the call, there it was, that prickling feeling on his nape.

The drive from Spokane to Angel Butte wasn't that long. His father could have set both fires. Maybe swooping in to recover his youngest boy and getting the Hales shut down wasn't enough for him. If he'd figured out that this was where Reid, too, had gone to ground all those years ago, he might like the idea of a punishment that, in his eyes, fit the crime. A little psychological torture might be just his style.

And if, in the end, some of the boys who lived there got torched, too, he'd figure they were getting what was coming to them.

Reid swore out loud.

CALEB SWUNG THE ax and watched the round of pine split in half. Man, his shoulders ached. Hearing voices, he immediately positioned one of the pieces and swung again. Truong and Diego appeared around the corner of the lodge. Working in silence, they filled their arms with another load of the firewood he had split. Instead of carrying it to the woodshed, they'd been ordered to start a pile under a sheltering eave on the other side of the lodge. Not until they were out of sight around the lodge did they start talking again.

So much for Diego being his friend, Caleb thought.

He stretched and groaned. It pissed him off that Roger was driving them all so hard. It was almost spring. They wouldn't need most of this firewood until next winter. Why not let it dry, and then they could split and stack it on a warm summer day instead of a shitty day like this, when each piece fell into slush and his feet were both wet and cold? Big brother hadn't mentioned his perfect sanctuary included forced labor.

In the days since the second fire, things had gotten really lousy. Mostly, everyone was looking at *him*. TJ was second in contention, no surprise—they were the two newest, and neither of them had a roommate, which supposedly made it easier for either to sneak out whenever they wanted. As if Roger and Paula weren't listening for them. And the front door of the lodge was heavy and thudded when it closed, while the hinges on the kitchen door squealed like a girl who'd just seen her best friend after a two-hour separation. And then there was the fact that TJ and him, they heard each *other* whenever they had to get up to piss.

Like last night. However quietly TJ opened his bedroom door, Caleb roused enough to notice. He'd waited to hear either the bathroom door or the toilet flushing, but instead there had been a long silence followed by...a creak. He knew that creak. It was the third step from the top. You couldn't avoid it without skipping the stair altogether. Tensing, he'd waited. Was that the back door? What happened to the squeal?

Wide-awake by then, Caleb had gotten up and peered out the window, but hadn't seen anything. No dark shape slipping around the side of the lodge, no orange glow of fire. He had thought about waking Paula or Roger, but TJ might have had some other reason for wanting to go out. Or maybe he had gone downstairs to the kitchen to get something to eat, or wanted to go online without anyone knowing. Things were bad enough between them already. Caleb wouldn't have admitted it to anyone else, but he was a little bit afraid of TJ, who was older, bigger and meaner than him.

It had to be an hour before he heard the soft sound of the bedroom door across the hall closing again. No squeak on the stairs. He'd remembered to step over that one this time.

Caleb had stayed awake for quite a while longer anyway, expecting…something. He'd seen the square of his window turning lighter before he'd dropped off again.

This morning, the first thing he'd done after going downstairs was to experimentally open the back door. No squeal. Heart pounding, he'd closed it and turned, only to find Roger right behind him.

"Somebody oiled the hinges," Caleb blurted.

Roger stepped past him and opened and closed it a couple of times. Then he studied the hinges, finally touching them. When he withdrew his hand, Caleb saw the thin streak of fresh oil on his fingertip. His expression when he looked at Caleb was hard.

"You're right. Somebody did."

Feeling sick, Caleb didn't say anything.

"You knew," the older man said.

"No, I—" A lump seemed to be jammed down his throat. "I just…opened it."

"Caleb, if you know something…"

"I don't!" he had yelled. "You think I'm stupid? I *want* to get burned alive?"

Roger had studied his face for a good minute before his jaw flexed and he'd nodded abruptly. "All right, son. Breakfast is on the table."

Halfway through the meal, Roger had said suddenly, "Thanks to whoever oiled the hinges on the back door."

Heads jerked up, including Paula's. Watching surreptitiously, Caleb saw only surprise or indifference. TJ had kept eating, his expression flattest of all. Caleb had gone back to his breakfast without looking at TJ again.

Now he wondered if Roger would call Reid and tell him about the door hinges. Whether Reid, too, was beginning to wonder about him, Caleb.

Filled with turmoil, Caleb swung the ax and then again when one of the two pieces remained standing. If TJ was doing all this crap, why hadn't *he* pointed his finger at Caleb?

Right now, everybody probably figured he and TJ were in it together. The fact that they detested each other…they could be faking it. Good theory, he thought bitterly.

He set the ax down and peeled off one of his gloves to inspect his stinging palms. Damn. One of the blisters had burst and it now seeped bloody pus.

"You'd better go put something on that."

Caleb started. He hadn't heard Diego approaching, but he was right there, looking over his shoulder.

Caleb shrugged and pulled the glove back on. Like a bandage was going to help. Without a word, he grasped another round and set it in place, then reached for the ax. Diego backed up, and Caleb swung.

Thud.

One thing you could say for this wood, he decided. As green as it was, it might not burn even if it was *saturated* with gasoline.

Good thing, since it was being stacked right underneath *his* bedroom window.

CHAPTER FIVE

ANNA PUT ON her boots while Reid pulled the skis and poles from the cargo space of his SUV and laid the skis flat on the snow. It was Saturday, clear and cold for the last weekend of March. Although the Nordic Center was still open, they'd agreed to try a trail she knew at a higher elevation, in Forest Service land. She'd been glad when they pulled in to see another couple of vehicles ahead of them. Untracked powder could be fun, but the last snowfalls definitely didn't qualify as powder. Slogging through a layer of heavy new snow sounded like hard work.

When they had lunch on Wednesday, she'd suggested this outing. She still didn't know exactly what he wanted from her, but he wanted *something*. Maybe just to be friends. She'd been intending to get her skis out once or twice more before real spring arrived anyway.

Reid's eyebrows had twitched, and then he'd said thoughtfully, "I haven't been in a long time."

"Do you have equipment?" she'd asked.

"No, but I've been meaning to buy it anyway." He'd nodded. "I'll do that tomorrow."

"Should be like riding a bike," she'd told him and had been shocked by his laugh. Oh lord, what it did to his face.

"Hoping I'll take a dive?" he'd asked, and then she'd laughed, too, because, okay, she might get some secret pleasure from watching Captain Cool floundering in the snow.

Watching now as he stamped into his bindings, tugged a black fleece hat onto his head and gripped his poles, Anna had a suspicion she'd been right in the first place. Skiing was one of those once-learned, never-forgotten skills. She was taking pleasure instead from looking at him. The stretchy, close-fitting pants clung to the long muscles in his legs and outlined a hard butt, presented when he bent to test his binding.

"Ready?" he asked, and she suppressed her sigh.

"Yep."

The track showed the passing of quite a few skiers before them. Initially, they climbed, using a cross-hatch technique. By the time they topped the rise, Anna's thighs were already feeling the burn and she was almost too warm in her close-fitted SmartWool jacket. Ugh. She hadn't been getting enough exercise. She'd either better start hitting the gym more often or make herself run, miserable weather or no.

Of course, Reid moved fast and effortlessly. *She* would have taken the hill at a slower pace, but pride wouldn't let her lag behind.

Reid stopped at the top, his head turning as he

took in the deserted white landscape around them. Above them arched a crystal clear blue sky. Any other skiers were hidden in the trees. From here they had a view north toward Mount Bachelor and the Three Sisters. The surrounding forest was silent, the evergreen branches bowed with a heavy weight of snow.

"Look." By instinct, Anna kept her voice low. She pointed the tip of her pole toward some animal tracks. Tiny ones.

"Hare, I'll bet." His face had relaxed amazingly. He inhaled deeply and with obvious delight. "God, it's good not to breathe in smog."

"Of course, it's probably eighty degrees in L.A.," she felt compelled to point out. "You could be running on the beach."

"True," he said, "but I'd gotten so I hardly ever did. Not like I could afford to live in Newport Beach on a cop's salary."

"You weren't a surfer."

His teeth flashed white in another of those rakish grins. "I took it up for a while." He shrugged. "You get busy, don't make time."

"Well, I try to keep making time to ski," she said. "This is more fun than killing myself on the elliptical at the health club."

"Yeah, it is." He gestured ahead. "Ladies first."

"You go first. You weigh more than I do. You'll run me down."

Besides—she'd rather look at *his* ass than know he was looking at hers.

He chuckled and pushed off, almost immediately bending to decrease wind resistance and go faster. Anna was right behind him, loving the exhilaration of the smooth glide, the rush of chilly air, the absolute silence but for the *shush* of their skis on snow.

They didn't talk much in the next couple of hours, only exchanging brief greetings when they passed two men returning on the same track. With his sharp eyes, Reid spotted some elk huddled beneath the branches of ponderosa pines. A hawk soared above them, searching for unwary hares or rodents.

Eventually they, in turn, decided to go back the way they had come rather than taking what she knew was a longer loop that would eventually return them to the parking lot, but add another couple of hours to the trip. She had an appointment this afternoon for a visit to a potential foster home, and Reid had said he was going to work, too.

During the last long glide to the parking lot, she realized she was tired but also happy, laughing out loud as she skidded to a stop and caught herself on the side panel of his Expedition.

"That was great!" she exclaimed.

He slid more deftly to a stop beside her and grinned. "Yeah, it was."

A ruddy glow from the cold slashed across his sharp cheekbones. Anna had the sudden, disconcerting realization that his eyes were the same deep green as the pines.

And she was staring.

Flushing—hoping it wouldn't show when her face was probably already red—she bent to get out of her bindings. When she straightened, he hadn't moved. He was watching her, no longer smiling. A couple of lines between his eyebrows had deepened, as if he was disconcerted by something.

He reached out and touched her nose with one gloved finger. "Rudolph."

Oh, great. Her nose glowed. Well, probably her cheeks, too, but *she* didn't have the same kind of elegant cheekbones.

"I have to be careful," she heard herself telling him. "My skin doesn't like too much sun, too much cold, most brands of soap or suntan lotion. I either flake or get a rash."

"It's sensitive." His voice was low, husky, his eyes intent on her face. "Soft."

Oh, God. The way he'd said the last word was sexier than a touch. Warmth flooded her, low in her abdomen.

"Anna."

She couldn't look away from him now. She wanted him to kiss her more than she could remember wanting anything in a long time.

His head bent slowly, either because he was giving her time to retreat or because he himself was hesitant. She quit blinking, only stared into his eyes.

And then his lips touched hers. They were cold, but his puff of breath warmed her face.

A sound seemed to vibrate in his chest, and he tilted his head to fit their mouths more closely together. Anna reached out and gripped the sleek fabric of his jacket, her knuckles bumping something hard. Was he carrying a *pistol* under there? How was it she hadn't noticed? But right this second, she couldn't bring herself to care. Her eyes closed and she reveled in the astonishing feel of him nipping at her lips, his tongue stroking the seam until she opened her mouth and let him in. And then it only got better. She wasn't cold anymore. All she felt was the stroke of his tongue, the scrape of his jaw, his big, still-gloved hand kneading her nape, the pressure of his muscled body against hers.

When he finally lifted his head, his eyes burned into hers. Anna was grateful for the bulk of the SUV behind her, given how wobbly her knees were and how jellylike her thigh muscles felt. Although, okay, that might be because of the unaccustomed exercise.

Only then did she hear voices and realize they were no longer alone in the parking lot. He must have stopped kissing her because he heard them first.

"You're carrying a gun," she blurted.

His lashes veiled his eyes and he let her go. "I usually do," he said, sidestepping away from her on his skis.

"But…why?"

"Habit." Face suddenly expressionless, he bent over and released his bindings, picking up his skis and shaking off loose snow.

Anna followed suit while he unlocked the rear of the Expedition. Their equipment stowed inside, he opened the passenger door for her and put a hand under her elbow to help boost her in. She was embarrassed to need the help. She really *was* in decent shape. It was only that her pride hadn't let her suggest they slow down.

He started the engine right away, then unzipped his jacket and stripped off his hat, tossing it onto the backseat. Anna began to shiver, waiting for the icy air coming out of the vents to warm. Unlike him, she wasn't willing to so much as lower the zipper on her coat.

Neither of them said anything. When she sneaked a peek sideways, it was to see him frowning straight ahead through the windshield. Why had her asking about his weapon annoyed him?

Or…was he sorry to have kissed her?

A band closed around her chest. Of course that was it. He didn't want to be attracted to her. She wasn't even sure he wanted to *like* her.

The knowledge felt…right, if unwelcome. Was it something about her? Surely he had friends. He couldn't have reached what had to be his mid-thirties without having a number of lovers. So…what was so wrong about her?

She clasped her still-gloved hands tightly together

and bent her head, focusing on them. The silence felt stifling.

The first warmth was seeping into the air when, with her peripheral vision, Anna saw him wrench his gloves off. The movement almost violent, he shoved the gearshift into Reverse. A moment later they were backing in a wide sweep, then following the tracks out of the small trailhead parking lot to the road.

Five minutes passed. Her shivers slowly abated.

"Better?" he asked.

"What?" Her head turned.

"Are you still cold?"

"Oh. No. I just felt chilled for a minute. I'm okay." Cautiously, she took off one glove, then the other, discovering the interior of the Expedition was warm enough now.

"Good."

Several more minutes passed.

"Does it bother you, knowing I carry a gun?" he asked abruptly.

She opened her mouth to say an automatic, polite no, but paused to consider. Did it? "No," she said finally, slowly. "I mean, I know you do on the job. I just didn't realize you had one today until I—" *Touched it.* "And then I wondered why you do." Before he could answer, she said, "It can't be simply habit. You must think you're going to need it."

"I don't think that. I've never yet drawn a weapon when I was off the clock." His frown had deepened, although he didn't look so much irritated as though he was brooding about what he was saying. "I suppose it's occupational paranoia. I've seen so much bad stuff happen to people at unlikely times and places—" His shoulders moved, half shrug, half discomfort. "I want to be ready."

"Do you keep it beside the bed at night?"

His gaze flicked sidelong. "Yeah."

"What if, well, you have children? You'd have to lock it up then, wouldn't you?"

"Of course I would." His jaw seemed to work. "I'm not sure I see myself as a father, though."

"Because of yours."

His breath gusted out. "Yeah. You are what you've been taught. You and I both know abused kids become abusers."

"Some do," she agreed. "Mostly ones who aren't self-aware. If you know what you *don't* want to be, you can guard against it."

"Do you actually know anyone who can prove your theory?" He sounded deeply cynical. "From my end, I see nothing but a never-ending cycle."

"I do know people," she said quietly. After a moment she lifted her chin. "I know myself."

He shot a look at her. "You said your mother wasn't abusive."

Oh, God, why had she opened her big mouth. "She wasn't."

After a minute, he said, "But someone was."

"A foster parent."

She watched him absorb that. "Were you there long?" he asked.

"A year and a half. Although I guess that isn't the same as spending your entire childhood with an abusive parent."

"How many foster homes did you have?" he asked.

Startled, she met his eyes when he turned his head unexpectedly, his gaze intense. "Um…six, I think. No, maybe seven. Plus a few receiving homes in there."

"That's lousy." He sounded angry. "Why so many? Do people just lose interest?"

She could answer this one as a social worker, not as a wounded child. "They do sometimes. Or they move out of state, or they have a baby and don't want a troubled older kid around. Sometimes it's just, well, not a good match. Or the caseworker suspects something is wrong."

"Like?"

"We had an instance recently where we discovered a woman was denying the foster girl the same quality of food her own daughter was eating. It turned out she hadn't been buying the girl clothes, either. She had one good outfit she had to put on whenever the caseworker was expected. Her drawers were just about empty."

"The woman was doing it for the money," he said with disgust.

"Yes. And sometimes we find out kids are being

punished inappropriately. The people might lack basic parenting skills, or they didn't understand what they were getting into with kids that came to them with so many problems."

"You're excusing them," he said flatly.

"No." Tension simmered in her, even talking about those instances. She herself had uncovered one especially egregious case of abuse, and after she'd removed the kids from the home and settled them in a temporary shelter, she had gone home herself and fallen to her knees in front of her toilet to throw up. Somehow she'd held in the nausea that long, but she'd had terrible nightmares that night and wondered why she'd chosen an occupation that so often reawakened her worst memories.

Like I had a choice. A vocation, remember?

She could tell Reid was still waiting for an explanation. "Understanding why something happens isn't the same thing as excusing. I *have* to understand why things go wrong if I'm going to weed out applicants who seem enthusiastic but can't be trusted with kids, or place children in the home that will be best for them."

"I get that," he conceded. He was frowning, though. "Do you have any foster parents who grew up in abusive homes themselves?"

"Yes. Several. One who has cigarette burns all over his back. He's the kindest, gentlest man I've ever met."

"You're friends." His tone was impossible to read.

"Insofar as it's possible, when I have to keep some distance as a supervisor."

He drove in silence for a few minutes. "I look like my father," he said out of the blue. "Gives me a chill sometimes, when I see my face in a mirror."

Didn't he know what an extraordinarily handsome man he was? But, no—to him, that didn't matter. He saw a face he hated—and, in that complicated way abused children think of their parents, possibly loved, too.

"I don't think appearance is one of the more important things we get from our parents," she said very carefully. "Quite often kids don't look much like either of their parents, or they take after one but not the other. But musical or athletic ability, a sense of humor, a gift for words, a tendency to like to think twice before speaking or, in contrast, to blurt out every little thought, those will be there anyway."

"I could make an argument about nature versus nourish."

She had relaxed enough to laugh. "You could."

They were entering the outskirts of Angel Butte, and traffic had picked up on the slushy roads. Reid drove with such relaxed competence, she guessed it was second nature.

Sneaking a look, she saw the moment his face tightened again.

"Physically, Caleb took after our father, too."

He might be hiding it, but she could hear how disturbed he was by what he'd said anyway.

"You could say he looks like you instead."

He opened his mouth, then closed it.

"What were you thinking?"

Reid grunted. "I was going to ask if that was any better."

"You look so confident," she said after a minute. "I'd never have guessed…"

His fingers flexed on the steering wheel. "That I'm a mess, like anyone else?"

"No, I knew that." The words out, she heard herself in horror. Dear lord. Had she actually *said* that? "I mean—"

To her astonishment, he was laughing. "No, don't spoil it. I like knowing you stick your foot in it sometimes like the rest of us mortals."

"Thanks," she mumbled, cheeks burning.

"Although I have to ask." A smile still played at his mouth, but he sounded thoughtful. "How did you guess?"

Did he really want to know? But Anna suspected it was too late to be mealymouthed. "You're so good at suppressing emotion," she said straight out. "Too good. Most of the time, when you smile, it's only your mouth smiling, not *you*. It's like…you're faking it."

He wasn't smiling anymore. In fact, his expression was so unreadable—no, his face was so *lacking* expression—that she thought she'd offended him.

"I am," he said abruptly. "I thought I was damn good at it."

"You are. I've had a lot of practice."

He made a sound she couldn't quite interpret.

They were only a couple of blocks from her town house, and she didn't know whether to be relieved she'd be able to escape, or to wish she had longer to somehow redeem herself.

Neither of them said another word until he turned into the alley that ran behind the block of town houses where he'd picked her up. The garages were accessed from the alley rather than the street, and she kept her ski equipment on a rack on one wall of the garage.

When he braked, she reached for the door handle, but paused. "I'm sorry."

"Sorry?" He looked at her, his eyes darker than usual. "You don't have any reason to be. I prefer hearing the truth. I've known since I met you I was risking having you see right through me."

"Is that why—" Oh, ulp. There she went again, not stopping to think before she opened her mouth. It wasn't like her.

His eyebrows climbed. "Why what?"

"Um. That time we had coffee. I don't know what I said, but you just…turned off."

"Ah." It was obvious he was debating how much to say. "I guess it was something like that. You sent up a flare for me."

Her heart beat so fast she felt a little light-headed. "But you keep coming back."

"Yeah." Slow and husky, his voice made her tingle. "I...can't seem to help myself."

Her lips parted, but she didn't know what to say.

He never looked away from her when he unfastened first his seat belt, then hers. Finally, he leaned toward her, his mouth catching hers in a quick kiss that seemed almost angry.

Before she could know what expression was on his face, he'd presented her with his back as he opened his door and climbed out. Anna's fingernails bit into her palms as she closed her eyes for a moment before getting out, too.

After she used the remote to open the garage, Reid carried in her skis and poles and hung them in place.

Whatever he'd been feeling, he had succeeded in pushing it down out of sight. "I enjoyed today," he said.

"I did, too."

This smile was one he didn't mean. She wondered how exposed he felt, knowing she could tell.

He kissed her cheek lightly, said, "Hope your afternoon goes well," and left.

She stood in the garage, waiting for the door to roll down, as she heard the sound of his SUV receding.

At least he hadn't lied and said he'd call.

FEELING RESTLESS AND claustrophobic in the small cabin at the old resort, Reid decided to take a walk around. He'd been in place out here at the youth shelter since a little after ten, once darkness had fallen. His watch told him midnight neared. The witching hour, time for him to be out and about.

He'd lied to Anna this afternoon; after leaving her, he'd gone straight home. Usually he didn't have much trouble falling asleep on demand; over the years, he'd worked erratic enough hours, and he'd learned to sleep when he could. This was an exception. Unsettled from talking to her and from thinking about that kiss—no, damn it, those kisses—it took him longer than usual to force himself to let go enough to drop off.

He'd gotten enough sleep, though, to be fine through the night. Since he'd slipped into the vacant cabin, boredom and cold had been more of an issue than drowsiness. This was the third night in the past week he'd managed to spend staking out the place, and he hadn't been spotted yet by any of the boys. Tonight, as usual, he had parked in the driveway of a neighboring house, currently unoccupied and for sale, and slipped through the woods to the cabin he and Roger had decided offered the best view of the old resort. By the time he got here, most of the boys had already been in their cabins, although they did some hooting and calling to each other from porch to porch. A couple of them didn't leave the lodge until after midnight, letting themselves out the back door. He hadn't needed the porch light to identify the two he knew were roommates. Apollo was black, and Isaac's beaky nose was distinctive when seen in silhouette. They talked as they walked past the cabin where Reid sat hidden, but their voices were quiet and he couldn't make out anything they said.

Roger, he knew, considered Apollo and Issac to be the least likely to be responsible for setting the fires. Isaac had been here for three years and would be turning eighteen in June, at which point he'd take his GED, then the SAT or ACT, and start applying to colleges. He was the math genius, Reid recalled. Apollo had been here for two years and was a steady, mature kid who'd stayed in touch with an older sister who hadn't been able to protect him from their father but had tried. Their longevity was a good argument in favor of both.

Problem was, most of the other boys had also lived here for a year or longer. Palmer and Diego had been here ten months, TJ five and Caleb just over three months.

"TJ's attitude is the worst," Paula had admitted, but reluctantly. She didn't like to say anything bad about any of "her" kids.

He thought he had to be the one to say this. "Caleb isn't going out of his way to make himself liked, either."

"No, he isn't," she agreed, "but that's normal

under the circumstances." She'd given him a wry smile. "You weren't loaded with charm your first few months here, either."

Reid had allowed himself a smile. "Was I ever loaded with charm?"

"I suspect most women would say you are." With a laugh, Paula had kissed his cheek. "You have your moments."

He had thought about Anna immediately. Reid doubted she would describe him as charming. Even now that she had been frank about seeing beneath his surface, he had no idea what she thought of him. Of how much she actually did see.

Obviously, a whole lot more than he'd have liked her to. All he could hope was that it wasn't as much as he feared. The truth was, he sometimes wondered who he really was, deep down. He'd hate to have to ask someone else to find out.

While he waited for all the lights to go off, he jiggled in place to keep warm. He forced himself back to business and mulled over what he knew about the boys who lived here.

Diego sounded like another good kid, always friendly and welcoming to newcomers. His roommate, Trevor, was a little more of an enigma, according to Paula. Reading between the lines of what she would and wouldn't say, Reid guessed Trevor might have been sexually molested, which could screw a kid up even more than physical brutality did.

Jose, Truong and Palmer hadn't taken on a lot of

personality in Reid's mind yet. Neither Paula nor
Roger wanted to see any of them as being twisted
enough to threaten the existence of the shelter with
arson. The only other kid they had grudgingly
agreed harbored some real anger was Damon, the
bullish-looking boy Caleb had fought with.

So far, the Hales were refusing to give Reid the
full names of their resident boys. While respecting
their reasons, he was becoming impatient. What
would it take to push them into admitting that the
boys' backgrounds needed to be investigated?

Reid stepped carefully as he crossed the small
porch, having already discovered that one board
creaked. A faint smile crossed his face. Maybe he'd
ask Caleb if the stair near the top in the lodge still
did the same.

Moving quietly in the darkness, he patrolled as
far as the last cabin to the west, then retraced his
steps. Twice he froze in place, once when a toilet
flushed, a second time when he heard a thump. It
was followed a moment later by a light coming on
inside one of the cabins. Through the small-paned
window, he saw a boy—Truong, he thought—lift
a glass to his mouth and take a drink. A moment
later, the light went out. Reassured by the continu-
ing silence, Reid resumed his rounds.

Down to the end of the line of cabins, the last several decrepit enough Roger was thinking of demol-
ishing them. The moonlight picked out the charred
hole in the roof of the damaged one, and the black

fan on the side where fire had burned through the dry old logs.

Reid had turned toward the lodge when he heard the muffled thud of a vehicle door closing. Not right out in front, but not far away, either. At a neighbor's? Could be, but it also might be out at the road.

His hand slid toward the butt of his weapon— "Habit," he heard himself saying—as he ran around one side of the lodge, cutting between it and the half-burned woodshed.

He stopped at the corner and scanned the front of the property, his gaze moving carefully over the black hulk of Roger's truck and several rusting pickups and cars Roger had the boys working on, the vast porch with its deeper darkness that spanned the front of the lodge, the driveway disappearing into overgrown woods.

Nothing. Not a hint of movement.

But as he waited, an engine started. And, God damn it, he'd swear it was at the road. Before he could move, the vehicle was already driving away.

Maybe a smaller SUV, but he suspected a full-size SUV or pickup truck. The sound was too deep.

"Shit," he muttered. If he'd started out five minutes sooner, he might have caught someone prowling.

Or, hell, it was equally possible that a couple of teenagers had pulled over to neck, or the sound really had come from the neighbor's driveway to the east.

He decided to risk using his flashlight and turned it on, scanning the yard and front steps. More nothing.

Turning off the light, he rounded the lodge. Just as he neared the back corner, he heard a sound that kicked up his pulse: a soft thud that this time he felt sure was the lodge's kitchen door closing.

Reid broke into a run, but when he reached the back of the lodge, the night was utterly still. No lights came on inside; he heard nothing from any of the cabins.

He turned on his flashlight again and swept the beam over the surrounding woods and the shadows between cabins. He tested the back door to the lodge and found it locked.

So somebody had been entering, not leaving. Sneaking back inside, he thought bitterly. Twice tonight, he'd been in the wrong place. Was it sheer chance that two people had been on the move, or had they been meeting? The timing suggested as much. And if so...one of those two people was either TJ or Caleb.

If there'd been a meeting at all, there were explanations that had nothing to do with the recent fires. Either boy could have told a friend where he was or conceivably have met a girl who had driven out here.

Brooding, he knew the possibility still existed that the sound of the car engine had come from a neighbor's or had been a vehicle stopped along the road for an innocent reason.

Given what had been going on here, though, Reid wasn't inclined to buy an innocent reason for either of the boys sneaking out in the middle of the night.

So—there had to be a reason.

With fresh resolve, he began walking again, worrying less this time about staying unseen and unheard. He checked every one of the cabins, the woodshed, the new pile of firewood along one wall of the lodge. And finally, he climbed the front steps to the deep front porch and swept the flashlight beam in a slow arc.

He had fire on his mind, so it took him a second to process what he did see. He brought the light back to shine on the huge old front door—and the wicked-looking hunting knife with a six-inch or longer blade buried deep in the wood. For one frozen second, he imagined the knife still quivering.

"Son of a bitch," he growled and took out his phone to wake Roger.

CHAPTER SIX

"IT WASN'T ME," Caleb repeated sullenly.

As if anybody believed him. The three adults at the table wore identical implacable expressions.

Paula cleared her throat. "Funny thing. TJ says the same."

Looking at her bothered him. Usually she was so together, but tonight he could tell she was scared.

The other times, with the two fires, she'd either still been dressed or had gotten dressed really fast before Caleb had seen her. This time, she wore some kind of ugly, lumpy fleece robe over a high-necked flannel nightgown. It was the first time Caleb had seen her hair loose instead of braided. It was, wow, down to her butt. Wavy from the braids, but mostly gray.

Roger's hair was wild, too, and he wore slippers, saggy flannel pajama bottoms and a faded Kansas City Chiefs sweatshirt.

Only Reid was fully dressed, in jeans, running shoes and a fleece pullover. Oh, yeah, and a shoulder holster holding a big nine-millimeter handgun. Thanks to Daddy, Caleb knew his guns.

They stared at him. He stared back.

"This was a threat, Caleb," his brother said.

He laughed. "Yeah, no shit."

"You think it's funny?"

"No, I don't think it's funny. What's funny is you thinking I'm stupid."

It was always hard to tell what was really going on in Reid's head, but right now was an exception. He looked sad. As if Caleb had let him down.

"You could try trusting me," Reid said quietly, his eyes holding Caleb's.

Temper and hurt flared. "Sure. Like you trust me?"

"I'd like to. Hard to trust someone who won't talk to you."

Caleb didn't have to say anything. His brother's eyes narrowed for a flicker, and then his face went blank. As usual.

Caleb swiveled toward Paula. "Are you done with me?"

They'd already asked whether he had heard anyone else up and around in the lodge the past couple of hours. Or anything unusual outside.

He'd said no. And no.

And tonight he *hadn't* heard TJ get up. For some reason, he'd been totally out. But he knew. TJ was going outside most nights. What Caleb couldn't figure out was what he was doing. Until this deal with the knife, there hadn't been any excitement in a week. TJ had had plenty of opportunity, so why hadn't he taken advantage of it until tonight?

When Caleb got upstairs, for once the other boy's door stood half-open and his light was on. Caleb hesitated, then stepped into the opening. So far, he'd kept his mouth shut, but he didn't like being judged because TJ was into some kind of shit.

Sprawled on his bed, TJ wore only a pair of sweatpants. He wasn't any taller than Caleb, who was already six feet, but he had some serious muscles. He had a man's facial and body hair, too. An unshaven growth of beard shadowed TJ's lean face. His brown eyes were always flat and cold.

When he saw that he wasn't alone anymore, his lip curled and he removed some earbuds. "That didn't take long."

"I said the same thing you did. I didn't have anything to do with it."

"Bet that's not what they wanted to hear."

"No. They wanted me to say I hear you go downstairs every night. That I know it's you who oiled the hinges on the back door so you can go in and out quietly."

TJ didn't move, but Caleb wasn't fooled into thinking he was relaxed. Just because he'd never seen a coiled diamondback ready to strike didn't mean he wouldn't recognize its state of mind when he did almost step on one.

"I could say the same about you," TJ said after a moment.

"But you'd be lying."

"You don't know anything, or you would have spilled."

Caleb made himself laugh, even knowing TJ wouldn't like it. "Yeah? Shows what *you* know."

TJ sat up so fast Caleb jerked backward in instinctive reaction.

"You're threatening me." The jerk snorted. "Or do you think I'll pay you to keep your mouth shut?"

"You don't have anything I'd want," Caleb scoffed.

"So what's the point?"

Caleb balanced lightly on his feet and readied himself, even though he didn't think TJ would attack him right now, not with Paula, Roger and Reid downstairs and alert. "I don't want anyone to die because you're pissed at everyone, okay?"

TJ laughed, an ugly sound. "Yeah, you *really* don't know what you're talking about. Go to bed, little boy."

Caleb never liked to back down. He was already mad at himself for flinching. He knew his stubbornness was rooted in all the times he'd had to duck his head and pretend to be submissive to Dad to avoid being hurt. Sometimes he wished he'd had the balls to refuse to back down. He could have taken whatever Dad threw at him. Or, better yet, killed the son of a bitch. Dad was careless with his weapons, a nine-mil Beretta and a Colt .38. A couple of times Caleb had seen one of the weapons lying on the kitchen counter and imagined himself grabbing it and just blasting away. *Bam. Bam. Bam.* Seeing the explosion of blood and the shock on his father's face followed by…vacancy. Caleb had wanted to do it so much, he'd shocked himself. *I won't be like him,* he'd told himself, but maybe that was just an excuse for being a coward.

What he did know was that he'd never give anyone that kind of power over him again. TJ might beat the shit out of him, but Caleb would rather that than know how gutless he was.

So he shrugged, real nonchalant, and said, "Keep telling yourself that."

Until now, he'd never seen anyone's eyes dilate so much they were pitch-black. But he held TJ's blistering stare long enough to satisfy himself, then turned and went to his room.

Which had no lock. He could stand up for himself when he was awake, but what if TJ sneaked in when he was sleeping?

After a minute, Caleb grabbed his desk chair and carried it to the door, bracing the back beneath the knob. At least this way he'd have some warning.

"WE MIGHT BE making a mistake to assume it was Caleb or TJ you heard going in," Roger observed, once they heard Caleb climb the stairs.

"That's occurred to me," Reid admitted. "It wouldn't be hard for any of the boys to get his hands on a key to the front door. He might be coming in that door, out the back, depending on what he thinks is safest. For that matter, he might have opened the door, heard me coming around the lodge or seen a spear of my flashlight beam, closed the door real quick and stayed in the kitchen. He could have let himself out later, once we were all out front."

There were enough other possible scenarios to give him a headache. He had an image of clowns in whiteface and bulbous red noses opening and closing doors, popping in and out with bewildering speed until the watcher was confused over who was where.

"But they're still the two likeliest," Roger said.

Reid grunted.

My brother.

Without a word, Roger heaved himself to his feet and disappeared into the kitchen, carrying his empty coffee cup. When he returned with it full, Paula shook her head.

"The caffeine will keep you awake."

He kissed her cheek, then straddled the bench beside her. "It's four-thirty in the morning. I won't be falling asleep again."

"Well, *I* plan to," she said with a sniff. "You two can stay up all night long if you want." She slid off one end of the bench, bent briefly to rest her head against her husband's back, then came around the table to squeeze Reid's shoulder. "Thank you for being here."

Reid, too, had just been thinking he could still get

some sleep if he went home. He doubted anything else was going to happen here in the waning hours of the night. But clearly, Roger had something else to say, so Reid didn't move.

"You're sure you don't want a cup?"

Reid shook his head. "You know something."

"What?" Roger looked startled. "No! Just that we've had more to do with local law enforcement than I've told you."

Reid tensed. "What do you mean?"

"You've heard the story on your predecessor's wife?"

That was an unexpected sideways jump. Reid cast his mind back. "She had amnesia because of a blow to the head. Came back to town years later, and the guy who'd whacked her the first time tried to kill her again."

"You knew one of those attempts took place out here?"

"You said something at the time," Reid said slowly, thinking it through. "That she'd had a boyfriend who lived here back when she was a teenager."

"Right. She drove out here without knowing where she was going because he'd brought her to see the place, way back when."

What Roger had never said, it developed, was that an Angel Butte police detective named Duane Brewer had found the shelter years ago. Not long after Reid "graduated," they figured out. This

Brewer had been a runaway himself who claimed he wouldn't have survived if not for the sanctuary given by a youth shelter. He wanted to help.

So he started mentoring kids, usually one at a time. Sometimes a girl, sometimes a boy. Only it turned out that he'd been sexually molesting those girls, a number of whom subsequently disappeared.

"We didn't worry as much as we should have," Roger said, his chagrin obvious. "You know kids walk out on us. We can't hogtie them to keep them here."

Reid nodded. His first year here, he'd thought about running away himself. He hadn't liked the restrictions or having to feel grateful. He hadn't wanted to trust anyone. During the three years he'd spent at the old resort, three—no, four—of the residents had taken off. One girl, three boys. Staying here, studying hard, keeping clean and abiding by the strict rules on any contact with outsiders wasn't easy. On occasion, Roger and Paula had had to ask kids to leave, too, trusting that they weren't angry enough to betray the shelter.

Reid had already asked if any kids who might be disgruntled had left in the recent past, but apparently it had been at least a year since the last had taken off. His choice, which made him unlikely for this campaign of fear.

"We know now that Brewer murdered those girls. It all came to a head when he tried to kill Maddie Dubeau—now Nell McAllister."

More of what he'd read at the time was coming back to Reid. Wherever he was living, he had always paid attention to news from central Oregon. Yeah, he'd known that after Brewer was brought down, Jane Renner, née Vahalik, had taken over as lieutenant in Investigations. What Reid had never read was any connection with the runaway shelter at the old Bear Creek Resort.

"How'd you keep your heads down?" he asked.

"With help from McAllister and Lieutenant Vahalik," Roger said. "That's what I wanted to tell you. They both know what we're doing out here and chose to keep their mouths shut."

Reid had trouble believing that. Going for blunt, he asked, "Why? Given their jobs, the ethical decision would have been to shut you down."

"In Sheriff McAllister's case, I think his wife begged him to stay silent." A frown gathered on his brow. "I'm less sure about the lieutenant. I guess I wondered—" He stopped.

When he didn't continue, Reid did it for him. "Whether she might have reason to sympathize."

"Yeah, that's it. There's something about her."

Funny, because Reid didn't yet know her well, but he'd had the same underlying sense. For all that she was, so far as Reid could tell, confident on the job, there was something…vulnerable about her.

The same something he'd recognized in Anna, he realized. *Ghosts.*

"Then, later," Roger continued, as if he were thinking aloud, "there was another cop. That one was with the sheriff's department. Sergeant Renner. He came out to ask questions about a kid that went missing on our road. I can't be sure how much he knew, but he said something about us doing a good thing, and if we ever needed help to call him."

"Clay Renner. He married Lieutenant Vahalik, you know."

Roger hadn't known. He and Paula read the local newspaper, but Reid doubted they paid attention to wedding or anniversary announcements, even assuming two cops would have bothered with that kind of thing.

"Why are you telling me this?" Reid asked. "Do you think we need more help?"

"Now? No." Roger shrugged. "But in case."

"I'll keep it in mind." Reid said his goodbyes and took off, his cover pretty much blown with the boys. But maybe that wasn't such a bad thing, as it might make their troublemaker hesitate.

Assuming the troublemaker *was* one of the boys rather than the driver of the car Reid had heard.

He realized how tired he was when he couldn't seem to make his mind grapple with what his next step ought to be. He kept picturing the knife, blade embedded in the door, and the ghosts in Anna Grant's eyes.

He heard Roger's voice, but it wasn't Lieutenant Jane Renner he pictured.

There's something about her....

And he was afraid he wouldn't be able to stay away from her.

ANNA PACKED A lunch on the Monday morning after the skiing expedition. In fact, she went to more trouble than usual, making a salad to go with a leftover burrito she could heat in the microwave in the staff room at Angel's Haven. She was pleased with herself when she plopped the insulated canvas lunch bag down on the passenger seat next to her purse. She could credit herself with some pride, at least. She'd be damned if she was going to make excuses to herself every day about why having lunch at the Kingfisher Café would be a really fabulous idea—at, of course, exactly the time she and Reid had met there.

Her phone rang before she backed out of the driveway, and she groped in her purse for it. What crisis now? But when she saw the caller's number, her heart gave a bump.

"Reid," she said, answering coolly but pleasantly.

"Good morning. I was hoping we could meet for lunch."

She almost groaned. Closing her eyes, she felt her pride melt like candle wax. Damn it. "The café? Or shall we shoot for some variety?"

"Are we talking Chandler's or A&W?" His amusement was apparent.

"Actually, either." Anywhere he wanted to go.

Her certainty shocked her, given that she hardly knew him.

No, if she were honest with herself, she didn't know him at all and wasn't sure she ever would. She had a very bad feeling that a woman could marry the man and spend the next fifty years with him while large parts of him remained closed to her.

"Chandler's is close to the police station, too," he said. "But your wish is my command."

She'd have to drive either way. She agreed that sounded good, and they set a time. After dropping her phone back in her bag, she looked ruefully at the lunch, debated taking it back into the house, and decided she could safely leave it in the refrigerator at work. It would still be good tomorrow.

Her morning was less than exciting, spent working on reports for state agencies. She never let herself feel resentful, unlike some coworkers. Anna believed deeply in concepts like compliance and accountability. On her watch, no child would ever fall through the cracks. No foster parent would go unvisited for too long. She encouraged the case-workers to make a certain percentage of their visits unexpected drop-ins, too. Foster parents with Angel's Haven were all warned that would be the case when they signed on.

She wasn't sorry to break at noon, however, hustling out of the office. The day hadn't warmed up, and the gray of the clouds had a milky cast, making her suspect they might get another snowfall whether this was supposed to be spring or not.

Maybe Reid would like to take his new skis out again this weekend.

But this time, he'd have to do the asking, she vowed. Pride. Remember?

Parking downtown was more plentiful than it was much of the year. The ski areas hadn't shut down yet, but would soon, snow or no. Once people flipped their calendars to April, their thoughts turned to gardening and summer sports. For locals, this was the best time of year to hit the slopes, with lift lines short.

She walked into Chandler's to find Reid waiting just inside. As usual, he wore a well-cut dark suit that made her think attorney, not cop. When he saw her, his eyes crinkled in a smile that barely touched his mouth.

The hostess signaled to them, and he gently touched Anna's back to steer her ahead of him. That slightest touch sent a shaft of pleasure through her.

She knew the menu at Chandler's well enough to barely need to take a glance, which left her free to study Reid as he read his more thoroughly.

Somewhat dreamily, she decided it was especially sad that he should have to hate to own a face so perfectly formed. The camera would love him if he wanted to be a model. He possessed the kind of hollows beneath the jut of his cheekbones that she'd seen only a few times before in real life. His nose was thin and straight, his jaw cleanly cut, his mouth just soft enough to suggest a sensual nature. And then there was the color of those eyes, so mysteriously dark.

To her horror, she realized he was looking right at her, amusement quirking his mouth. "Did I turn purple?"

"No, I was just, um—" *Give it up,* she told herself, and laughed even as she knew her cheeks had warmed. "I was admiring you. And thinking that if your brother looks like you, the girls are probably blushing when he so much as glances their way."

Warring emotions showed on his face. "Damn, I'd really like to kiss you," he said at last in a low, husky voice.

They stared at each other. Anna's entire body tingled.

"Hi, can I take your order for drinks?"

Anna started. Beside the table stood a curvaceous waitress in a snug, short black skirt and equally tight white shirt buttoned up barely high enough to keep her boobs contained.

Reid gave no sign of noticing the waitress's deep cleavage or the way she fluttered her lashes when she looked at him. After a questioning glance at Anna, he told the waitress they were ready to order their meals, then he and Anna did so.

"Wow," she mumbled, watching the ridiculously young and sexy creature saunter away. "Now I know why I don't come here more often."

Reid's eyebrows drew together. "What?"

"Every single waitress I can see is young, beautiful and buxom. Ours was flirting with you besides. That's tacky."

Reid laughed. "Do you know how disgruntled you sound?"

She pretended to sniff haughtily. "I was going for disapproving."

The grin made his handsome face breathtaking. "Jealous."

"I'm entitled."

"No, you're not. I'd guess that waitress was eighteen if this wasn't a brewpub and therefore I assume has to be twenty-one. She couldn't quite be my daughter, but closer than I want to admit. And no, until you pointed it out, I didn't notice her breasts."

"Really?" *Oh, beg, why don't you?*

It earned her another laugh. "Really. But I suspect you're right. Pretty waitresses probably are a draw. From what I hear, Mayor Chandler is a smart man. This is the kind of place where decorative staff helps the bottom line. What's more, he's also smart enough to offer a huge selection of craft beers *and* really good food, or people wouldn't come back."

"Well."

This smile definitely extended to his eyes. "You're too intriguing a woman to be so insecure."

No one had ever called her intriguing. "I'm a social worker," she said. "I don't have cleavage I could hide a passport in. My idea of makeup most mornings is sunscreen and maybe a brush of mascara. I can't be too witty, or I wouldn't keep scaring you away."

He'd remained smiling until then. The smile died abruptly and an uncomfortable moment passed. "But you notice I keep coming back," he said, a little deeper and rougher than usual.

"Oh, God, I can't believe I said that," she moaned.

"Why not?"

"Because I sound like I'm whining that you aren't calling me daily and sending me flowers. I didn't mean it that way."

His expression softened. The change would have been imperceptible to someone paying less attention than she. "I know you didn't," he said.

Their drinks arrived, and then salads. Probably to head off her next wretched outburst, he asked about the rest of her weekend, and Anna admitted her legs were a little sore.

"I punished myself by going to the health club yesterday." She grimaced, and he laughed.

"The elliptical."

"I swam some laps, too. And lounged in the hot tub. What about you?"

His frown came and went so fast, she almost missed it. "I did…something of a stakeout Saturday night."

"Aren't police captains above boring duties like that?"

"This was pro bono. Remember the friend who

had the fire? He's had some other problems. I lurked to try to catch whoever has it in for him."

That sounded more than a little strange to her, but maybe he thought it was fun. "Were you successful?"

"No." If he'd been having fun, he shouldn't sound so grim now. "He pulled another trick right under my nose."

"What kind of trick?" she asked, feeling apprehensive for no good reason.

"He stabbed a hunting knife into my friend's front door. A big sucker—" he measured the length with his hands "—black rubber handle."

"That's creepy!" Anna exclaimed.

"Yeah, no kidding."

"But— Were there fingerprints?"

"No. Isn't everybody older than kindergarten smarter than that these days?"

She wrinkled her nose. "Probably. And maybe even kindergartners, given what their parents let them watch on TV."

"There you go."

"This friend," she said tentatively. "Is he the reason you took the job here?" And—had he ever said the friend *was* a he?

Well, there might be a whole lot she didn't know about Reid Sawyer, but she felt confident he wouldn't be spending time with her if he was already involved with another woman. He was too honorable for that.

Still, she recognized how cautious his glance was.

"In a way," he said finally. "The couple are the reason I've spent time in the area before."

"Would I know them?"

"I doubt it." He took a long drink of his cola. "Roger's retired. They don't mix much."

So, not Reid's contemporaries. Friends of his father's? Um—the father he hated? Probably not. But even though nosiness did come naturally to her, she couldn't bring herself to press him.

"How'd your home visit go Saturday?" he asked abruptly, telling her she'd been right not to persist.

"Oh— It raised some concerns for me, to tell you the truth." She'd been disappointed, actually; she'd liked the couple, but the apartment had been too small to add an older child, and she'd learned that the husband was out of work and having trouble finding a new job. That made her suspect the stipend was a bigger part of their motivation than she liked.

"What do you look for?" he asked.

Since she could tell he was genuinely curious, she talked for a little about the kind of clues she sought on home visits, everything from the adequacy of the apartment or house to giveaways that might contradict something she'd read on the application or been told during the original interview.

"Everyone is sure I care deeply about dust or clutter, which is sad because I don't. In fact, some messes suggest active, interesting people live there."

"Sometimes you distinguish yourself from the

caseworkers, but you seemed pretty hands-on with Yancey."

She gave her introductory lecture about the web of interconnected services and supervision through the state, as well as private agencies like Angel's Haven, and explained that she did continue to take on some children herself even as she oversaw the foster program.

"Yancey is one, obviously. But we're not so big that I can't keep myself informed about all the children we're serving with foster homes." She went on to tell him about the other services offered: counseling for kids and for families, a "shop" where low-income parents could choose clothes for themselves and their kids, and a Christmas house for holiday gifts. "We also pair with a safe house for battered women by offering day care for their children as the women rebuild their lives. It's one way to help those kids stay with a parent and not need foster care."

"That's impressive," he said. "I'm guessing a lot of locals have no idea those services are even needed."

She chuckled. "I remember seeing an interview with your boss, Chief Raynor. He talked about how he'd chosen Angel Butte because he wanted a peaceful town for his family."

"After which his nephew was kidnapped by drug traffickers and corrupt cops to put pressure on him to throw a trial."

"There's some famous last words." She paused. "Did you think of Angel Butte as peaceful?"

"No." The lines in his forehead deepened when he met her eyes. "I don't delude myself."

No, she thought sadly, he wouldn't any more than she did. Abused children hardly ever grew up to be people who tried to believe the world was a kind place. They knew better.

"I've been wondering," he said. "Are you ever forced to return children to a parent or guardian when you suspect the situation there isn't safe?"

"Not often, but...occasionally." She fiddled with her fork, not wanting to meet those sharp green eyes. "DHS—the Department of Human Services," she corrected herself, remembering that he hadn't grown up in Oregon, "and we are encouraged to weigh in when the court arrives at decisions. But of course in the end a judge makes the call. Sometimes, in my opinion, the wrong one is made."

"So you just let the kids go."

Why did she feel quite sure that was a criticism? And even that he was angry, whether it showed or not?

"'Just'?" Suddenly, she was mad. "You say that as if it's easy. No, it's not. None of us like it. The truth is, though, that nobody is all-knowing. Maybe we're sometimes too close to the child to see clearly. And what do you suggest as a better system? We immediately lynch all abusive parents—and, hey, who is going to judge the evidence?—so there's no home the kid can be returned to? We set up an underground network to hide the kids? Of course, then the state wouldn't refer children to us in the first place, which would mean we can't help any kids at all."

"I didn't suggest—"

"Yes, you did. But before you judge, I'll tell you that we do our damnedest *always* to keep a connection open with children being returned to a home, whether we believe it's the right decision or not. We encourage the guardian to allow visits from the foster parents to ease the transition. We make sure the kids, if they're old enough, have phone numbers they can call if things go bad. If we have any doubts, we put a lot of pressure on judges to court-order counseling and maintain supervision by the state for a reasonable length of time." She stared fiercely at him. "We don't toss them back like a fish that isn't big enough and figure what the heck, win some, lose some."

Reid looked torn between consternation and amusement. "Was all that fury really ignited by a simple question?"

"It wasn't the question. It was the comment. 'So you just let the kids go.'"

"I'm sorry." He sounded gentle, as he sometimes could.

Anna's anger immediately deflated. Her shoulders sagged. "No, I am. You hit a hot button, that's all. Once in a while, we have to return a child to a home when we believe passionately it's the wrong thing to do. But I also believe our system is filled with caring people all doing the best they can. Perfection is a pipe dream."

"I suppose," he said after a moment, "all I wanted was to hear you're aware it happens and fight for those kids."

"You mean, you wanted to know whether I really care."

"No." Now she could tell he was troubled. "I already knew that."

She gave a little nod.

It was probably just as well that they talked about other things for the rest of their lunch.

And that a busy street only two blocks from the public safety building where he worked wasn't a place where he could do more than kiss her lightly and say, "I'll call, Anna."

Getting into her car, it occurred to her that this might be the first time he'd left her with a promise that she would actually hear from him again.

CHAPTER SEVEN

REID WOULD HAVE given a lot to be able to introduce Anna to Caleb. Paula and Roger, too. To get Anna's take on everything that had him roiling.

Yeah, he thought with black humor—everything except his feelings for *her.*

It was the crack of dawn Tuesday morning, and he was running. Despite the exertion, he was cold. He'd never in his life had to wear gloves and Polartec to run, but spring in central Oregon made new demands. For God's sake, this was the first of April.

And I moved here why?

Oh, yeah—for the kid who apparently detested him.

With each stride, his feet crunched rhythmically on the sidewalk, where leftover slush had frozen overnight. The resulting ice would make the morning commute a bitch, the cop in him thought. Pity the patrol officers.

He'd chosen a route that took him toward the butte that sat, so oddly, within the city limits. Because it was there, it set up a challenge in his psyche. He didn't run to the top every day, but he did at least two or three times a week. The more disturbed his night, the more likely he was to feel compelled to push himself come morning. A road spiraled up the red cinder volcanic cone to the crater rim, where the huge marble angel sat on her pedestal gazing blindly out over the town at her feet.

His muscles loosened as he picked up the pace. He was breathing easily, but knew his lungs would burn by the time he reached the top of Angel Butte.

With little traffic to watch out for, and having met no other runners, Reid found his thoughts reverting to Anna.

He should have stayed away from her. Those first instincts had been dead-on. Her profession alone should have been as good as a flashing red light. *Do not go here.*

He wanted her. God, he wanted her. If that was all it was, he might have been able to manage a casual, sexual relationship with her—a woman who supervised foster homes for a living.

As it was… Shit. He didn't know.

What would she do if she found out about the shelter? He had a bad feeling he knew. She might even be legally obligated to report it.

He'd already known his life was split in two: Caleb, the shelter and its problems, and his job and what little else remained. But by becoming involved with Anna, he had made matters worse. He had let himself be tempted into talking to her about Caleb, and now Paula and Roger. Even the threats. His job, present and past. With her and only her, he'd woven the separate parts of his life together. Which meant he had to do more than maintain silence about too much—he had to lie to her.

Reid didn't like to lie. He liked even less the idea of lying to Anna, with her clear-seeing eyes that held such pain.

He turned past the city-parks sign that said Angel Butte—Elevation Gain 474 Feet and felt the increased stress on his muscles as the climb began.

He should *not* call her. Not meet her again for lunch, or go skiing with her, or bring her back to the house he was renting for now, until he determined whether Caleb would settle in with the Hales and therefore whether he would be staying on with the ABPD. If he did any of those things, it could only be with the full knowledge he couldn't take their relationship any further than that. Sex was fine. Much of anything else wasn't.

He frowned, wondering why he was even having this talk with himself. He had sex. He didn't "take" relationships anywhere. He didn't *have* relationships. Friendships, sure, but even those had limitations. And he didn't combine real friendship with sex. His instincts said that would be dangerous.

He'd already gone too far down that road with Anna, which meant she should be off-limits for sex. As his lungs and muscles burned, he brooded about that even as he pushed harder, faster.

Then, for the first time that morning, he heard a thud of footsteps, these coming up behind him.

Knowing there was no reason to be competitive, still he shifted up a gear. The hell he'd let anyone gain on him, much less pass him. Not knowing who was behind him gave Reid an uneasy prickle between his shoulder blades. He resisted the impulse to look over his shoulder, though. That suggested he felt threatened. Anybody who was a real threat wouldn't be chasing him down on foot at seventhirty on a bloody cold morning.

Whoever was following him was no longer gaining, so he relaxed, letting himself slow when he reached the top, breathe in the cold, sharp air. Rolling his shoulders, he temporarily slowed to a walk as he circled to start back down.

Somehow he wasn't surprised to find himself face-to-face with Noah Chandler, mayor of the city of Angel Butte. Aside from their couple of games of racquetball, they had also passed each other coming and going on their morning runs, exchanging nods.

This time, Chandler slowed to a walk himself and nodded, then bent over with his hands braced on his knees. "Sawyer," he gasped between breaths.

Reid grunted a greeting. Were they going to have an actual conversation?

Chandler was at least Reid's height and built on the scale of a Mack truck. Not the usual physique for a runner. Reid had noticed before that Chandler's stride was powerful, but not smooth. Too many muscles got in his way.

"Hell of a view," the mayor said, straightening.

Despite the cold, sweat dampened his jersey and spiked his hair.

Reid spared the vista a glance. "Can't argue."

"Glad to see you like to stay in shape even if you are stuck behind a desk these days."

"I believe in setting an example."

"I do, too."

Feeling compelled to make conversation as they circled the angel at a walk then started back, Reid said, "Your wife not a runner?"

"She's a fair-weather runner." Chandler flashed a grin. "She's also been heard to remark on the idiots who want to run straight uphill."

His own laugh hit Reid by surprise. "I have to admit, I was thinking something of the same on the way up this morning."

"But you're here anyway."

"Yep." He threw a glance of friendly challenge at the mayor, who was, ultimately, his boss. "And not alone."

"Nope."

Without another word, they simultaneously broke into a trot, then lengthened their strides in unison. Reid made no effort to outpace Chandler. Running in unison felt strangely…companionable, he decided. He might even like this man.

They stayed together when they reached the flat, earning some glances from passing motorists who were more likely to have recognized the mayor than Reid. *Or not,* he realized belatedly, remembering that damn newspaper article complete with photo. He and the mayor didn't separate until he was only two blocks from his rental, which meant Chandler, too, lived in the old part of town along the Deschutes River. In fact, after lifting a hand in farewell, he continued straight on toward the river. As owner of three Chandler's Brewpubs in central Oregon before he went into local politics, he might even live in one of the handsome old houses built along the riverbank. Reid had coveted those houses when, as a boy, he had ridden his bike into town. He had a vague memory of seeing them as symbols of the kind of family and life he wished existed. Now he wondered if Noah Chandler might actually have that life. There had been something on his face when he talked about his wife.

Grunting in irritation at himself, Reid slowed to a walk for his cooldown. His rental was far more modest than the riverfront homes built by the wealthy early residents of Angel Butte, but it dated from not much later—1920s, at a guess. Two-bedroom, one bath, minimally furnished, it suited him for now.

Half an hour later, he'd showered and dressed for his day, eaten a quick breakfast and downed a cup of coffee. At eight-thirty, he stepped off the elevator on the second floor of the public safety building and strode down the hall to his office. Partway, he stopped to talk to Brian Cooper, his counterpart on the patrol side of the department. Brian wanted to meet with him later to discuss some issues with the new generation of patrol cars. Reid promised to have his PA check his calendar. Good excuse—it gave him time to research the Dodge Chargers that had been replacing the classic Ford Crown Victorias in the fleet. The department had gone in big in the past few years for Chevy Tahoe SUVs, too, something he had his doubts about. The hauling capability was impressive and the four-wheel drive was a plus in harsh winter conditions, but Reid had his doubts there was justification for the vastly larger and more expensive vehicles in a city this size—the SUVs didn't get comparable mileage to the standard patrol car. It would be interesting to see what Cooper thought.

Hey, maybe he'd already learned more than he realized.

The instant he opened the door leading into his outer office, he froze between one stride and the next. He was looking at a man's back, but that was all he needed to see. He knew this man. His response was visceral—a bowel-loosening moment of fear that he controlled after no more than a microsecond.

He saw his father turning and made sure his face had gone so blank it expressed utter indifference. He wanted to call a couple of underlings—rookies would be good, to achieve maximum humiliation—and have them escort Sergeant Dean Sawyer out of the building. Unfortunately, that would not only cause talk, it would give this contemptible man more weight in Reid's life than he deserved.

He let his eyebrows climb. "Strange place for you to show up," he said without interest, then looked at his PA. "Any important messages, Miranda?"

Her alarmed gaze flicked from him to his father and back. There was no hiding this relationship. "Um…no, sir. Captain."

He nodded. "Find time for me to sit down with Captain Cooper, will you? Give us an hour, if possible." Then he gestured toward his inner office with a glance at his father. "I assume you have something to say to me?"

Temper simmered in those eyes that were the same color as his. "You bet I do."

Reid didn't do him the courtesy of allowing him to go ahead. Instead he walked right by his father and into his office, going behind his desk before he so much as glanced back. The click of the door told him Dean had closed it behind him. Reid pulled out his desk chair and sat comfortably, leaving his father to stand on the other side of the desk glowering at him.

"I have a busy morning," he said mildly. "Say what you have to say."

"I know you have Caleb."

Exaggerating the motion, he looked around his office. "Where?"

His father planted his hands on the desk and

leaned forward, his expression ugly. "You're hiding him from me!"

Reid looked at this man he had once so feared and was relieved to discover that, once past the first shock, he felt nothing but contempt. So much, he resolved not to bother to lie.

No, you save that for Anna, whispered a voice in his head. He ignored it.

"You know, if you'd learned any lessons at all from me, I'd never even have known you had another son. It was your dates with a judge that alerted me."

"You're admitting you have him." Spittle sprayed Reid.

He reached in his drawer for a paper napkin left from one of his lunches on the go and wiped his face. "I imagine you've been by my house," he said conversationally. He saw from Dean's expression that he had. "Don't suppose you spotted a teenage boy."

His father straightened. "You're not stupid enough to have him there. He's stashed away somewhere."

"Think so?"

"I know so," his father snarled.

Reid told himself not to be stupid enough to taunt this man. That would be sinking to Dean Sawyer's level. But then he thought, *What the hell.* Turned out he'd been wrong; he did feel something more than contempt. He hated this man. Not because of what he himself had endured, but on Caleb's behalf.

If the son of a bitch had only stopped when he was ahead...but he hadn't. He'd wanted too much to have another whipping boy.

Reid leaned forward so suddenly Dean jerked back. "Then find him," he said very softly. After a moment, he relaxed again in his chair and let his lips form a mocking smile. "Shall I close my eyes and count to a hundred?"

With a roar of rage, his father grabbed the chair facing the desk and flung it to one side, then stormed out of the office, slamming two doors behind him so hard glass rattled in the frames.

As his door opened again and a panicky Miranda appeared, Reid reached for his phone and called the desk sergeant. Wouldn't you know, Sergeant Shroutt answered.

"A man who looks a lot like me but older just left my office. I'd like to make sure he leaves the building."

"You got it, Captain. Ah..." His voice changed timbre. "That would seem to be him coming out of the stairwell right now." There was a brief pause, then, "He's gone."

"Thank you," Reid said and set down the phone. "It's okay, Miranda. The excitement's over."

"Oh." Her gaze skittered to the chair lying on its side and the new dent in the wall. "Was that—"

"Unfortunately, yes."

"I see." She hemmed and hawed a little, finally telling him she'd conferred with Captain Cooper's assistant, and Reid and Cooper were to sit down together at ten.

He thanked her, and she left with a still-wide-eyed look over her shoulder.

Damn, he wished he could find the ideal candidate for his personal assistant.

After a moment, he picked up his mobile phone and called the Hales' number. It was Paula who answered.

"It's Reid," he said. "My father just left my office. He's here in Angel Butte. Claims to be sure I have Caleb stashed somewhere."

"Oh, no." She was silent for a moment. "Should I tell Caleb?"

"No." He squeezed the back of his neck, second-guessing himself. Was that a good decision? Bad decision? At his brother's age, would he have resented being protected from frightening news? That was a no-brainer: of course he would have. "I don't know, Paula," he said wearily. "Maybe we do need to. We can't afford for him to decide right now to sneak into town to see if there are any hot girls around."

She gave a choked laugh. "I hear Diego and Palmer did just that the other day. They picked up some snacks at the AM/PM two blocks from the high school right after it let out. Diego was sure some girl had her eye on him. Palmer told him he was imagining it. The girl was eyeing *him*."

God, that took Reid back. There were never more than a couple of girls living at the shelter at any one time. Paula and Roger were conscious of the issues bound to arise when they mixed teenage boys and girls. Sexual and romantic relations were strictly forbidden, and Paula especially seemed to have eyes in the back of her head and ears like CIA radar antennae.

"Tell him," he said abruptly. "We can't take a chance. And I'm going to have to be damn careful if I come out there at all."

"What if something happens?" she asked, and for the first time in his memory he heard a faint quaver in her voice.

He knew what kind of *something* she meant, and he felt a cramp of fear. What if they needed him, and he didn't dare chance leading his father to Caleb?

Or, if they needed him, did that mean Dean Sawyer was already out there?

After they hung up, he brooded. Could he have lied convincingly enough that Daddy would have gone away?

He shook his head even before he finished the thought. Of course not. Dean was counting on Reid leading him to his son. He had no other hope of ever finding him.

On the other hand, unless he planned to quit his job, Dean wouldn't be able to loiter in Angel Butte forever. *Wait him out,* Reid thought, knowing the only other option was to take him on in court, suing for custody of Caleb. Clearly Caleb's mother couldn't take on Dean.

Which would leave Reid the guardian of a boy simmering with hurt and rage. Yep, a recipe for disaster.

Great time to realize how desperately he wanted to see Anna.

Not to tell her any of this—he couldn't. Just to see her. The need was so primal, it scared the shit out of him.

You don't dare.

He told his voice of common sense where it could take its advice and picked up his phone again, scrolling to her number before he could have second thoughts. He could do this. Keep his cool and satisfy a craving.

ANNA KNEW HER eyes were red and puffy. This probably wasn't the best day for her to have agreed to have lunch with Reid. She didn't think he liked to deal with real emotion, and she was far from sure she could stay coolly composed, guarding herself. But, oh God, she'd wanted to see him, and she had felt such relief when he called that she couldn't resist saying yes.

He met her on the sidewalk outside the café, saw her face and gripped her arm, pulling her out of the way of passersby. "What's wrong?" he asked, voice low and urgent.

She'd mostly had herself together. This was what she'd been afraid of. The worry on his face undermined her composure. Tears flooded her eyes again.

"We lost a kid today."

"Lost—" His expression changed. "I heard there was a traffic fatality. The girl was in one of your foster homes?"

She sniffled and nodded. "I'm sorry. I should have taken a rain check, Reid. I'm not even hungry. Can we make it tomor—"

"Did you know her well?"

All she could do was nod, knowing tears were now streaming down her face. But instead of seeming appalled, he pulled her to him and wrapped his arms around her. Even as she buried her face against his chest, she felt him turning her. Shielding her, she realized, from curious gazes.

She cried quietly and only for a minute, the most she ever allowed herself. Then she straightened away from him and fumbled in her purse for a tissue. When her hand emerged with one, Reid took it away from her and gently patted her face dry before letting her blow her nose.

The next moment, he steered her to his Expedition, parked only a few feet away. "We'll get lunch to go," he said, opening the passenger door and urging her gently but somehow inexorably in. "I know you don't think you're hungry, but you may change your mind."

He closed the door before she could protest, and a moment later slid in behind the wheel.

"Go where?" she asked, as if it mattered.

He surveyed her even as he turned the key in the ignition. "My house. What do you say? A&W?"

He was making her want to blubber again, but instead she laughed. "Yes. All right. The bank says it's thirty-four degrees Fahrenheit, perfect weather for a root-beer float."

His quiet chuckle calmed her. "Why not? It's above freezing."

Anna didn't try to talk during the short drive. She laid her head back and closed her eyes, glad of the warmth pouring out of the vents and of the man beside her. She'd been so glad for his call.

She let him order for her at the A&W and was relieved when he seemed content with silence as they waited for their food.

The drive to his place was short. Reid pulled into the driveway of a small house with a winter-brown lawn and no landscaping. A rental, she presumed; surely, if he'd bought, it would have been something more inspiring than this.

She turned her head to see him glance in the rearview mirror. His expression hardened at something he saw there.

"Excuse me a moment," he said and got out.

Anna turned in her seat to watch as he strode down the driveway and across the street to where an equally large SUV was parked at the curb. He wrenched open the driver's-side door, and she half expected him to yank someone out. Instead, he must have said something. Given how inexpressive a person's back was, she had no idea what. An instant later, he slammed the door and walked back across the street.

It was strange how certain she felt that he was furious, given that he rarely projected his emotions and his stride was smooth. Maybe because the way he'd pulled open the door hadn't been smooth at all; her stomach had tightened at the violence of the act.

She hurriedly unbuckled her seat belt, grabbed her bag and both sacks containing their lunches, and got out of his Expedition so that she was waiting for him when he arrived.

He gripped her upper arm, his fingers uncomfortably tight. "Let's get inside."

"Who was that?" she asked as he hustled her up the walk.

"My father."

Anna blinked in surprise. The father with whom he had no relationship? *He* was sitting in a vehicle across the street from Reid's house, as if... Her mind groped for an explanation. As if he was conducting a stakeout?

Reid's house was no more prepossessing inside than outside. He must have brought the handsome leather sofa and recliner with him, but that was about it in the furniture department. He was currently using a wooden TV folding tray as an end table. A flat-screen television and DVD player sat atop a pile of plastic totes. Empty? Or maybe he'd lost interest in unpacking?

After shutting and locking the front door, he surveyed the room, as if seeing his home through her eyes. "Sorry. I haven't done much to settle in."

"I know when you live alone—" She gave up. She lived alone, too, but creating a real home for herself had mattered to her. It was her sanctuary. Reid's place was a sanctuary in the way the bleak confines of a prison cell might be for a lifer. All his, but hardly cozy.

"Have a seat," he said. His gaze lowered to the paper sacks she clutched. "Oh, you brought those in. Thank you. I was…distracted."

His eyes met hers, and she saw something that might have been shame.

"It's okay—"

"I wouldn't have brought you here if I'd known he was out there."

"It really is okay," she repeated. "Are you going to tell me what's going on?"

In the act of taking their lunch from her, Reid hesitated. Then he sighed and said, "I have bar stools in the kitchen. Why don't we eat there?"

She left her purse on the sofa and followed him. The kitchen was a standard rental house—adequate but unexciting. She couldn't imagine he often bothered to cook anyway. There was a Formica breakfast bar, which was a good thing, as the dining area lacked table or chairs.

"You didn't bring much with you."

Again he glanced around, seeming disconcerted.

"No, most of what I had didn't seem worth paying to have moved. I figured I'd buy new. Just haven't gotten around to it. I was waiting—" He stopped suddenly enough she knew he'd been about to say something he hadn't intended to tell her.

She automatically filled in the blanks. *I was waiting to decide if I wanted to stay in Angel Butte.* That had to be it.

He set out their floats and then the fries, burgers and napkins. "I hope you feel more like eating now."

Weirdly, she did, maybe because he'd successfully distracted her from her grief.

"Well, the float at least," she said, seeing a smile flicker on his mouth.

They sat side by side, his broad shoulder brushing hers. More distraction. She could peek down to see the way the fabric of his slacks pulled tight over impressive thigh muscles. Or sidelong to see his hands, large, strong, with long fingers and nails cut short. Hands she imagined touching her every time she saw them.

"Caleb ran away from our father's house," Reid said suddenly.

Startled, she stared at him. "But…why is your father *here?*"

"He's got it into his head that I have Caleb." A nerve jerked beneath one of his eyes. "How else could a teenager have made a successful getaway?" He continued to eat as if the conversation was trivial.

"They do it all the time."

"In his arrogance, he thinks his kid couldn't have escaped him without help."

She felt a strange tightness in her chest. She could be wrong, terribly wrong, but she'd swear he sounded pleased. Because he *had* helped his brother escape? Or only because his father was presumably enraged?

"Have you heard from Caleb?"

He looked at her. "You know I have."

"He's calling you."

"Yes."

"So you do know where he is."

"Yes." He peeled the top off the root-beer float and stirred the ice cream within, then slurped.

"Teenagers on the streets…"

"He's somewhere safe." The tension in his voice told her the casual way he was eating his lunch was pretense. "That's all I can tell you, Anna. Do you think I wouldn't have made sure of that much, at least?"

"No." That horrible sense of pressure inside her eased, but only a little. "No, I know you care."

"Maybe you think I should make him go home."

"No, not if your father is as awful as you implied he is."

"But you don't approve of keeping quiet about where he is."

She turned fiercely on him. "How do you know it's safe if it isn't an approved foster home? Who's monitoring to be sure nobody is hurting him there, too? Can you swear he'd tell you?"

He'd gone very still, and she knew the answer: *no.* There was too much strain between Reid and his brother for him to be certain of any such thing.

"I know these people," he said at last, slowly.

"Do you?" Hand shaking, she set down the cheeseburger she'd been clutching. What semblance of an appetite she'd summoned had deserted her entirely.

"Anna, decent people take in kids all the time without supervision by the court or social workers. You know that."

"Is he here in Angel Butte where you can see for yourself?" God, she felt sick.

Reid met her stormy stare with a face set in unrevealing lines. "This isn't my secret," he said finally.

"Sure it is. You're an adult. Your brother isn't."

He gave a short laugh. "That as an excuse would kill any trust dead in the water."

"Teenagers aren't always rational." Or should she have said, *Aren't* ever *rational?*

Reid only shook his head. "You don't know everything, Anna. Can't you trust me to have made the best decision?"

That stopped her. Could she? Okay, this was a hot-button issue for her, but if Reid had placed his brother temporarily with friends, was that so bad?

Reason said no. The terrible fear that always lived in her said yes.

"I know it's not my business," she mumbled.

"Unfortunately, it *is* your business," he said ruefully. "Why do you think I haven't said anything? Given your profession, you were bound to make a judgment."

"You think I'm rigid."

He shook his head. "I don't know. For Caleb's sake, I don't dare find out."

He didn't trust *her*. Of course he didn't. He shouldn't, she was afraid. If she was told too much, would she be able to keep her mouth shut? Anna truly didn't know.

She finally took a sip of her float, discovering the ice cream had mostly melted.

"Tell me about the girl who was killed," he said, the tenderness in his tone bringing a lump to her throat.

She talked about a child who'd come into the system when she was eight, after her father left her at a neighbor's, promising to be back within the week, but never reappearing. Nobody knew anything about a mother; the little girl thought Mommy had gone away when she was a baby. Dad was never located.

"Corinna was a little too old to appeal to people wanting to adopt, even assuming she'd have been freed for adoption. Plus, she had problems. Her father had moved them constantly, so her school attendance was spotty and she was way behind other kids her age. I think her father really loved her, though, so at least she was able to bond with people. Unfortunately, the first foster parents let her down. When they asked that she be moved, it was a huge setback. It took time, but she really thrived in the next home. This was her junior year in high school. She was a cheerleader. Did you know that?"

He shook his head, and she saw his compassion. For the dead girl? No, she knew, it was for her. Anna.

"She was talking about college. She was tutoring younger kids in the foster program and had decided she wanted to be a teacher. All that hope lost because her boyfriend wanted to show off."

"I heard that much. He's in critical condition, too."

Her first, vengeful thought had been, *He deserves to be.* But, of course, he was young, too. Only seventeen, swaggering the way boys his age did. If he survived, he would have to live with terrible guilt. Two tragedies for the price of one, she thought sadly.

"Was he speeding?" she asked.

"Yes, but under normal conditions it wouldn't have been dangerously so. With the ice, though…" He didn't have to finish.

She nodded.

"Eat," he said gently.

She did for a minute, not tasting what went in

her mouth, but what did that matter? It was a while before she said, "I want every one of them to have a chance at a happy life. Is that so much to ask?"

"No." Reid set down his own burger, braced his feet on the floor and drew her to him, between his legs. "No," he repeated huskily, rubbing his cheek on top of her head. "It's not too much to ask."

She let him hold her for longer than she should have. Anna wanted to trust him enough to stay in his arms forever, but she knew better than that.

When eventually he drove her back to where she'd left her Toyota downtown, Reid's dad followed behind them all the way in his SUV.

Anna got into her RAV4, waved and watched as Reid started forward again, his father crowding his bumper. Trying to make him mad. Anna couldn't help wondering whether, given their history, he would succeed. And if so...what would Reid do?

CHAPTER EIGHT

CALEB DIDN'T GIVE a shit about cars or what made them run. He wasn't old enough to get a driver's license, and now he wouldn't be able to go for one until he was eighteen. He didn't understand what made half the guys spend hours every day with their heads underneath the hood of one or another of the beaters the Hales kept around. Personally, he figured Roger messed them up as soon as someone figured out how to get one running, but Isaac said Roger and Paula gave a car or pickup to anyone who'd "graduated" from the Bear Creek Resort Home for Screwed Up Boys. They were able to drive away. Isaac said he wouldn't take one, though. Like Caleb, he didn't seem very interested in engines or brake linings or clutches. Since he was going to college, he said, he didn't expect to need a car for a long time. Which was probably true; the only reason Isaac ever got off the computer or put down a book was because he was expected to do chores.

Caleb wouldn't mind driving away when his time came, but not in some dented piece of crap.

Jose, Apollo and Damon had gone out to work on one of the old pickups. They'd gobbled breakfast because Roger had come home from town yesterday with the part they needed and they were excited.

Caleb didn't even lift his head when they went out the front door. Isaac had already taken over the computer that was in the corner. He was teaching himself some kind of programming that looked like gibberish to Caleb. Paula leaned over his shoulder as if she understood what he was doing. Who knew? Maybe she did. Roger was taking a shower. Caleb could still hear it running, which meant he'd be pissed if Diego and Trevor, who were on the schedule to clean the kitchen, turned on hot water before he got out. Caleb had had it happen—a blast of cold water. How come nobody got excited about plumbing instead of internal combustion engines? he wondered.

Only TJ and Caleb were still at the table, neither of them looking at each other. Caleb was reaching for another piece of toast when he realized the voices outside had risen in pitch. Suddenly footsteps thundered on the steps and across the porch. Caleb turned and was vaguely aware TJ and Paula had, too. Isaac, who knew?

Apollo burst in, the whites of his eyes showing.

"Roger's truck!" he burst out. "Somebody slashed the tires. All four tires."

Caleb felt as if he'd just been subjected to one of those blasts of cold water.

Some instinct made him turn his head to look at TJ. There was a flash of something on his face that might have been fear, until he noticed Caleb watching and blanked his face.

The other boys had followed Apollo in, too, and they were all babbling. Caleb tried to take it all in.

Without Roger's truck, nobody could go anywhere. They'd be stuck here unless Roger called a tire store and asked them to bring new tires out, and Caleb knew he didn't like outsiders to come here. Wait. No, he could call Reid—

Except...yesterday Paula had sat Caleb down to tell him his father really was in town and that Reid might not be out here for a while, because he couldn't risk leading their father right to Caleb. Yeah, so that left them... He experienced that weird chill again.

Trapped was the word whispering in Caleb's head, even though he knew it was dumb and melodramatic, 'cuz it was daytime already and there were neighbors and cars passing occasionally on the road, so it wasn't as if they couldn't get help.

He finally identified why he was so bothered. So, okay, they might not actually be trapped. But he was willing to bet that was the message the slashed tires were meant to send.

See what I can do to you.

AFTER HOURS SPENT brooding and then a nearly sleepless night, Reid was still angry at himself. The anger hardened into fury when he looked out his front window Wednesday morning and saw his father's Denali sitting there at the curb. Still.

Or again?

Gritting his teeth, he went back to his bedroom and dressed in athletic gear adequate for temperatures hovering around freezing. He finally let himself out the back door, hopped over a neighbor's rickety fence and went for a hard run through streets still messy from a melt-and-freeze cycle that wouldn't let up.

He had a sudden vision: himself running on the hard-packed, wet sand at the ocean's edge north of Malibu. The bluff to one side, the endless blue of the Pacific Ocean to the other. Seagulls dipping and wheeling and calling. The sun shining, a cooling breeze off the ocean, the crash of waves better than any music from an iPod.

When he lived down south, he hadn't gone out to the beach often enough. But when he wanted to, he *could* go. Now look at his options, and this was spring. Supposedly.

Neither the exercise nor the satisfaction of jogging slowly back to his front door and seeing his father's startled face at Reid's unexpected appearance allowed him to let go of his dark mood.

What he couldn't let go of was the reality that, yes, he'd been caught flat-footed by his father's presence yesterday, but that didn't mean he'd had to tell Anna the truth. He could have kept it simple. *My father wants to talk and I'm refusing. He thinks if he hangs around I'll relent. Not happening.*

Uh-huh. And then *she* would have said, *What does he want to talk about? You must have some idea.* If he'd said no, she would have looked at him with those eyes, which held all the compassion in the world and a hell of a lot of the world's pain, too, and told him it wouldn't hurt to find out, would it?

Staring at his dark ceiling last night, he'd run dozens of possible scripts, and none of them had turned out well. But wouldn't *any* of them have been a better option than admitting that, yeah, sure, he had stolen his fifteen-year-old brother and was hiding him from his legal guardian?

Did he *want* to spill his guts? he asked himself incredulously. Was that the explanation? Did he suddenly buy into a shining faith that confession was good for the soul?

A snarl erupted from him and he slammed his fist against the bathroom door frame. Swearing and nursing knuckles he suspected would be bruised, he stepped into a blisteringly hot shower and closed his eyes.

I'm losing it, he thought with shuddering dismay. He didn't understand what was happening to him, a man whose self-discipline had become absolute.

Not since that first tumultuous year with the Hales had he felt his composure fray like this until there were moments he could literally hear the ripping sound as it tore. He had never, as an adult, done anything like hammer his fist into a wall.

He'd never needed another person's liking, approval and touch with an ache that wouldn't leave him, either. And, damn it, this craving he understood the least. He and Anna had had lunch a few times. Spent the one day skiing with scarcely any conversation. He'd kissed her a few times. Held her.

Looked at objectively, she wasn't the kind of stunning beauty who could bring a man to his knees. She was prissy and judgmental. She still had secrets, and he had no idea whether she felt the same desperate compulsion to confess them to him that he apparently had to roll over and bare his unprotected belly to her.

She made Reid feel young and vulnerable and scared, and he hated it.

He especially hated having told her so much yesterday.

Swearing yet again, he turned off the water and grabbed for a towel. No, she wouldn't tell anyone what he'd said. He knew that much. But that wasn't the frightening part. It was that he wanted to tell her everything, and he couldn't.

Dressed for his day, he took a few minutes to scramble some eggs and eat them with whole-wheat toast before donning his weapon and badge and going out the door. He didn't glance toward his father. He hoped the son of a bitch *had* sat there all night and frozen his ass off. Too bad he hadn't asphyxiated himself with carbon monoxide.

When the GMC Denali fell in behind him, Reid's fingers spasmed on the steering wheel. Anna was one thing, but Dean Sawyer was another. He wouldn't give his father the satisfaction of knowing he'd riled him.

A slow thought crept in. It wouldn't be hard to make life in Angel Butte damn uncomfortable for Sergeant Dean Sawyer. No, Reid would rather his personal problems didn't become general knowledge, but it wouldn't take a whole lot of little jabs before his father would lose it.

Little jabs like traffic tickets.

Reid had a suspicion that his smile wasn't a pretty sight.

He parked and walked in to work without so much as looking back, though his internal radar never quit operating. He knew exactly where his father had parked and that he hadn't gotten out of his vehicle.

Instead of going straight to his own office, Reid detoured to Lieutenant Renner's.

"I have a problem," he told her.

She listened attentively and without comment. At one point, she turned to reach for a report and her blazer fell back. Her blouse rose enough for him to see that she hadn't been able to get the button at her waist fastened.

Damn, he thought. *Say something?*

No, wait. She probably didn't want other people knowing her business any sooner than was necessary. Generally, he felt the same. He was gaining enough respect for her, he hoped she intended to come back to work after a maternity leave.

Tuning back in, he heard her explain that, as was usual around Angel Butte, significant crime had plummeted with the recent crappy weather. Patrol officers were busy with fender benders and cars that had slid off the road; investigators had time on their hands. She could spare a couple of detectives as Reid needed them. She felt sure they'd be glad to help. She called two of them into her office. One immediately volunteered he had a friend patrolling Reid's neighborhood at night, too. He'd ask Officer Munro to drive by Reid's house often.

Reid thanked them all and went upstairs to deal with the usual morning phone messages and emails.

A call from Roger didn't improve his day. The creep had struck again, this time inflicting damage that would be costly. The tires had been slashed not only on Roger's truck, but on the three vehicles the boys had been working on.

Roger turned down Reid's offer to pay to replace them; a donation had just come in from another former alum that would cover the cost, no problem, he said. Feeling uneasy without transportation, he'd taken the opportunity to have a local tire store deliver four tires for his truck. According to Roger, he'd grumbled about vandalism, leaving the impression he'd already reported the crime.

His worry spiking, Reid felt even more unsettled. He had to get away from his father and stake out the grounds of the old resort again. He should have been there last night. If he wasn't going to get any sleep, he might as well be doing something productive.

Now, though, he'd have to do his best to know his father's whereabouts at night instead. Incidents had been staged somewhere around a week apart and, until now, only on weekends. Maybe chance, maybe not. Here, by unlikely coincidence, Dean Sawyer was in town midweek and, yes, they'd had another incident at the shelter. Patience never had been one of his virtues. Now that he was openly in town and showing his hand, if he was the one playing the tricks, he might accelerate the pace of his threats.

Reid almost wished he believed his father was behind the fires and all the rest. He'd positively enjoy arresting him. But he'd already put his finger on the source of his uneasiness. Dean not only wasn't patient, he also wasn't subtle. He lashed out when he was angry; he didn't taunt.

Although keeping Reid under observation 24/7 could be seen as a taunt. So maybe he'd changed in the past twenty years. It was something to think about.

Given his inability to concentrate on anything on his desk, Reid figured it was just as well that he'd scheduled a ten o'clock meeting at the sheriff's

department headquarters. On his way out, he made
a quick call to Detective Conner, one of the two detectives who had cheerfully agreed to provide one
of those jabs.

His father crowded his bumper again the minute
Reid pulled out onto the street. Now, *that* was his
style. In-your-face.

Not five minutes later, Reid had the pleasure of
seeing flashing lights appear two vehicles behind
him as his father was pulled over, surprised by an
unmarked car. Fun as it might have been to stay to
see the show, Reid kept going.

Strike one.

If he hadn't had the upcoming appointment, he
could have used the opportunity of having escaped
his shadow to drive out to Bear Creek. Not that he'd
learn anything. His mistake, he decided grimly, was
not being sure he knew where his father was all
night. He wouldn't make it again.

His talk with a major who headed the county
sheriff's department support services turned out
to be productive, and he was glad he hadn't post-
poned it. They were winding things up when the
major said, "Oh, I almost forgot. If you have time,
Sheriff McAllister asked if you'd stop by his office."

"Sure." Reid levered himself out of the chair and
asked for directions. A minute later, McAllister's
PA smiled and told him to go on in to the inner
sanctum.

He'd met the guy a few times, although their

conversations had been brief. Tall and rangy with steady gray eyes, Colin McAllister had to be close to Reid's age, maybe a little older. They shook hands and McAllister offered coffee, which Reid accepted out of politeness more than desire, since he'd just had a cup downstairs with the major. The PA took their orders and produced two cups with admirable efficiency.

When she stepped out with a final smile, closing the door behind her, Reid watched her go. "If I thought I could get away with kidnapping her, I'd do it. Keep her for a few days so I could suck everything she knows out of her head." There was more fervor in his voice than he'd meant to reveal.

McAllister laughed heartily. "What are you doing for an assistant right now?"

Reid told him. "I seem to scare the crap out of her. It's not getting better, either. And nobody I've interviewed feels right. Any suggestions?"

The sheriff had one. He'd been impressed with a clerk in Records. Leslie Needham. "The departmental head isn't going anywhere, which means no growth opportunity there. She's too sharp for the job, although selfishly I was glad to have her there so I could ask for her when I needed something. Try talking to her."

Reid made a mental note of the name. "I will."

McAllister wanted to know how things were going and whether Reid had any questions. Thinking about Anna's advice, Reid set aside his pride and admitted to some of his floundering.

"Take your time getting up to speed," he was told. "Nobody expected you to be well-informed on things like data management or evidence control. Never mind supplies."

"And fleet maintenance. I'm not a mechanic. I feel like a fraud."

The guy looked sympathetic. "Trust the people who work for you until they prove themselves untrustworthy. That was my philosophy. When I got promoted into that position, I came out of Investigations. I didn't have any more background for that side of the job than you do."

"At least you knew where the toilet paper was stored," Reid grumbled.

McAllister laughed again. "I did know that."

Reid studied the other man. He wondered if the Hales were right in thinking McAllister was fully aware of what they did. Would they have turned to him if Reid hadn't been in town?

If there was ever a time they needed to be marshaling resources, it was now.

"Paula and Roger Hale tell me they know you," he said.

The sheriff's expression immediately became guarded. "In passing," he agreed.

"How much do you know about what they're up to?"

McAllister considered him, not giving much

away. "How much do *you* know? I thought you were new to the area."

"They took me in years ago." Once he'd told Anna, it seemed it had become easier to be open about his background. "It's partly because of them I decided to take the job here."

"I see." The sheriff stirred after a minute. "I should have acted on what I learned, but chose not to. I hope that doesn't turn out to be the worst decision of my life."

"They're good people," Reid said.

"That was my impression. It's why I kept my mouth shut."

Reid smiled faintly. "Not because your wife begged you to? That's the version I heard."

McAllister gave a reluctant grin. "Might have had something to do with it." After an extended silence, he said, "I'm guessing there's a reason you raised the subject."

"They're having some problems right now. Nothing you can do yet, but...I'm testing the waters."

"You going to tell me what kind of problems?"

Reid did, including his own useless efforts to catch the perpetrator.

"So nothing lethal." McAllister frowned. "It sounds like the work of a troubled kid to me."

"That's been our assumption so far." Reid hesitated, not wanting to go out on a limb that might crack any minute. "It's crossed my mind that a pissed-off parent might have found the place." *Say, like Dad.*

"If so, why wouldn't he or she go to the authorities? Why play stupid games?" McAllister shook his head. "I don't see it."

"It's not likely," Reid agreed. "But I've heard the stories from the kids the Hales have taken in over the years. Some of those parents aren't wired right."

"I do realize that." The frown lingered on McAllister's forehead. "If there's anything I can do…"

Satisfied, Reid stood up. "I'll let you know."

"And feel free to call if you can't find the paper towels."

Reid was laughing when he left after a firm handshake.

Pulling out of the parking lot a minute later, he wondered how long it would take his father to appear in his rearview mirror.

IT TOOK ANNA twenty-four-plus hours to admit her reaction to Reid's part in his brother's getaway had been out of line. She knew how much he cared about Caleb. His determination to help his brother was the whole reason she and Reid had become…well, whatever they were. *Friends* didn't seem to quite cover it, not when she remembered the one passionate kiss, but she let it go for lack of any other word.

She of all people knew that sometimes there wasn't a good answer for a kid in his brother's situation. If the abuse had been going on for a long time and his father had convinced social workers and judges that it wasn't happening, Reid stepping in wouldn't necessarily turn the tide. How was he supposed to prove he'd been abused, too, all those years ago? Maybe placing Caleb somewhere safe for now *was* the best option.

She'd spent a couple of hours with Corinna Terrill's foster parents planning a funeral for a girl who was popular with her peers, and listening as they raged. The boyfriend's condition had been elevated from critical to serious, and she understood their anger even as she counseled them on what they dared be heard saying. Reporters were calling and ringing the doorbell. The principal of the high school had held a quick assembly this morning to offer grief counseling to students who wanted it. She was talking about waiting a week or two and then holding a second, lengthier assembly to hit hard on the subjects of safe driving and the perils of drinking and driving.

Anna wished her the best. This tragedy might actually chasten Angel Butte teenagers for a few weeks. An optimist would even hope for a month or two. But Anna knew darn well that by September and the beginning of a new school year, kids would have forgotten. Hormones would keep memories short. What kid ever thought anything bad would happen to him or her?

The ones who'd already had bad things happen, of course. But they would keep quiet, because that was what they did. They didn't want anyone to know how rough they had it at home. Mom might be a raging alcoholic and the fourteen-year-old knew no one else would feed her younger siblings if she didn't, but that reality would be hidden at school and even from friends. And, insane as it was, that same girl might well speed once she had her license, or think her boyfriend's reckless driving was cool. She might even have a sense of fatalism. Shit happened, and she knew she couldn't prevent it, so why not have fun?

Anna went home weary and seriously depressed.

She lasted through dinner before her conscience made her pick up the phone. She almost hoped to get Reid's voice mail, but instead he answered immediately.

"Hi," she said, feeling shy.

"Hey." His voice was low and gruff. "I kept thinking about you today."

"Me, too. I mean, I thought about you."

He laughed. "Good."

"I just wanted to, well, tell you I'm sorry for saying what I did about Caleb." She finished in a hurry. "I do trust you. And it's true that getting a kid involved in the foster-care system isn't always the best answer."

"Thank you for saying that." He sounded even gruffer. "The truth is, I'm afraid of losing if I take our father on in court."

"I know," she said. "Although—" Anna squeezed

her eyes shut. She'd sworn she wasn't going to pretend to have all the answers for him. Nobody liked a know-it-all.

"Although?" he prompted.

Now she pretty much had to say what she'd been thinking. "Just that having two of you saying the same thing might make the difference. That's all."

The pause made her wonder what he was thinking. "Maybe," he said at last. Typically unrevealing.

"Anyway, that's all I called to say. I get on my high horse easily. That's not what you needed from me."

Again there was a pause before he spoke. "Actually, I like it that you're honest with me, Anna. Don't pull your punches."

She gave a weak smile he wouldn't see. "I don't think anybody has ever said that to me before."

His chuckle felt like the slightly rough feel of his fingertips on her skin. "Have you eaten?" he asked.

"Yes. You?"

"Yeah. I could have used company."

"Did you have a bad day?"

"Not the best. You?"

They weren't saying anything special, but she realized they were both speaking in soft voices, as if… She didn't know.

"It was awful," she admitted. "Mostly fallout from the car accident. Um. Is your father still lurking?"

"Oh, yeah."

"I suppose he'd follow you if you came over here."
Oh my God. Was she suggesting…? The heat in her
cheeks told her that, yes, she'd just invited him over.

"Are you asking me?" The timbre of Reid's voice
had changed.

"If…well, you want to talk or anything." Especially *anything,* she admitted to herself. She didn't
do casual sex—but sex with Reid Sawyer wouldn't
be casual, not on her part.

"Yes, he'll undoubtedly follow me, but I don't
give a damn. Unless it'll bother you to have him
know where you live."

"He isn't a threat to me, is he?"

"No." His words came slower. "Not to you."

"You?" she whispered.

"Not anymore. If you mean it, I'll be there in
five."

Her heart was pounding, but that didn't stop her
from saying, "I mean it."

"Good," he said with some of the same intonation he had used earlier. His satisfaction was unmistakable.

Anna rushed to clean her kitchen before he arrived, as if he'd care, then sprinted into the bathroom to peer anxiously at herself in the mirror. Too
late to do much of anything about her appearance,
even if her suddenly slapping on a bunch of makeup
wouldn't be ridiculously obvious. She made a face
at herself. Obvious? No, just ridiculous.

In the end, she settled for running a brush through

her hair and changing out of her cozy but hideous cardigan into a loose-weaved sweater that clung to her body, making her look curvier than she actually was.

False advertising, she thought with a sigh, then jumped six inches when the doorbell rang. Pulse racing, she rushed to let Reid in.

He probably only wanted to talk anyway.

The breadth of his shoulders blocked any sight of his father's SUV. She hurriedly drew him in anyway. "Is he there?" Silly to be whispering.

He grinned, watching as she shut and locked the front door. "Nope. He likes to ride my bumper. Amazingly enough, he just got his second ticket of the day for tailgating. Which also means he lost me."

"Second of the day?" She stared at him. "You're responsible, aren't you?"

"Damn straight." The amusement was gone, the steel bared. "The son of a bitch is going to find out he can't terrorize me."

Maybe she should have an ethical problem with him using the police force for a personal vendetta, but… "If he's dumb enough not to have learned from the first ticket, he deserves what he has coming," she decided. "Besides, I hate drivers who tailgate."

Reid flashed another of those truly wicked grins. "Me, too. I'm performing a community service."

They were in the middle of her small living room

when she hesitated. "Would you like a cup of cof-fee? Or…?"

He took a step closer to her, lifting his hand as if to cup her face, but stopping before he touched her. His eyes had a dark glow that mesmerized her. "No coffee," he said. "All I want is you."

She tilted her head to nestle her face in his hand. "Yes, please," she said, her voice shaking.

He groaned, and the next thing she knew his hand had slid around to the back of her head and his mouth had closed over hers.

Anna rose on tiptoe and kissed him back with all the passion in her.

CHAPTER NINE

REID HAD MADE a resolution on the way over here. No matter how much he wanted her, this was just going to be sex. Good sex, he hoped, but he wasn't for one minute going to forget his limitations, and he sure as hell wasn't going to loosen the reins on his willpower. Which meant controlling even the kiss.

The fact that hunger rushed over him like a tsunami and had him devouring her shook him enough that he forced himself to pull his mouth from Anna's to string small kisses along her jaw, to nuzzle her neck, to nibble on her earlobe. He needed to get a grip. *Make it slow,* he reminded himself. *Give her pleasure. Don't push her up against the wall and bury yourself in her the way you want.*

God. That was something he'd never done before, but the picture leaped into his mind, shockingly vivid, and he had to grit his teeth to suppress a raw sound.

The next few minutes turned into something of a battle. She kept trying to capture his mouth; he'd let her win the skirmish, but would keep the kiss light and teasing. He didn't dare start to undress her. Touching her breasts through the nubby sweater and thin T-shirt was about all he could handle in slow-down mode.

Eventually, he raised his head. "Bedroom?" He sounded hoarse.

She stared at him almost blindly. "Oh. Um." Her head turned. "Upstairs."

God help him. He was so damn hard he didn't know how he was going to climb the stairs, but he wasn't going to throw her down on her sofa, either. He had something to prove to himself.

No, it wasn't that complicated. He just needed to make sure he didn't get mixed up about what this meant.

He grabbed her hand and led her to the foot of the staircase. It reared above them like Mount Rainier. He could see the sofa out of the corner of his eye. *No! Put one foot in front of the other.*

She took the initiative and led the way, tugging him by the hand. As he plodded, she laughed over her shoulder at him, her eyes alight. "Slowpoke," she teased.

"I have a handicap," he growled.

"Really? Is that what it is?"

No, it was the hard-on to end all hard-ons. He'd liked her better on the defensive, he decided.

No, this is good, he assured himself. *All she wants is to have fun, too.*

Was that what this was supposed to be?

The upstairs of her new town house had only two bedrooms. He saw through the first open door that she was using one of the rooms for a home office. The other, thank God, was her bedroom. He had an impression of warm colors and glowing wood, but all he really saw was the bed. Only a double, which suggested she might not entertain men here often. No footboard, so his feet could hang off the bottom.

When they reached the bed, Anna turned to face him. Those soft gray eyes searched his face, but she didn't say anything. Instead, she did a little shimmy and pulled sweater and tee over her head, ruffling her sleek dark blond hair and leaving her wearing only a bra that was presumably intended to be skin colored. Her skin was so white, it didn't work.

His question was answered about what she wore beneath her clothes. Utilitarian color, delicate cut, allowing a swell of female flesh above satin fabric. A guttural sound escaped Reid's throat, and he placed his palms right over her breasts and gently rotated. She bent her head and watched, hair fanning down to partially hide her expression.

Her breasts were considerably more generous than they appeared in her workday clothes. The truth was, she was so slender, with a narrow rib cage and tiny waist, the swell of what he guessed might even be C-cup breasts was erotic enough to cut off his breathing. He had to close his eyes for a moment.

You're in control. His mantra. He didn't usually have to remind himself.

His hands didn't wait for direction. One had

slipped behind her to unclip her bra so that, by the time he opened his eyes, the straps were already slipping off her shoulders and down her arms. She turned out to have small, taut nipples, rosy-pink.

Reid dropped to his knees in front of her and worked on freeing her from her slacks. The panties were tan, too, and damn skimpy. The soft curls he found beneath were a shade darker than her hair, a light brown. He eased slacks and panties down her long legs, until he helped her step out of shoes and clothes. The socks he had to peel off.

Then he explored her legs as he stroked his hands back up the way they'd come. Spectacular legs, slim with taut muscles. He'd already known how fabulous they were after seeing her in the skintight, stretchy pants she'd worn skiing. Her hips were almost boyish, but not quite. His thumbs explored the dip beneath her pelvic bones, then the jut of them covered by silky skin. Testing his self-control, he rubbed his cheek against her curls, feeling her fingers tangle in his hair and grip hard. When he licked between her folds, she gasped.

"Reid."

Oh, yeah. He liked the way she said his name.

He did it again, swirled his tongue a few times, closing his mind to everything but the amazing taste and sensations, the little sounds she made.

The fact that you're taking your time. Good.

He shed his shirt before he rose to his feet, and Anna immediately transferred her hands from his head to his chest. Every muscle in his body tightened at her exploring touch. In self-defense, he lifted her and laid her backward across the bed, planting a knee between her legs and pinning her hands above her head.

Better.

He made slow love to her, leaving his own trousers on. More self-defense. Only when her hips were rising helplessly and cries broke from her lips did he grab a packet from his pocket and get naked.

"Let me," she whispered, but he shook his head.

"Not this time."

Reid was shocked to see his hands were shaking when he donned the condom. Not a good sign.

He wanted her and that was okay. He was controlling the pace.

He went back to kissing her, his tongue deep in her mouth. She sucked on it, sending an electric charge through his body. Her legs were already splayed wide. All he had to do was position himself and push.

As slight as she was, he wasn't surprised to find her passage was tight. Move slow, when the roaring in his head demanded he plunge hard and fast. She squirmed, tilting her hips to meet him. By the time he was buried as deep as he could go, the very concept of self-control was beyond him.

Anna's fingers dug into the muscles of his back and she moaned.

At the small sound, he began to move.

He held on, although, God, he didn't know how, until he felt the first ripples of her climax. Only then did he let himself go, pounding into her once, twice, three times, the pleasure making him deaf, dumb and blind.

So damn good.

He didn't let himself sag on top of her the way he wanted to. Instead, he came down on his shoulder and rolled to the side, gently pulling her with him until her slim body was arranged the way he liked it.

It was a long time until he could think. Euphoria spread like a drug in his bloodstream. *Yeah, so what?* he thought as his brain gradually came back online. Sex was supposed to feel good. It had been too long for him. And, damn, he'd wanted her. He wouldn't make more of it than it was.

He should say something. What? Did he *usually* say anything at this moment? For some weird reason, he couldn't remember. Couldn't even quite picture another woman's head resting on his shoulder, the scent of another woman's hair. Something like panic squeezed him, but he stamped down hard on it. What an idiot, freaking because the sex was good.

It was Anna who eased herself away from him. She rose on one elbow and raked her hair back from her face. Her eyes searched his again, and this time he had no idea at all what she was thinking. There was a tiny crinkle between her eyebrows.

"Do you always like to be in charge?" she asked.

Stunned to know that she'd seen right through him, he let the silence go a little longer than he should have. "Yeah," he said finally. "It's the nature of the beast. Was it so bad?"

"You know it wasn't." But the tension evident in her voice and on her forehead didn't ease, either. "I just would have liked—" She didn't finish.

He caressed her face, slid his fingers into the silk of her hair. "Would have liked?"

Anna shook her head slightly but emphatically. "It doesn't matter." She laid her head back down, relaxing as if comfortable, but he wasn't fooled.

The panic was pressing upward, feeling a lot like heartburn. Stirred into it was a hint of wounded pride. That wasn't good enough for her? He knew she'd come, had heard her cry his name in astonishment. So what the hell did she want?

Resentment stirred. Power. That was what she wanted. To demonstrate her power over him. To know she could reduce him to sheer desperation.

Wasn't happening. If his brand of lovemaking wasn't good enough for her, well, there were plenty of women in a city the size of Angel Butte.

He rolled out of bed. "This was a mistake."

There was a discernible silence behind him before she said, "If you think so, then it was." She sounded cool, even indifferent.

Reid yanked up his knit boxers and the black

dress pants he'd worn to work. He had to look at her.
He didn't make a habit of slicing people deep without at least checking to see what he'd done to them.

Of course she wasn't looking at him. She, too, had
slid out of bed, but on the other side. As gutsy as she
was, he should have known she wouldn't try to wrap
a sheet around herself to hide her body. Instead,
with her head held high, she walked to the dresser.
While he still stood there feeling cruel and, God
help him, turned on by the sight of her slim, pale
body, she put on bikini underwear—petal-pink—
followed by a pair of jeans.

The bra she grabbed for didn't match. She probably didn't notice or care. Although she was keeping
her back to him, he could see her beautiful breasts
in the mirror above the dresser. Covered, then adjusted after she hooked the bra in back. A moment
later, she pulled a long-sleeved tee over her head
and at last turned to face him.

Reid hadn't moved. Even in the mirror, he'd seen
her eyes. For all her composure, he'd hurt her. Feeling sick, he asked himself if he'd meant to. *You
got what you came for, and now you want to make
damn sure she doesn't expect anything else or de-
ceive herself you'll be back for more.*

That, or he had lashed out because she'd hurt *his*
feelings.

The first option sounded more like him. He didn't
like knowing it, but he was capable of thinking that

coldly. Sometimes that was the only way he could protect himself.

The thought rattled him. Protect himself from *what?*

Feeling too much.

Reid thought of himself as a decent man. He didn't hurt people on purpose, although he'd like to make an exception for his father. He especially didn't hurt the women he had sex with if he could help it. But it had been easy to be a decent man when he didn't feel anything and had no need to protect himself.

Reid suddenly became aware he hadn't moved. His shirt lay on the floor halfway to the door. His socks and shoes were... He didn't know.

"I'm sorry," he said hoarsely.

Those extraordinary eyes met his. "You have nothing to be sorry for, Reid. I knew you didn't want to get involved with me. That's okay. But I'd like you to leave now."

"No. I didn't mean it." He almost groaned, the turmoil rising in him to fill his chest cavity. He couldn't afford to do this.

Anna crossed her arms. "What didn't you mean?"

"It wasn't a mistake."

"Obviously it was, or we wouldn't be having this discussion."

"No." God. A boulder lodged in his throat. "I was..." What? He knew, but could he say it?

"Afraid," he managed, sick that he'd bared himself to this extent. He remembered what he'd thought once, that for her he would roll on his back and expose his naked underside. That was what he was doing now.

The only reaction he could see was the slight widening of her eyes. "Afraid of what?"

"You were right. I do have to be in control. I didn't want to lose it with you. I needed to be sure—" He didn't know how to finish.

"I didn't get the impression I was anything special?" The bitterness was the first real emotion she'd let slip into her voice.

Oh, Christ, he thought, and, yes, he was going to do this despite the fear ripping at his gut. He'd found something more powerful even than his need to keep his distance from everyone and every emotion.

Anna.

He knew, somehow, that she'd been hurt in ways worse than what she'd told him. He could not, would not, add a layer, whatever the cost to him.

She was still waiting for him to finish the damn sentence. "I needed to prove to myself that you aren't." *Special* wasn't a word he could say. Implying was bad enough.

"Well, you succeeded," she told him, and the sharpness was still there. "Congratulations."

"No. I didn't succeed." He rubbed a hand over his face, willing it to stay impassive. "I hurt your feelings, and I didn't fool myself for a second."

Her forehead crinkled as she scrutinized him. "Do you have any idea how much I hate knowing that every time you call me, you wish you hadn't wanted to?"

"You can tell?" he asked in surprise, then winced at what he'd given away.

Her laugh broke. "Of course I can tell. I should never have asked you over tonight. *I* knew it was a mistake, but I suppose I hoped—"

He put a name to what he now felt: anguish. Or was it terror? Reid didn't know where he was going with her, or whether he wanted to go there, but walking away now would be worse.

"I owe you an explanation," he said.

"No, you don't."

"Please," he heard himself say. Beg.

The gray of her eyes darkened, clouded. His fault.

"All right," she said at last. "I'll go make some coffee." She detoured to her closet and thrust her feet into fluffy slippers, then walked right past Reid without looking at him again.

He didn't move until he heard her footsteps on the stairs and knew he was truly alone. Then he let his head fall back and strangled the bellow that rose to his throat. What emerged instead was a raw sound, nothing he recognized. He fought the desire to slam his fist into the wall again, too.

What was *wrong* with him? What was he going to say to her? Why hadn't he just left when he had the chance?

But he knew, and he wasn't being entirely unselfish. No, he didn't want to hurt her, but there was more. Adrift in so many unfamiliar feelings lately, he needed her. So quickly, she'd become essential. A lodestone. An anchor. He didn't really know, only that he wasn't sure he could maintain his sanity if he couldn't talk to her, touch her, see her.

And now there was a price to be paid.

He hated the price, but, even more, he hated feeling so mixed-up.

So out of control.

He'd been kidding himself. Tonight had been a pretense. He'd been pretending to himself a lot lately.

After a moment, he swiped his shirt up off the floor with an angry movement and thrust his arms through the sleeves. He sat on the upholstered rocker and put on socks and shoes, then looked around, feeling as if he was missing something.

His weapon. He rarely went without, but tonight he'd locked it in his glove compartment.

He had the ironic thought that he had come to her entirely unprotected.

THE COFFEE WAS ready to pour by the time Reid appeared in her kitchen. She'd heard the toilet flush upstairs, but couldn't help wondering what else he'd been doing. Searching her drawers? Hunting

for a listening device? God knew. He was paranoid enough.

Except she knew that wasn't right. The most im-
pregnable man she had ever met might also be the
most vulnerable.

Without comment, Anna filled two mugs, added
cream to hers and carried them to the small dining nook. The old table she had refinished was
made of sycamore, she'd been told, not one of the
more common woods. She'd hand-polished it to a
warm, rich color. She loved stroking the surface
and feeling the tiny indentations left by a century
or more of use.

She made sure to set the mugs down on woven
place mats.

The four chairs were antiques, too, with caned
seats. She let Reid take the one armchair, the most
substantial of the four. Picking up the sugar bowl,
she added a spoonful to her coffee and stirred without looking at him.

"This is something I've been thinking about recently," he said, then gave a grunt that might have
been intended to be a laugh. "Hard not to."

She waited to hear what *this* was.

"My life was on an even keel until I learned I
had a brother. I saw his name, that there'd been a
court proceeding, and I felt such rage. I'd forgotten
I *could* feel like that."

Anna finally looked at him, to find that he was

gazing down into his black coffee as if he'd find answers there. His hand cradled the mug.

"I told myself that was natural. I should have kept an eye on my father. That Caleb had suffered from his brutality for fifteen years was partly my fault."

Anna's lips parted, but Reid shook his head. So he was watching her, somehow.

"On a rational level, I know that isn't true," he said, before she could protest. "It's our father's fault. Entirely his."

"Yes."

"But something changed in me that day. I got in touch with Caleb, flew up to Spokane to meet him. Understood when he rejected me, said whatever I was offering was too little, too late."

Oh, she understood that, too. Had she ever believed anyone's promises again, the way she had before a betrayed promise resulted in her sister's death? Like Reid, she knew the angry man who killed Molly was really responsible, but in her mind she'd fastened on the young social worker who'd hugged them both and said, "I'll be by often to check on you. I promise."

A promise not kept, with fatal consequences.

"I lived for Caleb to call me," Reid continued. He sounded almost dispassionate, yet…not. "Once I'd met him, everything changed."

"You mean, *you* changed."

"Yeah." He met her eyes at last. "I quit my job.

I still don't know why. I don't know why I've done much of anything since then."

That stung. "Including starting something with me."

"No." His perturbation showed in eyes the color of an antique bottle. "Strangely enough, that's one of the few things I do understand."

She frowned. "What do you mean?"

"I saw you fighting for that kid. For Yancey. I wish I'd had someone like you. I never did. But there you were. I wanted—" he shrugged "—to understand why you were willing to put yourself out there for kids who weren't even yours, I guess. Talking to you helps me keep it together."

"But you're mad you need someone else to do that."

He grimaced. "Sometimes that's true. One more thing I'm not used to feeling."

Anna wasn't used to needing anyone, either. She did better at relationships than she suspected Reid did, but how much better? Once free of the foster-care system, she had never allowed herself to tell a soul that she'd had a sister. The reasons weren't subtle. As young as she'd been, she had blamed herself. She had tried to transfer all the blame to other people, but a small knot of guilt had continued to fester. She liked to think its existence, deep in her core, made her a better person. Better at her job. More caring.

But keeping the secret of a child's existence and her own guilt did not make her better at friendships, and she suspected it had something to do with the fact that she'd never let herself fall in love before, either. Opening yourself like that... She almost shuddered at the idea but was aware that Reid was already watching her strangely.

"Needing anyone," she said. "That's what you're not used to."

"Yeah." The word came out strangled. "I thought, tonight..."

"You don't have to say it." She didn't want to *hear* it. He didn't like knowing she was his mother confessor, so he'd tried to turn her into something else. A temporary sex partner, easy to dismiss. Maybe he hadn't even been that attracted to her. Men didn't have to be, did they? She was okay-looking, she'd invited him over here for reasons that weren't subtle. "Let's...leave it the way it was." *A mistake.*

His whole body jolted. "What are you talking about?"

"I'm happy to talk to you anytime you want, Reid." *Lie, lie.* "Let's not...confuse what's going on between us, okay?"

He shoved his chair back as if he was going to stand, but didn't. His hands gripped the arms of the chair, the tendons standing out. His jaw muscles spasmed. "I won't deny I'm confused, but I want you, Anna. Will you give me a chance?"

"A chance at what?" she cried, and now she was the one pushing her chair back. Fight or flight.

"I don't know!" he yelled. Then he bent his head for a moment. When he looked at her again, his eyes were dark. "Do we have to know in advance? Does anyone?"

It was weird how much shock she felt. No, of course the average man and woman had no idea when they met whether the attraction would go anywhere meaningful. What did she want, him to go down on bended knee? She imagined how suspicious she'd be if he did. They'd known each other a grand total of a month. Of course that was not what she wanted.

"You're not the only one who gets scared," she confessed in a low voice. "I'm trying not to be a coward."

"I've already hurt you. Saving yourself from more…that's not cowardly."

She moistened her lips. "Isn't it?

"No." He offered a sort of crooked smile. "It's common sense."

"Well, then, I'm just filled with common sense."

An emotion flashed through his eyes, too quick to pin down. "That's a no, then?" he asked.

Anna shook her head and smiled shakily. "No, that's a yes. You're right. When I invited you over tonight, I was willing to take a chance. I guess I still am."

"God." He was suddenly on his feet, yanking her up and into his arms. "I thought..."

She rested her forehead on his chest and shook her head. "You were right. I was trying to back away. Tonight...you didn't seem to want me all that much. It was so...scripted. It was like you didn't even want me to touch you. You stole my courage."

"I understand," he said hoarsely.

Did he? She supposed she'd find out eventually.

She took a deep breath and eased back, smiling almost naturally at him. "So. Want to go cross-country skiing this weekend?"

His laugh was ragged but real. "Yeah. I'd like to go skiing with you again. Only this time I think I may make you go ahead so I can enjoy watching you."

"And deprive me of the pleasure of watching you?"

Reid laughed again, his relaxation obvious. "How about if we take turns?"

"Deal."

He kissed her, so gently her bones felt as if they were melting. His lips were soft, whispering across hers, playing with them, teasing them. She felt him becoming aroused again, and she certainly was, but he finally ended the kiss by touching his forehead to hers and leaving it there. He breathed, and she breathed, and finally he stepped back.

Keep it light, Anna told herself. "I guess the question is, does your father have any Nordic equipment? Will he be able to keep up with us?"

Reid laughed again. "Unless he's taken up a new hobby, the answer is no. But it's a nice picture. He can sit and freeze his ass off in the parking lot instead."

The idea gave her the creeps. "Would he do that?"

He shook his head. "I keep hoping he'll get bored and go home. But God knows how much vacation time he's accrued."

"Does Caleb know what your father is doing?"

She sensed as much as saw Reid stiffen.

"He knows."

"He must be scared."

"I think he is," Reid agreed, "but he doesn't want to admit as much to me."

"He's a fifteen-year-old boy. Of course he doesn't. And to you, of all people."

His expression was odd. "Of all people?"

"You said he looks like you."

Reid frowned. "There's a resemblance."

She nodded. "Growing up, he must have heard about you."

"Probably nothing good."

"Sure it was. You escaped. You thumbed your nose at your father. You probably assumed heroic proportions to poor Caleb, who saw himself as a victim."

Reid stared at her.

"And then you swooped in and rescued him. He's

grateful, but he's resentful, too. How can he help it?" she asked simply.

His gaze didn't waver for a long moment, until he shook his head as if baffled. "I should understand him and I don't, but somehow you do. You make it sound…obvious."

"I could be wrong," she warned.

"No. You're not wrong. Tell me, oh wise one, how do I break through the resentment?"

How could she say this without revealing that she needed the same from him?

Keep it simple, she told herself. "You have to convince him that you need him, too. You're…so self-contained, it can be intimidating, Reid. And you two don't have the advantage of a lifelong relationship. He doesn't have the confidence to believe you love him. If he doesn't have anything to offer that you want, he'll assume he's nothing but an obligation you felt you had to take on."

He grunted as if she'd dealt a blow. For a moment, his expression was naked. "I don't know what I do feel for him. What I want from him."

"Don't you?" Anna rose to her tiptoes and kissed his rough cheek. He smelled so good she wanted to linger, but she knew the moment had come to let him go. He needed to recover his sense of self-sufficiency. Otherwise…*he* would resent her. "Sleep on it," she murmured.

He looked at her for a long moment. "I wanted you touching me, too," he said, then nodded and left.

CHAPTER TEN

REID GLANCED IN the rearview mirror. Annoyingly enough, his father hung well back while still keeping a visual. Evidently he'd learned something from the two tickets he'd received so far. Even farther back, Reid spotted an unmarked police car. Now that Dean knew he was a target, he'd have seen the car, too.

Too bad. Feeling an urgent need to get away, Reid tried to figure out how to open some distance between the vehicles. Or would that be a mistake? Might his father pretend to lose him, then manage to tail him out to Bear Creek?

The traffic light ahead had been green for a long time. Reid saw his chance. Dad wouldn't dare run a red light, knowing he was being watched. Too many tickets in too short a time could be made to have consequences beyond fines. Reid could ask Chief Raynor to call his counterpart in Spokane and say, *One of your officers is making a nuisance of himself in my town. I don't know what hair he has up his butt, but the way he's driving, he's a danger to the citizens of Angel Butte, and I want him gone.*

Reid eased his foot off the accelerator, biding

his time. Yes. The light turned yellow. He sped up just enough to glide through the intersection right as the light turned red. His father, hovering back with another cop behind him, had no choice but to brake. Reid stepped on it, staying inside the speed limit, but barely. His first thought had been to take evasive maneuvers, but he went with his instincts and continued driving straight, opening as much distance as possible, but not making any obvious effort to lose his tail.

In the mirror, he saw the Denali leap forward with the green light, while the unmarked took a right and disappeared. Shit. Detective Rogers, who'd been on him today, had probably taken a call. Strange, though, because Reid hadn't heard anything over the police radio.

His father's big black SUV closed fast. He'd seen that he had lost his pursuer and was taking advantage of the freedom. Reid was going thirty-five miles an hour; his father had to be pushing it at fifty or more.

And then, suddenly, flashing lights were there as a marked squad car burst out of a cross street. Chance? Or had Rogers taken the initiative to set up a trap?

Strike three.

Grinning, Reid imagined his father's fury as he slowed and pulled over—and watched his son vanish into the distance. Reid turned, then turned again, finally working his way back toward Arrow Lake, the city-operated airport and the route that took him out to the old resort.

Maybe this was stupid, but he kept thinking about what Anna had said last night.

Actually, he'd done nothing *but* think about Anna. When he wasn't remembering what she'd said, he relived the experience of making love with her. As a result, he'd been half-aroused all day.

Now he had to force his mind back to his plan.

Once she'd laid it out, he could understand all too well what Caleb must be thinking and feeling. Reid had always thought of his own, seemingly irrational resentment of the Hales in the early days as generalized anger. The minute Anna started talking about Caleb feeling like a victim, Reid had identified. Instantly, powerfully.

Yes. Reid, too, had hated the knowledge that someone else had had to rescue him because he was too helpless to get himself out of trouble. In fact, he'd loathed the feeling of helplessness so much, he'd determined on both conscious and unconscious levels that he'd never let himself need anyone as much.

Listening to Anna, he'd also understood immediately how crucial a feeling of reciprocity was. In his case, that had never been a possibility. The Hales *hadn't* needed him. They had come to care about him, but he was only one of many kids they took in. Succeeding with him would give them a feeling of validation, but Reid personally—the sullen teenage boy he'd been—had been more in the nature of a job to them than anything.

For all that he couldn't get it out of his head, Reid didn't like remembering last night's scene. He hadn't yet let himself come to terms with what it meant that he'd humbled himself for Anna. Or the fact that the concept of reciprocity wasn't only an issue between him and his brother. He knew he'd have to confront that truth eventually, but…one thing at a time.

Anna could wait. She'd said she would give him another chance. He thought she'd meant it.

Today, he needed to focus on Caleb. Reid felt an urgency to see his brother he didn't entirely understand. But now he had his chance and he was taking it.

No other traffic was visible when Reid turned off the road. Winter had deepened the potholes in the quarter-mile-long, overgrown driveway that ended in front of the old lodge. As usual, he saw a boy start to melt out of sight behind one of the derelict pickup trucks, then reappear when he recognized Reid behind the wheel. Roger's truck was missing, as, presumably, was Roger.

Reid nodded a hello to the kid—Palmer, he thought—as he got out, then took the porch steps two at a time. His gaze fell on the deep scar in the door left by the knife blade. Of the tricks so far, that one made him the most uneasy. He was frustrated, of course, because it had happened right under his nose. More than that, though, it had made plain the reality they weren't dealing just with someone who enjoyed setting fires, bad as that was. No, they were being taunted by someone who was saying, *I can get to you anytime, any way I want. Are you scared yet?*

Whoever he was, he could do much, much worse than he had so far. In fact, an escalation was inevitable. Somebody could die next time.

Reid grimaced. That fear might explain his intense need to see Caleb. To try to make things better between them.

He rapped his knuckles on the heavy door, then opened it without waiting for an answer. This being midday, half a dozen boys sat at various places along the long, cafeteria-style tables, while two others were planted in front of desktop computers. Paula had been leaning over Truong's shoulder pointing something out in a book open in front of him, but she straightened and smiled.

"Reid! Good to see you."

Caleb was one of the boys at the table with an open book and papers strewn about. His expression was first startled then wary.

"Paula." Reid nodded again as he cut between tables. "Boys." He grimaced at the sight of what Truong was studying. "Geometry," he said, feeling sympathy.

"Who ever uses this shit?" the kid asked plaintively.

Paula leveled a schoolmarm look at Reid, who made a valiant effort.

"Uh…engineers. Actually," he admitted, "even cops do sometimes."

"Cops?" Truong echoed in disbelief. Everyone stared at him.

Talking about a sharpshooter's calculations probably wasn't appropriate. Fortunately, there were other examples. "Yeah, you know when a major car accident happens? To understand how it occurred and which driver bears what degree of fault, we have to study the scene. We draw lines on the pavement. Take measurements. Determine things like speed and trajectory."

He'd helped do that, and it was a grisly job when there'd been fatalities. Nothing like trying to determine how fast a drunk driver was going when she crossed the highway median and struck another vehicle, killing a child. He didn't let any of that show on his face.

"Mind if I borrow Caleb for a few minutes?" he asked Paula.

"Sure, no problem. Caleb, did you finish the worksheet?"

He shrugged. "Except for number fourteen."

"I don't get it, either," another boy said. A third chimed in.

Paula smiled. "Then we'll wait and talk about it when Caleb gets back."

Caleb swung his leg over the bench and slouched his way to Reid, who led him through the kitchen to the back door.

"Let's walk along the creek," he said.

His brother grunted and reached for a down vest hanging in the mudroom that formed the back exit from the kitchen.

More snow lay on the ground at the lodge than in town, and last night it had frozen again. Right now, the sun felt almost warm, which meant slush. Reid wore boots, though, and saw that Caleb did, as well. Neither had on gloves. Reid shoved his hands into the pockets of his parka. For a few minutes, the squelch of their footsteps was the only sound.

"Dad's still in town," he said finally. "He's doing his damnedest to follow me everywhere I go."

Alarm flared on his brother's face. "Then why'd you come out here?"

"I shook him." He smiled grimly and explained his strategy.

"He's gotten three tickets?" Caleb was clearly savoring the idea. "That's awesome!"

Reid let himself grin. "I thought so. I'm hoping he'll have had enough soon and go home."

"If he's following you, that means he still doesn't know where I am."

"Likely," Reid agreed, "but it's also conceivable he's playing us. Setting up his innocence."

"Is that what you think?"

They passed the last cabin. From here, Reid could see a rooftop across the creek and downstream a hundred yards or so. Otherwise, the landscape was pristine, painted in white and the deep green of pine boughs and the clear gray of running water. He took a breath of the cold, clear air and felt a primitive kind of satisfaction. He'd missed the Northwest.

"No." He paused to look out at the stream. "I don't. Tell me if you disagree, but I don't see him having any patience or subtlety. To the contrary, one of his problems is having lousy impulse control. I could never figure out why it hadn't gotten him in trouble on the job."

"It has." Caleb kicked a rock and they both watched as it rolled with a small splash into the water. "He's been suspended twice in the last, I don't know, couple of years. The union goes to bat for him, but he was demoted not that long ago."

"And took it out on you." Reid's jaw set.

Those still-too-thin shoulders jerked.

"I want you to know that no matter what, I won't let that son of a bitch take you back." This was the first and maybe most important thing he knew he must say. "I thought you'd be better off here with the Hales and other boys your age than you would be with me, but if need be, I won't hesitate to go for custody."

Caleb kept his head down and didn't respond.

Reid cleared his throat. "I'm not good with emotion. But there's something else I want you to know." He waited until his brother lifted his head to look at him. "It's lonely not having family. I don't usually let myself think about it, but since I found out about you—" It was hard not to squirm like an awkward kid. Man, this was hard to do. Lying in bed last night, he'd rehearsed and revised this speech a dozen times. To his own ears, he sounded falsely hearty, but he was doing the best he could. "I moved to Angel Butte to be near you because I hoped we'd be family. You may not want that. If not, you don't owe me anything." That part was important to get out. "But think about it. Unless your mom comes back in the picture, we're pretty much all each other has."

Caleb stared for a long time. He seemed...stunned. Who could blame him? Reid thought. Unless he'd been a lot luckier than Reid, he wouldn't be any better at talking about how he felt.

"You're saying this because you think you'll soften me up so I'll tell you stuff I wouldn't otherwise," he said finally with acute suspicion.

That stung a little, but Reid kept his stance relaxed and shook his head. "No. I owe the Hales. Now that I live nearby, for them and for the other boys, I'd be trying to find out who's doing this no matter what. But I'm here because of you, and my biggest priority is keeping you safe." Holding that long, disbelieving stare took an effort of will, but Reid managed it despite the discomfort.

Anna had damn well better not have misled him.

But suddenly Caleb ducked his head again. "Okay," he mumbled.

"You want to keep walking?"

"I guess."

"I've been seeing this woman," Reid heard himself say, before the jolt of shock hit. This wasn't anything he'd rehearsed. He had no idea if talking about Anna to Caleb was a good idea or a really, really bad one.

Caleb snuck a look at him. "You ever been...like, married or anything?"

"No." *God, no,* he thought, but didn't say. That wasn't what he wanted for his brother—to grow up believing himself incapable of commitment and love. "I never thought I'd want to get that close to someone," he said, speaking slowly.

Hearing the past tense jarred him. The fact he'd used it meant something.

Caleb looked as astonished as he felt. "But she—this woman—is making you think about it?"

"I...don't know." A sharp pain crept up his neck toward his skull. *Hell.* "Anna has shaken some of my assumptions, though."

Caleb's nod was awkward.

They walked in silence for a good five minutes, until they emerged into a clearing surrounding a house. No one appeared to be home, but in concert they turned and started back.

"There's one guy who kind of freaks me out," Caleb said suddenly. "He's... I think he goes outside at night sometimes."

Careful not to jump on that, Reid nodded. "Is this the one who lives in the lodge, too?"

"TJ. He's really tense. Mad all the time. He doesn't like me and I don't like him."

"Do any of the boys talk about their parents?"

"Not really. I mean, you see stuff." Caleb was quiet for a minute. "I don't like Damon, either, but he's got some majorly horrible scars on his back. Someone beat him bad."

A kid. Reid's hands balled into fists in his pockets. "A few years ago, I was one of the investigators looking into a religious sect. Anybody who 'sinned' was whipped in front of the whole congregation. A teenage girl who sneaked away and had sex with her boyfriend was stoned to death."

Caleb whispered an obscenity.

"Caleb." Reid hesitated. "I'm going to ask to see the files on all the boys here." This time, he wasn't taking no for an answer. "I need their last names so that I can find out what's in their pasts."

"You mean, like, if any of them have set fires before."

"Right. Certain kinds of abuse make someone more likely to act out in specific ways, too. I'm telling you this in confidence. Asking you to keep it to yourself."

"Oh, yeah," the teenager scoffed. "Because telling everyone my brother is investigating them would make me most likely to be elected prom king."

Reid had to laugh. "No, it probably wouldn't make you everyone's best friend."

Caleb didn't look at him. "Are you going to start with TJ?"

"I will. The other thing I'm going to do is try to locate their parents or guardians. Are they where they should be? Or could one of them have found him?"

Caleb stopped dead. "But *how?* I mean, Dad found you. But if you hadn't come to Angel Butte…"

"I've been thinking about that. How many of these guys have stayed in touch with someone from home? Brother, sister, mom, girlfriend? Do any of them sneak out to meet someone?"

Caleb started walking again. Out of the corner of his eye, Reid watched him struggle with his conscience.

"Maybe," he said at last. "But I think a couple of the guys might have met girls in town. You know? There isn't exactly a rule against it, even though Paula and Roger don't like it."

Reid nodded. "I remember." His second year here, he had gotten something going with a girl he'd thought was hot. For a couple of months, she sneaked out, he sneaked out, and he'd had sex for the first time. Inevitably, she got tired of the sneaking thing and found someone else. His heart hadn't been broken, but he'd really enjoyed the sex. "That's not what we're looking for," he said. "It's someone from the past who could have let the wrong thing slip."

His brother nodded his understanding.

"Do you think TJ is meeting someone?"

"I don't know. I haven't heard voices or anything like that."

"All right. Don't try to follow him. He could be dangerous."

Damn. When Caleb didn't say anything, Reid began to wish he hadn't asked that last question. Trailing TJ was exactly the kind of thing he'd have done in Caleb's place.

The lodge was in sight again. Reid clapped his brother on the back. "Time for you to get back and figure out problem fourteen."

"Math sucks."

"It wasn't my strong suit," Reid admitted. "Until calculus. For some reason, I liked calculus."

Caleb gave him an incredulous look.

Roger had returned and was putting away groceries when Reid and Caleb came in the back door. His gaze moved over the two of them, and his eyes warmed.

Reid squeezed his brother's shoulder even though such a simple act of intimacy felt uncomfortable to him, then watched him head back to the main room. Only when he knew he and Roger were alone did he say, "Can we talk?"

ANNA WASN'T SURPRISED when she didn't hear from Reid over the weekend. Their agreement to go skiing one more time had been forgotten, maybe just as well since the warming trend was turning the snow to mush. Despite the fact he'd asked for another chance—or *because* he'd been driven to ask for that chance—she had expected him to retreat. Truthfully, she wouldn't have been shocked if he never called again.

He was good at covering. Way better than the kids she dealt with on a day-to-day basis, but she still recognized more of his subterranean fears and motivations than he liked. They both knew that was partly what attracted him to her, but also what made him leery of feeling anything for her.

Had he seen how much they shared? That she had the same fears, that like him she was often driven by her past in illogical but emotionally rooted ways?

Probably. Anna admitted somewhat ruefully to herself she wasn't nearly as good at faking it as he was.

Monday morning she was on her way to visit foster homes in Klamath County when her phone rang. Seeing his number, she chose to pull over rather than put the phone on speaker.

"Reid," she said cautiously.

"Hey. Any chance of having lunch? If not today, tomorrow?"

"Tomorrow would be better." She told him where she was.

"Okay. I'm sorry we didn't make it out skiing."

"No, that's okay. It's probably too late in the year anyway."

"I see the girl's funeral is scheduled for Saturday. I was thinking I'd come," he said.

Her heart skipped. Was he offering because he thought she might need him? "I was hoping there'd be a police presence," she said, trying for calm.

"I think there will be. Having a local kid get killed hits everyone hard."

"Yes." Damn it, her eyes stung. "Thank you. I'd… like it if you were there."

"Then I will be."

They set a time for lunch tomorrow and he was gone. Anna sat for a minute, dealing with the heart-pounding effect of his promise before she could put her signal on and merge back into the traffic on the highway.

To her astonishment, that was the beginning of an amazing week with him. They had lunch twice and planned dinner for Friday night.

At Tuesday's lunch, he told her about the speeding ticket given to his father on top of the two for tailgating, and that Dean had taken off afterward, not to be seen again. Reid wasn't sure yet whether the man had gone home or only retreated to lick his wounds. She'd had to laugh at his grin when he had said that.

Thursday, she asked if he'd learned any more, and Reid said, "Yeah, I talked to one of Dad's cronies at the Spokane P.D. He's definitely home, back to work."

"Poorer, too," she said cheerfully.

He'd laughed again. "Yep. Close to seven hundred bucks poorer in traffic fines alone."

"Do you think...well, that he's given up?"

The pleasure left his face. "I doubt it," he said shortly. There was something grim in his voice that made her wonder what he feared. Was his father angry enough to want to hurt his own son? Anna couldn't help remembering when she'd asked Reid if Dean could be a threat to her, and the way he'd hesitated, then said, "Not to you." Had there been an emphasis on that last word that implied he thought his father might...what? Attack him? That seemed crazy, but his expression didn't invite more questions.

Friday night, she cooked dinner for him. Neither of them had their minds on food. Leaving dirty dishes on the table, they barely made it upstairs before shedding their clothes and making love.

Reid let her explore his body, too, this time. She loved the contours of muscles laid over bone and reveled in the responses her stroking hands evoked. Every jerk he made, every groan and sucked-in breath, heightened her own arousal. In the end, he still took control and she knew he'd held back, but she was satisfied they were making progress. Satisfied in every other way, too, but then she had been the first time, however depressed she'd been to feel essentially alone in the storm of passion.

Reid didn't say much as they cuddled afterward, or when he got up, dressed and kissed her goodnight, either. Anna had secretly hoped he would want to stay the night, but she knew she should have expected that was too big a commitment for him. His slightly brooding air as he departed left her wondering if he was unhappy about having surrendered as much of himself to her as he had.

It also made her wonder if he wouldn't make an excuse tomorrow not to show up at the funeral. Anna grimaced at the thought. She could hardly blame him if he did. *She* was dreading the darn thing. And, for him, it would be a commitment of another kind: appearing at her side in public and in a big way. People would have to know he was there only for her sake.

Once she thought of it that way…Anna resigned herself to going alone.

GOD, HE HATED FUNERALS. His mother's had been the start. Later, Reid had attended more than his share of them, first as a young officer who felt obligated to make an appearance after he'd scraped somebody off the pavement, then later when he made detective as part of investigations. Who showed up at a funeral could be telling, as could how everyone behaved once they were there.

This funeral was held in the New Hope Assembly of God, one of the largest churches in Angel Butte. Reid arrived before Anna.

As she'd warned him she might, she showed up in company with the foster parents, familiar to him from interviews on local television news. One look at their faces told him they were taking this as hard as any biological parents would. Parents wanted to believe it was possible to protect their children. Finding out, so harshly, that you couldn't...

Reid shook his head. Sometimes he wondered if his father would have grieved if he'd been killed in a car accident. Could a willingness to hurt your kid exist right along with the need to protect? Reid couldn't imagine.

Anna saw him and steered the older couple his way. The black suit she wore was formfitting enough to avoid being dowdy, especially with the addition of black high heels. Although he doubted that was her intention, black was a good color on her, with her honey-blond hair, pale skin and misty-gray eyes. He was disturbed at how aware he was of her lithe body inside that sedate suit.

At least he could be confident his expression didn't give away his thoughts. "Anna," he said and kissed her cheek, seeing her startled glance and flush of color. "Mr. Lund. Mrs. Lund." He shook hands with each in turn. "I'm Captain Reid Sawyer, Angel Butte P.D. You have my sympathy."

The woman's eyes filled with fresh tears. "Thank you."

Seeing that they were the focus of several television cameras, Reid moved to block the grieving couple from the cameras' eyes. Mrs. Lund's sister appeared and the two women hugged, then he got them all moving into the church.

Letting the others go ahead, Anna took his arm

and leaned in so that no one else could hear her. "Tell me your father hasn't reappeared."

He was able to shake his head. "Nope."

"Thank goodness."

He smiled at her vehemence, not letting her see the worry he was holding on to. Yes, Bob Sarringer had confirmed his buddy Dean was back at work. He'd even gone quiet for a minute, then said, "He was in a rage when I saw him. He said things—" There was another pause. Then, "Damn, I'm sorry, Reid."

Reid had felt a burst of rage hard to quell. Sarringer was sorry *now?* He managed an insincere "Thank you" and learned that Dean normally had weekends off.

Which meant there was nothing to stop him from having clocked out yesterday then driving into the night to pull another ugly trick in Angel Butte. Just because Reid hadn't seen him yet today didn't mean he wasn't here in town again.

Reid had put out the word to patrol and plainclothes officers alike to watch for his father. He had felt less reticence this time. He'd been…touched, he guessed was the right word, by the enthusiasm with which his officers had originally taken on a job that, realistically, was a waste of police resources, not to mention the skill level of detectives. They'd made plain that while he might be new on the job, he was one of them. The attitude had played a part in the shift he'd felt just this week toward the move to Angel Butte and whether he saw a future here.

When he and Anna entered the church, he forced thoughts of his son of a bitch of a father and even the future from his mind.

Reid shortly found himself anchoring one side of the front pew, with Mr. Lund on the other and the three women between them.

Large as it was, the church filled up fast. A shiny pink casket sat front and center, almost buried in flower arrangements. The scent of the flowers was overpowering. Reid was grateful the lid was closed.

The service opened a floodgate of grief. A dozen members of the congregation spoke about Corinna Terrill. A church choir sang. The pastor talked about the open gates of heaven and about how she'd be there waiting for her loved ones.

By long practice, Reid had armored himself well. His armor had a fissure today, though: Anna. Most of the emotion here flowed over and around him, but he felt Anna's. She never broke into sobs; instead, she comforted the foster mother, who wept from beginning to end. But every so often Anna had to swipe at her own cheeks. Mascara he'd hardly been aware she wore flowed with the tears. Reid, who had come prepared, pressed tissues into her hand. She gave him an astonished look, then blotted the tears. Seeing the dark streaks that remained caused an unfamiliar ache in his chest. He waited until the service ended to surreptitiously spit on another tissue, hoping she didn't notice, and turn her face up to his to gently wipe it clean.

Anna's tremulous smile made the ache grow until it was all he could do not to rub at his breastbone in an effort to relieve it. She tipped her head against his shoulder, the merest touch, but more than enough thanks, then stood when the pastor came to comfort the grieving parents.

Reid stepped back, waiting until Anna was ready to go. He'd seen a number of police officers, city and county, all wearing uniforms, sitting near the back. His department was well represented without him. In fact, he'd seen surprise when his presence was noted. No wonder, when he was so new on the job and hadn't been involved in any way with the investigation into the cause of the accident. And yet here he was, sitting beside the grieving family.

All he knew was that Anna had wanted him here, and that even as she spoke to other people, her head turned frequently, as if she needed to know he was still there. Reid felt no impatience. None of his usual discomfort at the idea of being needed by another human being.

Caleb, and now Anna. Her inclusion on a short list that was new to him might scare the shit out of him later, but not yet.

Finally, she murmured to the Lunds, then came to him. "Shall we go?"

He searched her face and found, not peace, but an easing of pain. He crooked his elbow, waited until she laid her hand on it, and walked her down the very long aisle and out of the church.

Outside, she turned to him. "You don't need to go to the reception with me if you'd rather not. I mean, you didn't know Corinna."

"But I know you."

"Oh, damn it," she mumbled, then clapped a hand over her mouth before casting a wild look around. "Did anyone hear me?" she whispered.

He chuckled, low and quiet. "I don't think so. Could have been worse. At least you didn't take the name of the Lord in vain."

"You're going to make me cry again."

"The last thing I want to do." He laid his free hand over hers, still resting on his arm. "Would you rather I not come, Anna?"

She stared up at him, her eyes red-rimmed and puffy. "I'm capable of doing something like this on my own."

This determination to do something that would normally repel him had come out of nowhere. All he knew was she'd given him more than she'd guessed, and he wanted to give back.

"Today, you don't have to," he said.

She bit her lip, nodded and sniffed. "Thank you."

As they walked across the parking lot to the enormous hall, where the church housed a preschool as well as meetings and celebrations, he had the passing thought there wasn't anywhere else he would want to be.

CHAPTER ELEVEN

THE RUSH OF WIND cold on his face, Caleb pedaled hard on his bike. No way was he going to let TJ pass him or Diego pull too far ahead. So far, the three were staying in a line, all listening for any traffic coming up behind them. The curves and lack of a shoulder made 253rd a dangerous road for walking or bike riding. As if they had any choice; it was the only way to get anywhere, and none of them could drive.

Caleb hadn't set foot off the grounds of the old resort in at least a month, so even though he was weirded out that TJ had come with them, Caleb felt exhilarated. Dad was back in Spokane. The relief he'd felt when Reid told him had been huge. At least now it was safe for him to go out, do something different.

Damon, who'd been out earlier, said the county park on Bear Creek had opened after having been closed all winter and that some girls' sports team was having their end-of-season deal there. He'd shrugged when Diego asked what kind of sport. Ski team? Basketball? "Who cares?" was what he'd said. There were girls their own age.

They'd built a big fire and were roasting hot dogs, and Damon had seen boxes of graham crackers on the picnic tables along with a row of trophies, so he guessed there'd be s'mores, too. They'd let him have a hot dog, and he was mad because he'd had to come home because he was on the schedule for tutoring with Isaac—and Paula had zero tolerance for anyone being late for a special tutoring session. Sunday was a day of rest, but not Saturday. This late in the afternoon, though, Caleb, Diego and TJ were all done with their schoolwork. Dinner was still a couple of hours away.

Diego had grabbed Damon's mountain bike and grinned at Caleb. "Man, let's go!" His gaze fell on someone behind Caleb. "You want to come, too?"

Caleb was still surprised TJ had agreed. He wasn't very friendly with any of the other guys. But he was older than Caleb, who still hadn't made a serious move on any girl and hated the fact there weren't any around to at least *look* at. TJ might have even had a girlfriend before he came here. He'd looked surprised to be asked, but said, "Yeah, sure." They'd left word with Apollo and within minutes were on their way.

Visions of a roaring bonfire, a hot dog with the skin splitting open and a pretty girl smiling shyly at him were dancing in Caleb's head like sugarplum fairies when he heard the deep-throated rumble of an SUV or a truck coming up behind them. They'd just gone around a curve, and when he looked over his shoulder, he couldn't see the vehicle. He hesitated, not sure whether to pedal faster or stop or what. TJ was glancing back, too. Looking ahead again, Caleb saw Diego was still pedaling, so he did, too, trying to speed up. It would be better if they reached a straight stretch.

The sound of the engine grew louder, and then he heard TJ yell. Even though it probably wasn't safe, Caleb looked back again. A big silver grille and a monster black vehicle coming fast were all he could see except TJ, who'd swerved off the road and whose bike was skidding in the gravel. Still holding the handlebars, TJ was diving toward the ditch.

Beyond a shocked awareness that the truck wasn't even slowing down, Caleb didn't have time to react. He saw the face through the windshield. There was more yelling—TJ and maybe Diego, too.

And then the bumper hit him and he thought *I'm flying* and *It's gonna hurt.*

REID READ WITH dismay what he'd gleaned about Truong. That poor damn kid. No, it wasn't any worse than his own history, or Caleb's, for that matter, but that didn't make it any better. He swore out loud. How could police and family-court judges be so blind? And if they saw—how did they live with themselves after making the decisions they did?

After all their foot-dragging about giving up the last names of the boys they sheltered, Roger and

Paula had finally seen the necessity. In turn, Reid had asked permission to bring in someone else. His goal was to make sure that police inquiries didn't lay a trail of crumbs straight to Angel Butte. Again, they agreed after he promised not to explain who the boys were or the reason for his investigation.

His closest friend in Southern California worked Computer Crimes for the Orange County Sheriff's Department. Detective Phil Perez had listened in silence to Reid's request a couple of days ago when he'd called. Accepting the fact he was to be kept in the dark, he had agreed to find out what he could about the nine boys. Telling himself trust had to go two ways, Reid left his brother's name off the list. If anyone could confuse the issue of who was asking the questions, it would be Phil. Reid mentioned his interest in the parents and guardians, too, especially their current whereabouts.

The information was already pouring in. Reid hadn't expected Phil to make his request a top priority, but clearly he had.

After he left Anna's bed last night, Reid had driven to the resort. He'd alternated patrols with hour-long naps. Fortunately, nothing had happened.

And today, once he and Anna had escaped the reception following the funeral, they'd parted ways. Anna had planned to drive the Lunds home and stay long enough to make sure they were okay, which left him on his own. Tempted though he was to go home and hit the sack, he'd decided to go into the station to check his email. Worry was driving him. It was the weekend again.

He was still scrolling through the information Phil had unearthed on Truong when his cell phone rang. Preoccupied, he glanced to see that the number was the Hales'. *Oh, damn.* He'd started dreading their calls. And this was Saturday. They were due for the next incident. Picking up the phone, Reid told himself that so far, everything had happened during the night, and he knew nothing had occurred last night. This might be something trivial or even Caleb could be calling because he'd thought of something Reid should know.

"Reid here."

"It's bad news." Roger sounded distraught.

Reid's heart thudded.

"Three of the boys decided to ride their bikes down to the county park because Damon found out there were teenage girls there," Roger continued. "TJ leaped on his bike and made it back. A pickup truck or SUV ran two of them down. TJ was at the back. He says he swerved and fell off the bike into the ditch or else he'd have been the first hit." Roger hesitated. "The truck didn't even slow down. It hit Caleb and Diego. Caleb is unconscious, Reid." His voice got heavy. "I'm out here waiting for an aid car. It doesn't look good. Diego's got some broken bones. A leg and collarbone for sure. He yelled for TJ to go."

"The driver didn't stop?" Reid sounded eerily calm to his own ears.

"No. TJ swears it was deliberate. He didn't get a look at the driver. From the way the bikes are mangled, there might be some minor damage to the vehicle. I don't know. A car stopped, but he didn't see the accident, just came on the boys lying on the road."

"Jesus," Reid breathed.

A faint wail of a siren came through the phone. "Listen, I've got to go—"

Reid was already on his feet. "I'll meet the ambulance at the hospital."

"How are you going to explain that?"

It took a few seconds for that to penetrate. "You're not claiming the boys," he said, momentarily shocked.

"If I have to, I will, but you know what I'd be jeopardizing."

Reid understood even as he was suddenly, blazingly angry. All he could think of was Anna and what she'd say. No, that wasn't all; he heard himself swearing to her that Caleb was safe.

The anger transmuted into something more violent than Reid had ever felt before. If his own father had run down his son, Reid wanted to kill him. Slowly, painfully.

"I'll think of something," he repeated and ended the call. Moving fast, he was grateful that it was Saturday and the assistant wasn't at her desk, so he didn't have to bother with an explanation. He was half running when he left the elevator on the ground floor.

"Captain Sawyer." Even in the act of lowering a gurney from the back of the aid car, one of the EMTs threw Reid a wild look. "Somebody must've called you. Hit-and-run. I don't know if this kid is going to make it."

Caleb.

They were moving so fast, he didn't get a look at his brother's face before the gurney was whisked inside the emergency room entrance. Hospital workers were helping pull the second gurney from the back. Diego lay on it, his face contorted with pain. His dark eyes met Reid's, desperation in them, but he didn't say anything.

Reid laid a hand on his shoulder and walked in with them. "Did you get a license number? See the driver?" he asked.

Diego shook his head. "No."

And then he, too, was hustled through another set of doors and Reid was left standing in the emergency room.

The woman behind the counter said, "May I help you, sir?"

He showed her his badge. "I'm told this was a hit-and-run."

"I'm afraid I don't know anything yet."

He was barely keeping it together. "I need to go back, find out how the boys are and what they know."

"Officer, you have to let the doctors work." Her tone suggested she'd said this so many times, it came by rote. "I'll call back and let them know you're waiting."

At the sound of the outside doors sliding open, Reid spun on his heel. Roger ran in, his hair disheveled, his expression frenzied. "Do you know anything?"

Reid gripped his arm and drew him away from the receptionist's curious gaze. They walked down a wide corridor that led to the rest of the hospital.

"Diego pretended not to recognize me, but he's conscious. He said he didn't see the driver. No license plate." A lump formed in his throat. Forcing words past it, he said, "I didn't get a look at Caleb. They were moving too fast."

"God." Roger sagged.

Reid put an arm out to hold him up. "You okay?"

"No." He braced both hands on the wall and bent over, panting for breath. "I'm sorry. God, I'm so sorry."

Reid gritted his teeth, trying not to say, *What the hell were you thinking to let them go?* The only thing stopping him was his own memories of how many times he'd biked or jogged along that same road to get to town, or just away from the shelter and the claustrophobia he sometimes felt.

In the kind of foster home Anna supervised, the boys would have been riding a bus every day to school. Roger could be openly picking them up from after-school activities. He and Reid wouldn't have to be standing here now, terrified and yet having to pretend they didn't know either of those boys.

"Will Diego tell them?" The question was torn from him.

"The first thing he said was that he wouldn't. That's why he told TJ to go. He didn't want him to get pulled in."

Reid nodded. He'd seen enough already about Theodore James Haveman's background to know he didn't want the boy's father to get his hands on him again.

But maybe there was another way. The words whispered to him. And he knew: he'd been wrong to send Caleb to the Hales. He should have stood up to their father. Stood up for his brother, given him a home. Found a way to keep him and his mother safe, if she could be located and Caleb preferred to live with her.

A man who hadn't bargained with God since he was a boy and found out it didn't do any good, he begged now for a deal as he paced the hall, waiting. *I will do anything. Give him a chance. Please. God, please.*

He ached to call Anna, but how could he? Anybody looking at him right now would wonder why he was so upset. For the sake of the other boys at the Hales', he needed to hide his personal fear.

Cover. That was what Anna called it. When had it quit being automatic for him?

"Um…sir?" It was the woman's voice.

He swung around to see her hovering at the head of the hall. "There's another officer here."

He nodded, took a couple of deep breaths, then started after her. He paused long enough to grip Roger's shoulder and squeeze. "I'll come back out once I know something."

The responding officer had arrived. The sight of Reid startled the county deputy. "Captain Sawyer?"

Oh, hell. The accident had happened outside the city limits. It would have occurred to Reid if his head wasn't clouded with fear.

"I know Roger Hale, the guy who called 911." Reid nodded toward Roger, who had turned to stare. "Listen. Any chance you can get Sergeant Renner here?"

"Uh…I can try." He made a phone call, and Reid could tell he'd reached the sergeant. He looked at Reid as he talked, telling him what had happened. Then he said, "Yeah, Captain Sawyer is here. He asked for you." Pause. "Okay. Sure. I'll tell him. Yes, sir." He ended the call. "The sergeant says he's on his way."

"Thank you." Reid heard how ragged he sounded.

Would Renner be willing to keep the Hales' secret once he knew who the boys were? Or should Reid even tell him?

Maybe, he thought, this was a secret that shouldn't be kept anymore.

The deputy was talking. "No skid marks at all." His voice was flat, but anger seeped through. "The boy who is conscious said he didn't think the driver even braked, and I'd have to agree. One of the bikes flew off the road. It's all twisted. The other one is flattened. The son of a bitch just kept going."

"Did you get names?" Reid asked.

"First name only. Diego."

"So we can't call parents."

The door opened and a nurse in pink scrubs stuck her head out. She was looking at the deputy when she said, "The doctor says you can ask some quick questions now."

Reid cut him off. "I'll do that if you wait for Renner out here." He followed her, leaving the poor deputy flat-footed. He was lucky the nurse accepted his presence without realizing he had no jurisdiction.

The nurse led him to Diego, and Reid realized they must have given the boy some pain meds, because his gaze was bleary. A young woman doctor turned to Reid when he stopped at the foot of the bed.

"He has a mild concussion and a number of broken bones and abrasions." She gave details.

"He's already had X-rays. Next step is casting his leg and arm, but I thought under the circumstances this might be a good moment for you to get some information. Right now we're operating without parental permission, which we're not crazy about."

"The other boy? Do you know how he is?"

"I'll go find out," she promised and left the two of them alone.

When Reid moved to Diego's side, the boy's hand shot out to grab him. "They'll call my dad, won't they?"

"We'll have to, but I'll make damn sure he's not allowed to take you."

"But you don't know anything."

"I do. I've been looking into all your backgrounds."

"Because of the fires."

He nodded.

"You swear?" Diego begged.

Reid took his hand and held it, praying he could keep his word. "Yes."

"Okay," he whispered, his eyes drifting closed.

"Wait!" Reid got his attention again, but learned next to nothing. Diego thought the vehicle that hit them was a pickup with a canopy rather than an SUV, but he wasn't positive. It all happened so fast, he said, sounding ashamed. Black. Yes, he was positive about that much. Maybe TJ saw more.

Reid shook his head. "TJ was rolling in the ditch when the two of you got hit. Roger says he's scraped up pretty bad. TJ also said the vehicle was black, but that everything happened so fast. He saw Caleb in the air, and the way he landed—" Reid couldn't finish. Couldn't say the dreaded words. *He thought Caleb was dead.*

Diego did. "He's dead, isn't he?"

"No!"

Reid didn't realize he'd yelled until he saw the kid shrink away from him. He passed a shaking hand over his face. "I'm sorry."

The glass door slid open and the doctor reappeared. "The other boy is hanging in there. Do you have a name for him?"

"Caleb. I think he might be my brother. Caleb Sawyer." Christ. He wasn't having to fake anything—not the tremors, not the ragged voice, not the expression that had the doctor staring. "They're runaways. Diego—this boy—says Caleb was looking for his brother. That's why they came to Angel Butte. I need to see him."

"Oh, no." She shook her head, not in refusal, but in shock. "Yes. All right, come this way."

He barely recognized the figure surrounded by medical personnel. Caleb's face was raw and grotesquely swollen. He'd been intubated and was being given oxygen. There was no life at all in him beyond the faint rise and fall of his chest.

Life support.

Despite having known what he would see, Reid staggered, barely righting himself. "It's him," he managed to get out. "Caleb."

IF IT HADN'T been his number on her screen, Anna wasn't sure she'd have recognized Reid's voice.

"Your brother?" she said, stunned. "He's here? In town? And injured?"

"They're working on him right now. He's unconscious. He doesn't look good, Anna."

"I'm on my way. I'll find you, Reid."

She'd been at the health club when her phone rang, getting dressed after a workout. It had been cleansing after the funeral and the strain of trying to comfort the Lunds when she felt such grief herself. Although she was dressed, she hadn't yet dried her hair, but she didn't care. She hastily stuffed workout gear into her duffel, slammed the locker and all but ran out. The drive to the hospital couldn't have taken five minutes, but it seemed like forever. Every red light, every flicker of a brake light in front of her, made her want to scream.

She parked at the hospital and raced into the emergency room. "Captain Reid Sawyer," she snapped to the receptionist. "He's in back with his brother. Caleb Sawyer."

The woman frowned and perused her computer. "I'm afraid I don't have a Caleb—"

"It was a hit-and-run."

"Oh. Yes. Why don't you take a seat? It'll be a minute."

"He asked me to come." That was a lie, she realized with sudden shock. She hadn't even given him a chance to ask. What if he'd been about to say, *I don't need you, but I wanted to let you know what was happening?* Oh, dear God. What was his brother doing in town?

Looking for Reid, of course. What else could it be?

What if he died?

Pacing in an agitated circle right in front of the double doors leading to the back, Anna tried to blank her mind to the possibility. She'd seen the pain he bore already. A loss like this— What would it do to him?

But she knew. Oh, God, she knew.

The door burst open and he was there. His expression was terrible. She'd wanted to see naked emotion on his face, but nothing like this.

"Reid." Anna flew to him. His arms closed hard around her even as she held on to him with everything she had. "I'm so sorry. Oh, Reid. How is he?"

"They…don't know yet. He's unconscious. There's swelling in his brain. Some broken bones, too, maybe some internal bleeding. They aren't sure yet. He looks really bad, Anna."

She pulled back enough to look up at him. "He must have told them his name."

Reid shook his head. "No. He's with another boy. Diego Ramirez. They were traveling together. I haven't figured out yet where they were staying or where they got the bikes they were riding, but he says Caleb wanted to see me." A shudder ripped through him. "I let him down. He wasn't safe."

"No." She tightened her arms again, laying her cheek against his shoulder. "It's not your fault, Reid. You'd have done anything for him. I know you would. He wouldn't have been looking for you if he hadn't decided to trust you."

This shudder was worse than the last. Or was it a sob? Shocked anew, she saw tears running down his hard cheeks. She held him while he cried, trying to protect him from curious stares as he'd done for her that day on the sidewalk in front of the café. Anna heard herself talking but didn't even know what she was saying. Just a mishmash.

I'm so sorry. He may be fine. Just because he was knocked on the head doesn't mean he won't come out of it. It's okay, Reid. Let it out. It'll help. It will.

She didn't know if any of it was true. *Please don't let this boy die.* It would destroy Reid. She knew that much.

He pulled himself together fast, retreating from her physically and emotionally. He used the wool sleeve of the fine suit coat he'd worn to the funeral to wipe his face. She stared at the now-closed double doors, giving him the space he obviously wanted to resume his usual facade.

"Thank you for coming," he said after a minute, his voice only a little gravelly.

"Of course I did." She shot him a fierce look.

He gave a broken laugh. "Of course you did." Then his gaze went past her and she turned to see that he was looking at an older man who looked upset, too. There was blood on his flannel shirt, she saw, and the knees of his canvas carpenter's pants were dirty, with bits of grit clinging to the fabric. His gray-streaked dark hair looked as if he'd been wrenching at it, and maybe he'd been pulling at his beard, too.

Reid kept an arm around Anna and led her over to the other man. "Anna, I've told you about my friends here in Angel Butte. This is Roger Hale. The boys were hit on the road not far from his place. He was one of the first on scene."

"You must have recognized Caleb," she said.

"I—" His eyes met Reid's. "No," he said after a minute. "He was bloody, and…it didn't occur to me. I called Reid because the driver who hit the boys didn't even stop."

"Unfortunately, the accident scene is out of my jurisdiction," Reid put in.

She gaped at him. "But it's your own brother. You wouldn't have wanted to investigate anyway, would you?"

The ferocity of the look he turned on her made her quail. "Want to? Yeah, I want to." The vulnerable man he had let her see earlier was gone. "In fact," he continued in a hard voice, "I'm going to call my father right this minute."

She pressed her fingers to her mouth. He couldn't think— Could he? But obviously he did. He had his phone out and was scrolling for a number. He found it and pushed Send. She and Reid's friend—

Roger—both waited. Anna could hear the rings, but with the phone pressed to Reid's ear, she couldn't make out the voice that answered.

Like a knife, Reid's voice sliced. "All right, you son of a bitch," he said. "Where are you?"

"HERE'S THE OTHER kid's story," Reid told Anna. He called up Diego's court records on his smartphone. After explaining what Diego had told him—*you mean, lied to her, don't you?*—he handed her the phone and said, "Take a look."

She read in silence for a minute, scrolling down. When she finally looked up, he would have been reassured by the fiery light in her eyes if his fear and his guilt hadn't been so bottomless.

"First thing I'll do is call in a Child Protective Services worker," she announced. "I need to talk to Diego myself."

After being told the boy was moving upstairs to a regular hospital room, Anna decided to accompany him. "I think I can block any immediate attempt to return him to his father. That'll give us time to work."

They both knew that by now Hector Ramirez, yet another winner in the parental stakes, had been called and might be on his way from the Portland area to Angel Butte. They were in a race.

Reid nodded. Being able to talk at all was getting harder for him.

Eyes soft again, Anna hugged him, rose on tiptoe

and pressed her lips to his cheek. "I'll be back," she murmured. "Hang in there."

He couldn't even nod this time. He'd never been so scared in his life. He expected to be summoned any minute and told the worst.

Instead, the outside doors glided open and a man entered. Reid knew a cop when he saw one, even if he wore a suit and tie. The guy walking toward him was powerfully built with an angular, rough-cast face. It was the walk that gave him away—had to be cop or ex-military. The way he scanned every-one in the waiting area and then zeroed in on Reid was familiar, too.

When he got close, Reid saw the badge on his belt. He held out his hand. "Sergeant Renner?"

"You're Captain Sawyer. Jane has described you."

"I won't ask what she said."

The grin was quick and then gone. "You want to tell me what this is about?"

Reid hadn't been sure until now how much he wanted to say. Before agreeing to go home, Roger had said the decision would be Reid's. "We're at a crossroads," he said bleakly. "Too many people know we're here now. Maybe it's time to give it up."

Reid felt the same, yet couldn't forget his own desperation when he came to the Hales. He thought of all the kids since, the ones who'd stayed safe, earned their GEDs, gone on to good lives thanks to Roger and Paula.

But his conscience wouldn't let him forget the

others, too. The ones he never let himself think about. The girls murdered by a serial killer given access to them by the Hales. The ones who'd run away even from this sanctuary, any safety net lost to them.

He drew a deep breath and said, "Yeah. I asked for you because the Hales tell me you're aware of their operation."

Comprehension was immediate. "The hit-and-run was on 253rd, wasn't it? Well, shit." Renner looked around. "Let's find someplace private. The cafeteria?"

"I need to stay here."

Clay Renner nodded. They ended up choosing a couple of chairs in a corner. Reid braced his elbows on his knees and let his head hang for a minute. "It's a mess," he warned.

"It almost has to be."

He straightened, unwilling to evade those sharp blue eyes, and started talking. Talked until he was hoarse. "I owe them my life," he said finally. "We can still leave them out of this, if you're willing. Right now, I don't know what's right or wrong. I will tell you, I think this was deliberate. A murder attempt."

"Aimed at your brother."

"Maybe, maybe not. The boy who was riding behind Caleb is a possibility. It sounds like he'd have been hit first if he hadn't dived for the ditch. It's also possible whoever this is didn't care which boys he killed. He hates the Hales and this was just part of his campaign of terror."

Furrows had long since formed on Sergeant Renner's forehead. "I wish you'd come to me sooner."

"I did talk to your boss."

"My boss?"

"The sheriff. Until today, nobody had gotten hurt. The incidents were no more than taunts. Nasty, but there was no attempt to harm anyone."

"Yeah. Okay." Renner sighed. "Forward me everything you've got on these kids and their parents or guardians. The first thing we need to do is pin down where everyone is."

"I'm pretty damn sure my father—Caleb's father—is here in Angel Butte." Reid's voice had thickened.

"Ah. Have you tried to get in touch?"

"I called. He claimed he'd just crossed the Oregon border, that he didn't leave Spokane until midmorning. I don't believe him. No matter what, he's on his way here. Like I told you, he was here last week when the tires were slashed. He has weekends off and could have been here when the fires were set, too."

"Would he do this? Try to kill his own boy?"

"He killed my mother. It was in the middle of a fight. He hit her, she fell against the corner of a kitchen cabinet. But he was cold-blooded enough to set it up as an accident. I saw him pour some water on the floor to make it look like she slipped."

Renner's harsh features hardened. "Then he's at the top of my list."

"The Hales?" Reid had to ask.

Renner let out a huff of air. "I don't know. I'll talk to them and the other boy. Let me think about this, okay?"

Reid only nodded. He'd been doing a lot of that. It occurred to him then that his career was over if this all came out. He'd been breaking the law. He probably hadn't done anything he'd be charged for, although Roger and Paula would be, however fine their intentions and however much good they'd done. Reid would hate to see that. At the moment, he couldn't seem to make himself care about the fallout for himself personally.

Renner left then, and Reid stood watching until he went through the door and was out of sight. He not only had never been so scared before, he'd never felt so helpless.

CHAPTER TWELVE

REID HAD JUST finished forwarding everything he'd gotten from Phil to Renner—with Phil's name and email address wiped out—when someone came out from the back to tell him Caleb was being moved to Intensive Care, and would he care to go to that waiting room instead.

Once he'd arrived there, a different doctor emerged to say they didn't believe Caleb had any internal bleeding, which meant surgery wasn't currently necessary. He did have multiple broken bones in his shoulder and upper arm, as well as his collarbone. They were attempting to immobilize much of his upper body.

"Of course, it's the head trauma that has us worried," the doctor said unnecessarily. "The damage to his shoulder may be good news, in a way. Clearly it took a significant amount of the impact when he hit the road."

Instead of his head. Or, *Instead of* only *his head.*

"I wish I could give you a prognosis," he continued, "but it's too soon for me even to speculate. I know how hard this is, but all we can do is wait and see."

Right now, Reid wouldn't let himself think about the possibility of brain damage. He just wanted his brother to open his eyes. Squeeze his hand.

"Yes. I understand."

"Perhaps you should go home," the doctor suggested. "I feel sure he won't regain consciousness before morning at the very least."

"Not yet. I'd like to sit with him as much as possible."

His expression kind, the doctor said they couldn't have him back there all the time, but would give him a few minutes perhaps every half hour.

Another nod.

Left alone, Reid paced. Despite near numbness, fury was a hot spark waiting to be lit by his father's arrival.

ANNA WAS TROUBLED by the time she left Diego to sleep. The caseworker from DHS had come and gone earlier, but Anna had stayed to try to mine more details from the boy. There was too much wrong with his story.

He and Caleb had "borrowed" the bikes, he said. They planned to return them later, after they'd ridden into town and found Caleb's brother. He claimed not to remember exactly where they'd borrowed them from. When she asked how the boys intended to return them, he mumbled, "Maybe we could find the place. Or leave them in front of the police station."

Where Caleb's brother worked. Genius plan.

Diego was vague about where he'd been living since he disappeared over a year ago from his own home. Another mumble. "You know. On the streets." He'd met Caleb in Portland, he said. Anna guessed it was possible that was where Reid's friends who'd taken in his brother lived. But how had he come to meet a street kid and become good enough friends for them to take off together? Why, since he was in regular communication with Reid, hadn't he just called him? Borrowed the money for a Greyhound bus ticket instead of hitching over here with some street kid? What did he expect from Reid?

And why the lousy memory? Was it an effect of trauma…or was there a whole lot Diego didn't want to tell her?

Once he was snoring softly, she'd taken the bag containing his clothes and everything he'd had on him out of the closet and dug through it. No wallet, no money, no keepsakes. There was absolutely zilch in his pockets. The clothes had gotten dirty and bloody in the accident, but otherwise appeared almost new, and she'd bet they had been freshly cleaned before he put them on this morning.

"We were sort of camping in the woods," he'd said. "We left stuff there."

Where was that? She offered to pick up their things to keep them safe. He'd pretended to fall asleep, a pretense that did, a few minutes later, become reality.

Wondering if he'd told Reid any more, Anna headed for the elevators. Last time she'd talked to Reid, he'd said there hadn't been any change in Caleb's condition. She could find him either in ICU with his brother or right outside. He told her a Sergeant Clay Renner from the sheriff's department was investigating the accident.

He sounded so remote, she ached for him. And, selfishly, for herself. Sometime during this wretched day, she had accepted that she was deeply in love with Reid. *Hopelessly* came to mind, especially if his brother died.

The moment she stepped out of the elevator, she saw Reid just outside the doors leading into ICU. He was talking to two men, one who, from the scrubs and a mask pulled down around his throat, must be a doctor. The other one was about Reid's age, also wearing a suit. He stood with his hands on his hips, which pulled the suit coat back, allowing her to see a holstered pistol. Maybe he was the sergeant Reid had mentioned?

She heard her heels clicking on the floor as she walked toward him. The other cop glanced her way, but instead of turning toward her, Reid looked down the broad corridor leading from the E.R. She had almost reached him when she saw the man approaching.

Oh, dear heaven. It could only be Reid's father. He was…not as tall as his son, she thought, and had thickened around the waist and acquired the beginnings of jowls. Something about his face made her think he was a heavy drinker. But otherwise...the resemblance was shocking.

In fact, the other two men were staring now, too. Reid stood absolutely still. She wasn't even sure he was breathing.

Driven by a sense of impending disaster, Anna hurried.

"Ah, this would be Caleb's father...?" the doctor began.

"How dare you show your face here?" Reid snarled. "Don't think I'm letting you get within touching distance of Caleb."

Anna reached him, but if he noticed her, he didn't indicate it. He vibrated with fury. His lips were drawn back from his teeth and his hands were fisted at his side. She knew every muscle in his body was taut, ready to fling him forward.

"You tried to steal my boy," his father snapped, "but you're not getting away with it. You're not speaking for Caleb. I am."

Anna willed Reid not to attack. He needed to keep his cool. Devastate with words, not fists, however much he wanted to punish and hurt this man.

She took a chance and touched his arm. A jolt went through him and he looked down at her hand, then at her face. And then his furious stare returned to his father.

"Sergeant Renner here has questions for you," he said in a voice that chilled to arctic. "You're now a person of interest in the attempted murder of Caleb Sawyer."

Dean Sawyer's face suffused with dark color. "What the hell—"

"We already know you can kill, don't we, Dad? And so cold-bloodedly, you have no trouble staging the scene to look innocent."

Reid's father flung himself forward. Anna had been oblivious to what the sergeant was doing, but with seeming effortlessness, he caught Dean Sawyer in a headlock and pulled him away from Reid.

"Captain Sawyer is correct. I do have questions for you. Attempted assault now will not help your cause, sir."

Reid's father yanked free of Sergeant Renner's loosened grip. A stare filled with hate arrowed in on his son. "Threats will get you nowhere. I'm going to be taking Caleb home with me."

"No." All the tension was still there in Reid's body language, but he spoke calmly. "I will be filing for custody, and I will have no difficulty at all proving the horrific abuse you visited on me and Caleb. You're not at home now, where your cronies support you no matter what the evidence says. Home court, Dad. The judge here is going to hear the truth and believe it."

With a face that was nearly purple, Dean looked as if he was going to have a stroke any minute. A vein throbbed in his neck. Whatever he saw on Reid's face had him retreating a step. "Any weight of truth is on my side," he blustered. "Do your worst, and I'll slap you down in court as fast as I would anywhere else."

"Yeah, you did a lot of that, didn't you, Dad? Except you tended to use your fist instead of your open hand." Reid shook his head and looked at Sergeant Renner. "He's all yours." Then he turned his back on his father.

The sergeant gripped Dean's arm and said, "Please accompany me now, sir. I do have some questions and will need to take a look at your vehicle."

Reid's gaze seemed blind when it met Anna's. "I'm sorry you had to see that."

She wanted to tell him she'd been right where she wanted to be: at his side. But he wouldn't like hearing anything like that. "I'm not," she settled for instead.

Reid looked at the doctor, a thin man with salt-and-pepper hair. "I'm sorry you had to see that, too, Dr. Stafford. But I'm going to ask that Caleb's father not be allowed any access to him. First thing in the morning, I'll file for a restraining order."

The doctor looked perturbed, but finally nodded. "I think I can agree to that. Although, given the accusations you made, you'd better be prepared with persuasive evidence."

The muscles tightening in Reid's jaw was his only reaction. "I am."

Anna turned her head to see Sergeant Renner escorting Reid's father away. After a few more reassurances about Caleb, the doctor vanished into the ICU.

"Would you like a cup of coffee?" Anna asked in lieu of the comfort she wanted to offer. "If you'd rather not go to the cafeteria, I'd be glad to get you one."

His mouth quirked, but as smiles went it was weak. "How about a root-beer float?"

Almost choking up, she said, "Even better."

He squeezed his eyes shut for an instant. "Let's sit down."

Once they took a pair of chairs some distance from the only other occupants of the waiting room, a family group huddled together in a corner, Reid reached for her hand. He held on with a tight grip.

"I keep expecting—" He couldn't finish.

"Don't." Anna bit her lip. "Do you have any updates?"

He shook his head. "They come out to talk to me every so often, but they're not saying anything new. 'Wait and see.'" He said that almost violently.

"That's pretty normal for a head injury."

His eyes met hers. "You should have seen him. Raw and bloody, and his head swollen grotesquely. He must have bounced like a goddamn basketball."

Her stomach clenched. "How could someone do that? Just aim at a group of boys and run them over?"

He shook his head, obviously baffled, though,

given his job, he must have seen as bad or worse repeatedly.

Anna couldn't bring herself to question him about Diego yet. Instead, they sat together, mostly quiet. He was allowed to go back to be with Caleb for a few minutes and told her she didn't have to stay, but when she shook her head and said, "I'll be here," his relief was obvious.

Perhaps an hour after leaving, Sergeant Renner returned. He nodded at Anna, but said to Reid, "Walk with me."

Anna pushed herself up from the chair. "If you'd like privacy, I can—"

Reid touched her shoulder. "No. Stay put."

The two of them strolled toward the hospital proper, disappearing around a corner. Anna sat again, but tensely, worrying. There'd been something on the sergeant's face. He had something to say he didn't expect Reid to like. What?

Feeling fidgety, she got up and walked around herself, the tingling in her legs telling her she'd been planted on her butt too long anyway. Her entire being was concentrated on the hallway where the two men had disappeared. Reid didn't need one more devastating piece of news.

It was a good ten minutes before they returned. When they did, his face was utterly expressionless. Anna didn't kid herself it meant he'd regained some of his equilibrium.

He came straight to her, the sergeant still beside him.

"Don't look so worried. Sergeant Renner has been able to determine that it wasn't my father who ran down Caleb and Diego."

"How?"

"A receipt for a gas purchase in Umatilla."

Anna knew Umatilla to be a town just on the Oregon side of the Columbia River. If Dean had been driving down here from Spokane, the logical route would have taken him across the Columbia there.

"They looked hard at the front of his SUV, too." He sounded almost numb. "There'd almost have to be some damage from hitting a pair of bicycles. Nothing there."

She nodded, seeing compassion on Sergeant Renner's face. He took his leave, and Reid stumbled to a chair, sitting with his elbows on his knees and his hands gripping his head. His knuckles showed white. All she could do was sit beside him and gently rub his back. She didn't wonder why he wasn't glad that his father hadn't done this particular vile thing. Besides…now they were left with *no* idea who had tried to kill a pair of teenage boys.

Not much later, a woman Reid introduced as Lieutenant Renner from Investigative Services arrived. She seemed too young to be a lieutenant, and then there was the ponytail, bouncing as she walked.

Wait. Renner?

The lieutenant saw Anna's surprise. "You must have met my husband. He told me what's going on."

"Oh. Yes. I didn't realize…"

She and Reid went for a walk, too. Anna was beginning to wonder what he knew that he wasn't telling her. She didn't like this feeling that she was being stonewalled not only by Diego, but by Reid, as well.

Maybe it was nothing that would affect how she handled Diego's case. Law enforcement officers did tend to keep quiet about details of an investigation.

Recognizable from photos and television news, Police Chief Raynor appeared next. He shook Anna's hand when Reid introduced them, and, gee whiz, the two of them left her, walking down the hall that ought to be developing ruts by now. Anna was less sure this time that Chief Raynor had anything special to say, beyond sympathy. An air of restless energy surrounded him, making her suspect he wasn't any better at just sitting than Reid usually was.

After that, a succession of plainclothes and uniformed Angel Butte officers came and went. It seemed there was hardly a moment when one or two weren't sitting near Reid and Anna, letting him know they were there for him. Watching Reid thanking them broke Anna's heart. She could tell he was moved by the support, even as it was killing him to have to answer questions and thank them for coming. She wanted to snatch him away and just hold him.

Twice she left to go upstairs and check on Diego, but both times found him still asleep. Or pretending to be asleep—she wasn't positive which.

What didn't he want to tell her? Even as she stayed focused on Reid, the question nibbled at the back of her mind. Diego was a runaway, fifteen years old. What could he possibly have to hide?

The answer came to her suddenly, in an *oh duh* moment.

Diego and Caleb hadn't been alone. *Weren't* alone. Diego couldn't send her out to get his stuff because she would have come across another runaway. Even several other runaways.

Had they been close by enough to have heard the sirens and thereby guess why Caleb and Diego hadn't returned? Or were they—or only one scared boy on his own?—currently huddled in the woods somewhere, or maybe in an empty house the group had broken into, wondering what had gone wrong?

Thinking about it, she was seized by pity, but also frustration. Diego's history was a good lesson in why some kids did go on the run. Every single person who could have made a difference had let him down. The brutal parent was only the beginning. From what Reid had said, Caleb was another example. Anna knew full well that too often adults in a position of power in particular evaded any reckoning. Cops were classic, but they weren't alone. She'd had a boy briefly in a receiving home who had been sexually molested for years by his father, a juvenile probation counselor. No one would listen to the boy, even when he attempted suicide twice. Deeply troubled, he was now in a group home. His father had known how to work the system, how to make his kid look like a liar.

Like Reid's father did, she thought, anger hardening inside her.

It was almost one in the morning when Reid emerged from ICU after having spent ten or fifteen minutes sitting at Caleb's bedside. Anna was the only person left out here. Weariness and despair altered his face into someone less handsome and more human.

He shook his head even before she could ask if there'd been any change. "We both need some sleep. I can come back first thing in the morning."

Almost as tired as he looked, Anna pushed herself to her feet. "That's a good idea. You need to take care of yourself. Especially if you're going to file for a restraining order in the morning, too."

"God, yes. If it's possible on a Sunday." He ran his fingers through his already disheveled hair. "Let's go."

They walked silently toward the parking lot, Reid escorting Anna to her RAV4. They seemed to be completely alone, their footsteps the only sound. Once at her vehicle, she unlocked the door, then turned to him.

"Do you think you can sleep?"

"I don't know." He swallowed. "Anna."

She stepped forward and wrapped her arms around his waist, laying her head on his shoulder. "Oh, Reid."

"Will you come home with me?" The question sounded as if it had been ripped from him.

Surprised, she lifted her head. Before she could respond, he made a ragged sound.

"No. You've got to be beat, too. You've done enough, Anna. I'm sorry."

"Of course I want to come home with you," she said almost steadily.

Shadowed from the yellow-tinted sodium lamps, his eyes searched hers. "You mean that."

"You know I do."

There was another of those sounds, so uncharacteristic for such a guarded man.

"Do you want to ride with me?"

"I'd better follow you. You'll need to see an attorney first thing tomorrow."

He frowned, but finally nodded. "Yeah. Okay."

At this time of night, the drive was short. Thank goodness, his father wasn't parked across the street from Reid's house. That would have been the last straw.

Reid unlocked his front door. The sight of his partially furnished home made her wish she'd suggested they go to her place instead. But then she remembered what he'd said to his father: *Home court, Dad.* Maybe Reid needed his own refuge, however bleak it looked to her.

He'd no sooner closed the door than he turned to her. "You're sure about this?" His voice was hoarse.

Her eyes burned and she reached for him. He came to her fast, yanking her against him, pushing aside her hair to nuzzle her neck. She felt the edges of his teeth, the tautness of his body. The hard ridge that pressed into her belly. With no warning, her own body shot into full arousal. Weariness was forgotten.

"I need you," he growled, backing her up against the door. "Say no if you're going to. *Now*."

"Yes," she whispered and yanked at his suit coat, momentarily trapping his arms.

His kiss seared her. His wall had been dynamited, leaving a desperate man whose hands shook as he tried to strip her. Her parka fell to the floor along with his suit coat. Reid got her blouse partially unbuttoned before giving up. He lifted her and suckled her breast through bra and shirt alike. The sensation was electrifying. She heard herself crying out. Her back arched, pushing her hips against him.

He was talking as he pulled up her skirt and yanked tights and panties down. Anna's brain wouldn't parse what he was saying, only fixated on his voice, the roughened nap of velvet. And his hands, oh God, his hands, still shaking, sliding against her bare skin then squeezing. He had his trousers open when he went completely still.

"No!" she moaned. "Why are you stopping?"

He seemed to be struggling for breath, his eyes dark and intense. "Need to get a condom."

"I'm on birth control."

The sound he made then was indescribable. He lifted and spread her in one movement, filling her before she could snatch a breath. The weight of her body pushed him deeper than he'd ever been, making her cry out again. She was helpless in this position. All she could do was hold on and ride the current of his need.

"Now, Anna."

She did hear that, said from between gritted teeth. It wasn't necessary. Her body imploded, and then he thrust hard a couple more times, pulsing inside her.

Anna knew she was sagging in his arms. He leaned against her for a moment, flattening her to the door, and she couldn't have protested if she'd wanted to.

Instead of releasing her, Reid sank to his knees still holding her tight. They leaned against each other, swaying.

"We can't stay here," he mumbled, sounding drunk.

Anna wanted to topple over. But Reid gently smoothed her skirt down, then staggered to his feet. He adjusted his trousers, zipping them, but not bothering with the button or belt. When he bent and lifted her, she managed to help. *She* felt drunk. Totally done for. Even so, she managed to totter the short distance into his bedroom and stood like a child as he disrobed her. She was totally naked when she crawled into bed and already half-asleep by the time he joined her. She snuggled close, instinctively seeking his warmth, laid her hand over the hard beat of his heart and her head on his shoulder, and dropped off.

REID HAD NEVER felt anything like that before. He'd never slept like that, either, so deeply he wasn't sure he had dreamed.

The idea made him wince. Was Caleb dreaming? Hearing voices? Or was he just…gone? Lost in blackness? Was a coma like death, except the heart continued to beat?

Reid groaned and bent his head under the hot, pounding water from the showerhead. It was the one bit of remodeling he'd bothered with after moving in here—no low-flow showerhead for him. He needed the closest thing to a massage he could get before he went out the door every morning.

The word echoed in his head.

Needed.

That was what he'd said to Anna. *I need you.*

It shook him, how frantic he'd been. How…naked.

And damn if it wasn't the most explosive orgasm of his life. Cause and consequence. Simple.

She could destroy him.

But he kept seeing her face as she sat in that waiting room watching him. The softness and the worry and, God, something else he'd never seen on a woman's face before, not when she was looking at him. Maybe love. Was that possible?

His chest tightened. What was with him, that he kept thinking things like that? Imagining...

Don't, he told himself harshly. At least...not yet. Get through this first. Protect Caleb from their father while waiting for him to wake up—or not. Keep lying to Anna.

He stumbled over that one.

From a practical standpoint, it was likely the story would unravel. Clay Renner hadn't committed to keeping his mouth shut yet. It might be different if this was a random hit-and-run—some guy out driving too fast, comes around a bend and takes out a couple of bicyclists, decides in a panic to take off. But Renner, like Roger, had believed TJ, who swore it had been deliberate. The lack of skid marks was compelling, too. And if the driver had been trying to kill or at least maim those boys—he almost had to be the same person who'd set the fires, slashed the tires, buried a knife blade in the front door of the lodge. Someone with a burning grudge.

Once they caught him, it would all come out.

I have to tell her the truth, he realized. Not liking it, but not liking any alternative, either. The lies to her, of all people, hadn't sat well with him from the beginning. He remembered thinking that she was the person who came closest to knitting together the parts of his life. The ache when he wanted to talk to her and couldn't.

The risk was huge that she'd turn them all in right away. As he stepped out of the shower and toweled himself dry, Reid mulled over steps he'd take to protect the Renners and Sheriff McAllister. What they'd known and ignored didn't have to be part of the truth he told her.

He hoped she'd cool down before she took action, though. Really listen. She'd understood why Diego had gone off the radar, why Reid had helped his brother escape their father even if he'd done it in a way she didn't entirely approve of.

He stared at himself in the mirror for a moment, but his decision was made. He'd tell her everything. Almost everything. But later. Now he needed to get moving if he intended to have that restraining order in place before his father showed up at the hospital.

With a grunt, Reid reached for his electric shaver.

CHAPTER THIRTEEN

AFTER DELIVERING THE restraining order to the hospital, Reid was allowed into the ICU to sit with Caleb, whose condition had been deemed unchanged.

His brother appeared dead, but for the steady rise and fall of his chest. Cold comfort came from knowing that he was breathing on his own. Some part of his brain was still functioning. It seemed to Reid that the swelling might be going down, although the livid color of the bruises made Caleb look as if he'd been made up for a horror film. Too extensive and vivid for real life, Reid's eye tried to tell him.

A different doctor this morning explained that they were keeping Caleb sedated. They didn't want him to wake up yet. Reid had a vague feeling he'd been told that yesterday. It just hadn't sunk in. So maybe he was being artificially kept from opening his eyes and saying, *Reid! Man, what happened?*

Left alone with his brother, Reid took Caleb's hand in his, remembering the comfort of holding hands with Anna last night. Not just physical contact—it had felt more like the hookup between two computers. Signals flying back and forth. Maybe, wherever Caleb was lost, he'd feel the same kind of connection.

"Dad can't get to you here. I got a restraining order," Reid said, his voice sounding unnaturally loud. He cleared his throat. "No problem. That doesn't necessarily mean clear sailing from here on out, but the judge was sympathetic. It was a woman, pretty new on the bench, I'm told. I went in with my dental records and I got yours emailed first thing this morning. Lucky you'd told me where he took you to get that bridge. She said the number of dentists he took me to over the years was a red flag that should have been noted when I was a kid." He paused, watching for a twitch of reaction. *Nada.* "Dad hasn't showed his face yet. I think I shook him up yesterday. I…really thought it might have been him who'd run you down, but it doesn't look like it was." His voice gained urgency. "I sure as hell wish you'd wake up and tell us what you saw."

He rambled for a few more minutes. He didn't talk about Anna, although he wanted to. Figuring out what to say was too tricky. Not when part of his turmoil concerned sex.

Making love.

The sight of her still sleeping in his bed before he left this morning had stirred him in unaccustomed ways. He'd had the fleeting vision of waking up with her every morning. The idea didn't scare him as much as it should.

He did tell his brother that he had to go out to the Hales' because TJ wanted to talk to him. "I'm meeting Sergeant Renner there, too. No way around it. It's his investigation. Uh…I told you about him last night. So far, he seems okay. I guess I'm not surprised, since he's married to Jane Renner, who works for me, and she's good."

He squeezed Caleb's hand. "I'll be back in a couple of hours at the most. Later today, the doctors are going to start tapering off on the sedatives. Your head will feel a lot clearer. In the meantime—" God, he sounded like an idiot "—you just rest, okay?"

Was he imagining the tiny flexing of those too-chilly fingers? Yeah, he decided, staring down at them, he must be. Reid hesitated, then lightly touched the less-damaged side of Caleb's face. "I'll be back," he repeated and strode out.

IT WAS DISORIENTING to wake up in someone else's bed. Anna lay still for a minute, until she remembered where she was. Then she opened her eyes and turned her head to see she was alone. The small house was quiet. So he was gone— Then her gaze fell on the clock and she squeaked. 10:54? No wonder Reid was long gone!

She leaped for the bathroom, where she found a note laid on the closed seat of the toilet, hard to miss.

Hope you didn't have to be anywhere early.
I figured you needed the sleep. I'll see you at
the hospital.

Signed, *Reid.*

Not that she'd expected any *Love, Reid,* but…

She huffed. Sure. Dream on.

After a shower, she ate a quick bowl of cereal and left, using the push-button lock, but unable to turn the dead bolt without a key. Somehow, she kind of doubted today was the day someone would break into Reid Sawyer's rental house and steal…what? There weren't a lot of goodies on display.

At the hospital, she spotted a strongly built, very dark-skinned Hispanic man near the nurses' station on Diego's floor. Even from a distance, his fury was obvious. Wonderful. He'd been told he wouldn't be allowed to see his son. Talking to him was a peachy way to start the day.

Fortunately, his anger already had a target: the DHS caseworker, who cast Anna a grateful glance when she joined them. They took him into a small conference room, where they explained that given the allegations of abuse, they had requested a dependency hearing. In the meantime, his son had asked for no contact.

Hector leaped to his feet with a roar. "You know nothing! *Women.*" He spat it like an epithet. "Don't think you'll keep my son from me."

The painfully young DHS caseworker shrank back from him, an enraged male standing above the two women with his fists balled. "You'll receive a fair hearing…."

"And this time, so will Diego," Anna was unwise enough to say.

Snarling, he picked up a chair. She saw in his eyes how much he wanted to swing it at her. Cave in her head. Smash her. She sat frozen, instinct telling her not to stand up, not to move at all. That same instinct said, *He's fooled half a dozen caseworkers and as many family court judges. If he lacked all impulse control, he wouldn't have managed that.*

She was right. His eyes never leaving hers, he set down the chair and walked out of the small room. The caseworker was shaking, and Anna was disturbed to realize she was, too.

After that, she went in to talk to Diego, who, sitting up in bed with the TV on, was undeniably awake. He looked wary. "Miss Grant."

"Yep, I'm back. I just met with your father."

The wariness became fear. "He's *here?*" He looked past her at the door. "I can't stay. I can't." He shoved the tray table aside and struggled as if he thought he could swing the heavy cast over the edge of the bed and leap to his feet. "I won't go back with him. I'll kill myself first!"

"Diego." She laid a hand on his arm. "He can't come in here. We've filed a court order preventing him until the allegations you've made can be investigated. The nurses and doctors are aware of what's going on. They won't let him get to you. I promise."

His face contorted and he bent his head, trying to hide tears from her, but his shoulders heaved with a sob. Anna sat on the edge of the bed and wrapped her arms around him. He cried against her, in that raw, unpracticed way of boys and men. When he finally pulled away, she saw his shame. In his eyes, he hadn't been manly.

Without a word, Anna handed him a box of tissues and he wiped his face and blew his nose.

"You know what?" she said. "I need a Pepsi or Coke. How about you? Would you like a soda?"

He sneaked a look at her face. "Can I?"

"Sure you can. What do you want?"

She had to go all the way down to the cafeteria to secure two tall bottles of Pepsi, chilly and beaded with moisture. The look on his face when she handed one over was her reward.

She bided her time, letting him gulp a quarter of it down and sipping her own before she said, "We need to talk, Diego."

His alarm flared again. "I told that other social worker everything."

Anna nodded. "I know you did. She's going to request medical records and call everyone whose names you gave. I'm more interested in, oh, getting to know you so I can put you in the right foster home if it comes to that." She paused, watching his guard lower before adding, "I need to know more about your recent history. There's a whole lot you aren't telling me, isn't there, Diego?" she said gently.

He was tough, but also only fifteen years old. Anna's experience trumped his stubbornness. Even so, she didn't get everything, but he did admit enough to make apprehension, anger and a sense of betrayal tangle in her until she could hardly draw breath.

Reid had lied to her. He must have. Unless his *dear* friends had also taken in Caleb and probably other boys, too. None of whom could have been court supervised, or said caseworker would have noticed the boys who *weren't* on her list of foster children who belonged in the home.

"You've already met Caleb's brother, Reid, haven't you?" she said casually.

Diego's mouth opened and then closed. His eyes were dark and worried. He didn't have a face meant to keep secrets.

Anna laid her hand on his arm and squeezed. "It's okay, Diego. I know you're trying not to get anyone else in trouble, and I understand. We'll leave it there for now, okay?"

He gave a jerky nod. "What if my dad sneaks in?"

"Scream." She let him see that she meant it. "Raise a ruckus. Help will come. I promise."

Diego's head bobbed. "Okay."

She was almost to the door when, behind her, he said, "Thank you."

Anna turned in surprise. The look on his young face was heartbreaking.

"I mean, for believing me."

She swallowed a lump in her throat before she could get out a word. "I do believe you, Diego. So did Ms. Hinton. We're on your side."

She almost said, *To the death,* but didn't, because that would sound bad and send the wrong message. She didn't even exactly mean it. There were legal avenues to save this boy, and she believed in those, heart and soul. She of all people knew what came of not following the guidelines.

Then, feeling sick—no, worse than that, *grieving*—she headed for the elevator that would take her down to the ground floor and ICU.

DURING REID'S VISITS to the Hales', TJ had remained a closed book to him. His looks alone were daunting to the other boys, who noticeably kept their distance.

Although barely seventeen, TJ looked to be in his twenties. He topped six feet, and unlike the other boys, had already developed a man's muscles, long and ropy. A man's growth of beard, too. The stubble was paired with shaggy dark hair that often hung over his equally dark eyes and hid his expression. Reid had never seen the kid look anything but sullen. From what Paula and Roger had said, his attitude was lousy. And yet, he'd stayed.

After reviewing his records, Reid could see why. Theodore James Haveman's father didn't just have anger-management problems. He held grudges and possessed a mile-wide streak of cruelty. He harbored a hell of a lot of anger, but didn't necessarily lash out the way your garden-variety abusive parent did. No, this guy would bide his time, let his kid think he'd gotten away with something or that an offense had been forgotten, and then he'd punish him viciously. Even creatively. Unfortunately, he was smart enough to do it in ways that didn't show on the surface. Bruises and scars might tell a story. Electrical shocks didn't. Killing the family's pet didn't. Hurting Mom to punish the kid, that didn't, either. Apparently, he could count on his wife to keep her mouth shut.

Reid hated this guy. He despised him. Unfortunately, Reid was left wondering how sane the son could be after a lifetime of such treatment. There was no way he'd been behind the wheel of that pickup truck, but he still could be the arsonist who was also fond of knives.

Renner had said TJ seemed genuinely distraught over the hit-and-run. The kid was seriously shaken, and no wonder. Riding along the shoulder of the road, TJ had had a bull's-eye on his back, escaping only because of sharp ears and quick reflexes.

Reid grimaced as he got out of his Expedition in front of the lodge. TJ had probably had a hell of a lot of practice in evading pain. He'd learned to trust instincts he should never have had to acquire.

A dark green Jeep Cherokee was already parked in front. Was somebody else here, or had Renner driven his own vehicle?

Reid took the steps two at a time and went in without knocking. Four heads turned. Clay Renner, Paula, Roger and TJ were seated on benches on each side of one of the long tables rather than in the more comfortable living room setup around the river-rock fireplace. No fire burned in it today. The weather had actually turned a corner, and the day almost felt like spring. Memories of the winters he'd spent in Angel Butte made Reid suspect the almost-balmy day was only a trick to make them think winter had released its grip.

No sounds came from the kitchen. The other boys were absent, probably huddled in their cabins.

At the sight of him, Roger swung a leg over the bench. "Coffee?"

He flapped a hand. "Don't get up."

Nobody else wanted a refill when he offered. When he returned, he chose to sit right across from TJ.

"Any update on Caleb?" Paula asked anxiously.

Reid told them what the doctor had said about keeping Caleb sedated. "We'll see once they taper him off." He raised his eyebrows, his gaze on TJ. "All right. What's this about?"

"Can't I talk to you alone?" The boy had a man's voice, too, deep and even gruff.

Renner didn't look happy, but didn't raise an objection.

Reid took his time thinking how to answer. "TJ, unless this is unrelated to the safety of everyone here at the lodge, I don't see how we can keep what you have to say from Paula and Roger. And if it has to do with the hit-and-run—" He stopped as soon as he saw from the boy's expression that it did. "I think you'd better just come clean."

TJ slid a glance at Paula, took a deep breath and nodded. "Everything happening... You know. The fires and shit. Stuff," he corrected himself. His Adam's apple bobbed hard. "I think it's my dad."

"What makes you believe that?" Reid asked, keeping his voice calm. "Did that look like his truck?"

He'd already checked and knew that Randal Haveman was the registered owner of two vehicles, neither of which was black.

But the boy shook his head. "No. I mean, I don't know. He might have gotten a new one. Or borrowed it or something. Before he had a Yukon. It didn't have the right kind of grille. Besides, it was like a 2007 or 2008. Whatever it was that hit Caleb was really shiny and new. You know?"

Reid nodded. "It's a help that you were so observant."

"Oh, sure. You mean, like how I got the license number?"

Reid held his gaze. "You saved yourself. That's pretty damn impressive."

The boy ducked his head for a minute. "Everything that's happened, it's just like Dad," he mumbled. "He likes to scare people. When he was in a really good mood, I knew he was setting us up for something. And Dad really liked fire. He has this, like, monster grill on the patio. He owns a whole chain of stores that sell grills and woodstoves and saunas. You know, like that. At home he had this brick circle in the backyard to have fires, too. He'd get these *huge* ones going with sparks floating toward the neighbors' roofs. They called the cops a few times." His eyes were dark and desperate. "After the guy who lived next door complained, Dad slashed his tires. I saw him coming back in with his knife."

"Son, why didn't you tell us this sooner?" Roger asked, somehow keeping his voice kind.

"I thought maybe I could catch him. Or at least see him so you'd believe me." He looked from face to face. "It's me that oiled the hinges on the back door. I've been sneaking out at night, watching for him. The night he stuck the knife in the door, I saw someone running away down the driveway. But when I started after him, there was someone else there." His shamed gaze met Reid's. "I didn't know it was you. I'm sorry. I sneaked back in."

"I heard the door."

"You think your father was trying to hit you, and Caleb and Diego were collateral damage?" Renner asked.

"He wouldn't have cared if anyone else got hurt."

"Has he ever actually tried to kill you before?"

"No, but I sort of ducked my head and tried to get by. He…came pretty close this one time when I ran away and was brought back."

This wasn't the time to ask *how* the son of a bitch

had "almost" killed his son in retaliation for the sin of trying to escape. "I've been trying to check out your father's whereabouts," Reid said instead. "It's turned out to be a challenge because he has a dozen stores, including ones in Bend and Klamath Falls, which gives him good reason to be in our neighborhood. He's traveling a lot. Pinning down his whereabouts hasn't proved easy."

"I should just go," TJ said in despair. "If I'm not here, he won't have any reason to keep doing this stuff. That's what I wanted to say." He hunched his shoulders. "And that I'm sorry about Caleb. It's my fault."

"No." Reid heard how hard his voice was. "It's not. TJ, if your father is really behind all this, *he's* responsible. Him and no one else. Caleb would say the same thing. And no, you're not going anywhere. You're a victim as much as Caleb is. More. We're going to find a way to keep you safe. You hear me?"

The boy stared at him, seemingly stunned.

Paula scooted along the bench until she could wrap her arm around the boy who looked like a man. "Of course you're not leaving us," she said softly.

"Don't even think about it," Roger echoed.

TJ's face crumpled and he began to sob.

Throat working, Clay Renner stood and jerked his head toward the door. Embarrassed that his eyes were burning, Reid nodded and went with him.

Outside, the two men stood on the porch. Both of

them stared out at the woods that shielded the old resort from the road and neighbors. Renner let out a gusty sigh at last.

"God damn. Sawyer, I don't see how we can protect the Hales, not if Haveman is behind this. It would involve a shitpot full of lying, and that would only work if he keeps his mouth shut."

"Which he won't do," Reid said flatly. "He's going to claim he's over here on a legitimate mission to try to get his boy back from renegades who hide runaway kids from their legal guardians. Shining the spotlight on the Hales will suit his purposes."

"That's what I think, too." Renner turned his back on the view and leaned a hip against the porch railing. "What do you suggest?"

"We find the son of a bitch first."

A crack of mirthless laughter came from Renner. "Good plan."

Reid grinned reluctantly. "I don't have jurisdiction."

Renner's face sobered. "No. I'll call every one of his stores and his home. We'll nail down his schedule."

"Which will tell him his son is here in Angel Butte if he doesn't already know."

"Yeah." Renner's regret was obvious. "It will. That doesn't mean he'll be able to touch him."

"No." Reid ran a hand over his head. "Let me know what I can do to help."

"You helped, cracking the kid open in there. You should be focusing on your brother."

"There's...not much I can do, until he opens his eyes." *Until* was such a positive word. He wished he entirely believed it.

"You hear about Jane's sister?" the other man asked unexpectedly.

Reid turned toward him. "No."

Renner frowned at the woods. "Melissa was in a car accident. No, it was more complicated than that—her kid was grabbed and held hostage. Turned out Lissa had been blackmailing her boss, who was using his trucking outfit to run drugs." He slanted an apologetic glance at Reid. "Sorry. None of that's relevant."

"Some part of it must be." He kept stumbling over other melodramas. It probably said something about him that he felt better to discover these colleagues—maybe new friends—had suffered through deep shit of their own. Maybe that was why they were sympathetic to the Hales—and to him.

"She was in a coma. Lasted for days. We weren't sure she'd make it or who she'd be if she did open her eyes."

Reid winced.

"Thing is, she's fine." One side of his mouth lifted in a wry smile. "Serving a prison sentence, but that's a whole other story."

"I wouldn't mind hearing it one of these days."

Renner clapped him on the back. "We'll have you to dinner once Caleb's home with you."

Reid winced again.

Renner's blue eyes were friendly. "A little worried about becoming parent to a teenager?"

"You could say that."

"Is that what you have in mind?"

Reid drew a deep breath. "Yeah. Yeah, it is. He needs me." *I need him.*

"Good. Keep me updated on his condition and I'll do the same on what I learn."

"Thank you."

With an amiable nod, Renner departed in the Jeep Cherokee. Reid stayed where he was for a few minutes, not looking forward to going back in and talking to Paula and Roger, looking forward even less to the talk he had to have with Anna when they met up again.

REID'S FIRST REACTION at the sight of Anna rising from one of the chairs outside ICU was pleasure. The second was dismay.

That discussion would have to be *now,* before things blew up and she learned the truth some other way.

And then he got a good look at her face and thought, *Oh, shit.* She knew. Maybe not everything, but something.

"Hold whatever you're thinking," he said abruptly. "Let me check on Caleb."

No change. He stood at his brother's bedside long enough to gather himself, not talking this time, just gripping his hand. Finally he said, "I'm here, Caleb. Whenever you're ready." Then he walked out.

Anna was waiting. They were alone out here, but for the elderly volunteer who sat behind a desk guarding the inner sanctum. He took Anna's arm and led her far enough away so they wouldn't be overheard.

"Diego's father here yet?"

Disgust and maybe a hint of fear flashed across her face. "Oh, yeah. He considered assaulting me, but thought better of it in time. It's almost too bad."

Reid ground his teeth. *Almost* assaulted her? "That son of a bitch," he said.

She shook her head. "Not the first time, won't be the last." Her eyes swam with emotions he didn't want to decipher. "You lied to me."

Crap. Wearily, he sank into a chair. "Yeah."

She stood over him, anger and hurt undiminished. "Let me rephrase that. You've *been* lying to me. All along. Over and over."

"I didn't want to." He knew how weak that sounded, and said it anyway.

Anna didn't even bother scoffing. "Why?"

"Because I knew you'd turn the Hales in."

"The Hales." Recognition dawned. "Roger. The man who was here at the hospital."

Reid nodded. "The hit-and-run happened a few hundred yards from his place."

"He heard it?" she said slowly.

Oh, man. "No. A third boy was there, Anna. He… dived into a ditch and didn't get hurt beyond a few bruises and scrapes. Diego had enough presence of mind to tell him to go to the Hales'. TJ…has one of the worst parents of all."

Her face was ghost pale. After a moment, she sagged into a chair. Not the one next to his. The empty seat between them felt like, and was meant to be, a chasm. "All," she repeated, sounding shocked despite whatever she'd thought she knew.

"They have…had ten boys," he told her. His voice was robotic. "The Hales are good people, Anna, whether you want to believe it or not. They've been doing this for years."

"Hiding children from their legal guardians and the authorities."

"Hiding children from viciously abusive guardians. Children who, no matter what the allegations, were sent home over and over again." His voice gained passion as he willed her to understand. "Children no one listened to. Refused to believe." His jaw tightened. "I was one of those children."

She stared at him, unblinking. "An underground shelter."

"Yes."

She shook her head. "And you truly believe this is the right way to rescue these kids."

His "Yes" lacked as much force as he wanted to inject into it.

"Foster parents being overseen by no one. Who could be abusive themselves, but have kids too scared of their alternative to speak up or take off."

"They're not—"

Her hand chopped off his ability to speak.

"Foster parents whose background has never been investigated. Who, even assuming *they* have the best will in the world, are robbed of any ability to investigate adults *they* introduce to the kids."

Reid was held silent by the memory of police lieutenant Duane Brewer, who had mentored, raped and murdered girls from the Hales' shelter—a man whose past they couldn't check out. In fact, the very secretiveness of their operation left them vulnerable to unspoken blackmail. Brewer had been a cop; he could have exposed them if they hadn't welcomed him as a volunteer, let him take kids anywhere, anytime, he wanted.

Whatever hurt Anna felt was no longer apparent. All he saw was ferocity.

"Foster parents who had no recourse when a kid chose to take off. They couldn't go looking for him, the way I did Yancey."

Reid had thought of that, too. Imagined kids who couldn't cut it at the Hales doing something as desperate and stupid as thirteen-year-old Yancey had been about to, preparing to hitch across the country in search of a relative who would have rejected him if he'd ever gotten that far. In search of a dream.

"Do you know what happens to kids when there

is no oversight?" Suddenly, her voice shook. The pain in her eyes was back. "Let me tell you."

"Anna—"

"No," she said sharply. She sat on the edge of the seat, her back ruler straight. "I had a sister. Molly."

The grief on her face was a blow to his midriff. He reached for her hand, and she stiffened and shrank away. *Don't touch.* After a moment, he let his hand drop to his side. He wasn't sure he could say anything.

"She was two years younger than me. We were... I don't know. On our second or third foster home. We had a new caseworker. She insisted that this was a wonderful family. They had acreage, and dogs, and even a pony. She would visit often. She *promised.*"

For all his experience, Reid had never heard a single word said with such shattering pain. She didn't have to tell him what had happened, but she did.

"She lied. Or forgot because she got busy. Who knows? What *I* know is that we spent a year and a half in hell. I was in first grade. I should have told my teacher what was going on, but I didn't. I saw how much she liked them both. We were lucky girls to have a home with them, she said."

His throat unlocked. "She didn't know."

"No. She didn't. Maybe she would have listened. But I was only six, and I kept thinking, Miss Byrd *promised.*" There it was again, a lethal slice of pain. "She'll be back and I can tell her and she'll take us somewhere else. Someplace safe. Only—" Her voice broke. "She didn't. Not in time." Anna breathed hard, and then she glared at him as if it was all his fault. "He killed my little sister, and I have to live with the guilt because I should have told someone. Anyone. I should have—"

Reid stood and reached for her.

She leaped up and retreated, her expression wild. "Don't touch me. Don't!"

His fingers curled and uncurled. "Please. Anna, let me—"

"*That* is what you encouraged. Condoned."

There was no good answer. It was true. All of it.

"Condemned your brother to."

He felt the first stirring of anger. "I visited often. I promised I would, and I kept that promise."

"Lucky Caleb," she said, bitterly scathing. "What about all the other kids? *Years'* worth of other kids?"

"I lived with the Hales for three years. I know what kind of people they are. They saved a lot of kids."

"Every one who came to them?"

There was no doubt she could see the answer on his face.

He tried one more defense. "Have *you* saved all the kids who came to you?" The question came out sharper than he'd intended, and no sooner had he spoken than he realized how unintentionally cruel he'd been. She hadn't been able to save the one child who meant the most to her: her own sister. And she would never forgive herself, despite the absurdity of a six-year-old child taking responsibility for protecting anyone else. "I didn't mean that the way it sounded. I'm sorry," he said roughly.

Anna only shook her head and backed away. "I thought at least we were friends."

"We were." Desperation swept through him. "We are. Anna—"

Tears ran down her cheeks. She took an angry swipe at them, turned and walked away. Her walk became faster and faster until she was almost running by the time she disappeared from sight.

Reid dropped into the chair again, feeling as if he'd been shot.

I love her. I would do anything—

He buried his face in his hands. Anything. Like tell unforgivable lies.

Anna, Anna.

CHAPTER FOURTEEN

ANNA WENT HOME.

She didn't tell anyone where she was going. She didn't let herself worry about whether Diego might need her. She couldn't imagine going to work tomorrow. What would she do? Lie, like he had? Claim to be sick?

I am sick.

At first she did nothing but sit on her sofa and stare at the wall, remembering every lie Reid had ever told her. Every flickering expression that crossed his face when he told those lies.

He hadn't known her. Not well enough to realize what those particular lies would mean to her.

I don't have to be fair.

No, she didn't. She wouldn't be. She was *obligated* to report the Hales. How could she not, even knowing what that would do to Reid?

She was hugging herself for warmth when it occurred to her she hadn't adjusted the thermostat. It took her another five minutes to make herself get up and do it, then grab a fleece throw from the back of a chair to wrap around herself. A cup of tea would be nice but…would take more effort than she had to give.

Inevitably, her mind started clicking again, starting with a slide show. All Reid.

The man she'd first met, who was so good at hiding what he felt, she'd wondered if he *did* feel anything. The smiles he began letting loose. The thousand other emotions he'd let her see since.

And she remembered how much he *had* told her, even as he kept secrets. His wretched childhood, his bafflement over how to reach the brother he hadn't known he had. His clumsy attempts to create a relationship she could see he craved, for all he didn't want to need it—or to let anyone else see what he must believe was a weakness. His honesty the night they first had sex. *Made love.* She couldn't imagine he'd ever revealed as much to anyone. The tenderness and passion he'd given her since, not easy for him, but a part of the man nonetheless. His cold anger at his father. His terror when he heard about the accident. The awful look in his eyes every time he came out of the ICU after sitting at Caleb's side.

The even worse look in his eyes when she backed away, rejecting even his touch.

I love him, she thought miserably. *I threw him away.*

I think he might love me.

Oh, dear God. Was she really going to let the horror of Molly's death justify a loveless life?

Curled in a tight ball on her sofa, Anna didn't know. Had no idea how to let go of the guilt and anger and grief that had made her who she was. Or even if she wanted to let go.

WEARY TO THE BONE, Reid still made himself drive back out to the shelter that evening. When he walked in, all the boys except TJ were in the main room. Heads turned, and he saw that the sight of him scared them. *As it should,* he thought bleakly. He had a feeling their reaction had more to do with how he looked than with recent events.

Paula emerged from the kitchen, her eyes locking on Reid. "Boys." She spoke sharply enough to gain their attention. "Time to say good-night. Everyone to their cabins."

Except for a few minor grumbles, they complied, shooting backward glances until they were all gone.

"TJ?" he asked.

"Upstairs. Do you need to talk to him?"

"No. You and Roger."

"He's—" They both heard the back door open and close again. "That'll be him," Paula said with relief.

Now he was scaring her, too.

"Just taking a walk around," Roger said on seeing Reid, who suggested they sit down.

They chose the table closest to the kitchen and the farthest from the stairwell. Reid would rather TJ didn't hear what he had to say.

"Your cover is blown," he said bluntly. "We expected it would be once Sergeant Renner caught up to Haveman, if he's our guy. But it's happened sooner than we expected."

Roger looked stoic, Paula stricken.

"Diego tried, but he let enough slip—" No, damn it, he would not lay the blame elsewhere. "When I spoke to Anna Grant, the social worker for Angel's Haven who is trying to place Diego in a foster home, I told her the whole story. I think she'll report you."

Neither said a word for a long time. Finally Roger bent his head. "I told you to use your judgment."

"She was…angry," Reid said with difficulty. He told them enough of her story for them to understand. "It doesn't help that I've been, uh, seeing her." Sleeping with her. Falling in love with her. "Talking to her about Caleb, but telling a pack of lies, too. The fact that this is personal for her may not help your cause. I'm sorry," he said simply.

"No." Paula's gaze had never left his face. To his shock, she reached across the table and laid her hand over his. "*I'm* sorry, Reid. If we're responsible for damaging a relationship that meant something to you…"

"My fault." He couldn't keep the bleakness from his voice. "Doesn't matter."

"It does."

He only shook his head.

They were all silent for a time again. Roger was the one to speak up.

"Should we try to find places for the boys to go?"

"I can't advise you on that. None of this will help my career, but actively involving myself now in any action you take to hide the boys would cross a line. I can't."

Both nodded.

"But if you want my advice?"

"Of course we do," Paula said warmly.

"Then I'd sit tight. What I can and will do when it all comes out is my damnedest to defend and support you. *And* to make sure these boys' stories are heard. My guess is you can count on Sergeant Renner, too. I don't think any of the boys will be returned to their former homes. And, for all that she's angry at me, I know Anna will fight for your kids."

A nerve twitched beneath Roger's eye. Paula abruptly bent her head to hide her face.

God damn. This was hard. Reid felt as if he was betraying them, as he'd betrayed Anna and maybe Caleb, too.

"I need to get back to the hospital," he said. "Caleb was looking a little more active. Twitching. Even moving a little."

"That's good news," Roger said heavily.

"I hope so." He flattened his hands on the table to shove himself up, then stood for a minute, feeling as if each foot was encased in cement. Actually walking out felt beyond him.

Caleb, he reminded himself.

"I'll keep you informed," he said, nodded a good-night and left.

WAKING AND SLEEPING were versions of the same nightmare.

Reid had asked permission to stay with Caleb, and the latest doctor had okayed it. Caleb was struggling toward consciousness, and nobody liked the idea of him waking to unfamiliar people on top of an alien environment.

He was no longer on oxygen, but was still wired for monitoring. His slightest movement caused beeping and a wild disarrangement of one of the squiggly green lines that ran across a screen. The beating of Caleb's heart became part of Reid's waking and sleeping dreams, along with visions of Anna's face while she told him about her sister.

He killed my little sister.

Reid wondered how. He'd seen enough bodies of young children to be able to envision too many possibilities, all graphic. God, had six-year-old Anna seen it happen? Discovered her sister's body afterward?

Promises meant everything to Anna.

He hadn't made one to her. He hadn't broken a promise. Not to her, not to anyone. Reid didn't ever remember making a promise beyond the most casual, the "I'll call this afternoon" variety, until Caleb had come along.

Didn't matter whether there had ever been an explicit promise, Reid realized. He had known how much Anna would disapprove of what the Hales were doing. No, he hadn't known why, but his gut had told him she had a powerful and very personal reason. He'd lied anyway, because what else could he do?

By morning, he felt like hell. His neck was stiff and his skin grimy. Yesterday morning's shower and shave were a distant memory. He clenched his teeth against the jab of another memory, that of Anna sleeping in his bed, nestled in the middle because she'd been cuddled up to him until he'd eased himself away. That had been yesterday morning, too.

He stood and stretched until his bones cracked, after which his eyes focused on his brother, who lay quietly as if sleeping. The swelling that had made half his face grotesque had noticeably gone down. No, the sleep wasn't peaceful, he saw then—there was a lot of activity going on beneath Caleb's eyelids. Dreams? Or a semiconscious battle?

"I'm still here," he said quietly. He gripped his brother's hand again. "You're in the hospital, Caleb. I'm going to feel one hell of a lot better when you open your eyes and say my name."

The movement under the boy's eyelids intensified, even seeming agitated. His lashes fluttered—and his eyes opened. He closed them as quickly, opened them again, but squinting this time. Well, on his good side—on the battered side of his face, the remaining swelling allowed barely a squint anyway. What Reid could see of his eyes looked…blank.

Feeling a thrill of fear, Reid said, "Caleb?"

That uncomprehending gaze very slowly turned to him. And then his brother's misshapen mouth twisted into what might have been a stab at a smile. His mouth opened and closed a couple of times. His tongue touched chapped lips. Finally, he formed a word. "Reid."

"You heard me."

The mouth formed another word, almost silent. "Yes."

"God." Reid dropped like a stone onto the bedside chair. "You scared the crap out of me. You've been unconscious for damn near two days." He ran a shaky hand over his face. "I need to let the nurse know you're awake. Hold on there, kid. I'll be right back."

He would have sworn Caleb said, "I know," although he might have been mistaken.

Within moments, Caleb's bed was surrounded. Reid was banned to the waiting room for the next while. Exhilarated, he didn't mind. He walked the hall outside the unit until his muscles loosened, then took out his phone. It was early, but…he couldn't imagine anyone else had slept much better than he had.

He called Anna first. The call went to voice mail. *She might still be asleep,* he told himself, but he knew better.

"Caleb's regained consciousness. He said my name. I thought you'd want to know." Despite the glorious relief, he became aware of the huge hollow beneath his breastbone. "Anna...will you talk to me? Will you listen?" For some reason, he waited, as if she might pick up even though he knew that was impossible.

After a minute, he touched End, then called Clay Renner, who did answer, sounding alert.

"That's good news," he said. "Has he been able to answer questions yet?"

"No. The doctor is in with him now. They kicked me out. But he's all here, Clay." His voice had thickened. "He said my name."

"I'll come straight there," the other man said kindly. "See you in fifteen."

Paula answered the phone at the lodge and began to cry when Reid gave her the news. "Thank God," she said. "Thank God."

He'd barely finished that call when Clay Renner arrived, a manila folder in his hand.

"Will they let us question Caleb?" he asked.

"I don't know." Reid rasped a hand over his jaw. "If he's up to it, I don't know why they wouldn't."

Renner eyed him. "I've got an electric shaver in my glove compartment. You want to borrow it?"

A reluctant grin broke on Reid's face. "That bad?"

"Some people look good with stubble. You're not one of 'em."

It felt good to laugh. "Yeah, if you wouldn't mind. I itch."

Nobody had emerged from ICU to summon Reid before Renner returned with the razor. Reid headed to the nearest restroom, laid out paper towels to catch the whiskers and shaved. When he was done, he eyed himself, not sure the whole picture had improved. The lack of sleep showed. His hair, never cooperative, was doing strange things. He wet it down and tried to smooth it, but wasn't sure he hadn't made matters worse. With a shrug, he gave up, tossed the wadded paper towels and went out to join Renner.

"They're ready for us."

For some reason, Reid's heart gave one hard beat. He didn't know why.

The doctor cleared everyone out of Caleb's cubicle when Renner and Reid went back. His brother's eyes were closed, giving Reid another brief scare, but when he said, "You awake?" and touched his hand, Caleb looked at him.

"Hey." He sounded a little better. A cup of ice chips sat on the bedside table, so maybe just moistening his mouth had helped.

Reid introduced Renner, who smiled. "Glad to see you looking a lot better," he said.

Caleb slowly lifted the hand that the IV was inserted into and gingerly touched the damaged side of his face. "Yeah?"

Renner's smile widened. "Didn't say you looked good. Just better."

Caleb laughed and then winced. His gaze turned to Reid. "Shaved."

He rubbed his chin. "Yeah."

"Thought you might be growing a beard."

"God, no." He stood looking down at his brother, wondering how much of what he felt was on his face. "I didn't go home last night."

"Oh." Caleb seemed as vulnerable and uneasy about the unspoken emotions as he felt.

"Do you remember the accident?" Reid asked abruptly. "Neither Diego nor TJ saw much."

Caleb didn't move. Reid saw him absorbing the fact that, in addition to himself, at least two other boys had now been exposed. "They're...okay?" he asked at least, cautiously.

"Yes. TJ made it into a ditch. Diego is here in the hospital, too, with a broken leg and some other broken bones. No head injury, though, unlike you. You took the hardest hit."

"He drove straight at us." The horror of the memory was in his eyes. "We were on the shoulder. As far over as we could go. He swerved to take us out."

"Neither of the others was sure what the vehicle was. They didn't get a license plate or see the driver, either."

He looked at Reid. "Wasn't Dad."

"We know." Reid took his hand again. "Sergeant

Renner questioned him, but he was able to prove he wasn't in Angel Butte."

Caleb nodded slightly. "Dodge Ram." Long pause. "They've got…kind of a different front grille. You know? My friend Ian's dad drives one."

"Ah." Renner sounded pleased.

"Did you see the driver, Caleb?" Reid asked.

"Yes. Don't know him."

Renner said, "I brought some photos to show you, Caleb. No, don't try to sit up. I'll hold them so you can see them."

Reid recognized the faces enlarged and printed in color that Renner had fanned out at the foot of the bed. He said nothing, but approved when Renner chose to start with Trevor's uncle, deliberately skipping the photo of TJ's father and moving on through several others before he held up the driver's license photo of Randal Haveman.

Caleb's whole body instantly stiffened. "Yes!" he hissed. "That's him. Oh, man. Who is he?"

Reid kept his mouth clamped shut. Renner's eyes met his briefly before he looked again at Caleb. "Can you keep it to yourself?"

"Yes."

"TJ's father. He's…been afraid it was his father. I guess he's been sneaking out at night hoping to catch him red-handed."

"Oh. I thought…" Caleb closed his eyes, leaving his suspicion unspoken.

"We'll find him," Renner said, voice hard. "You'll have to testify in court, Caleb."

"I will." His fierce stare held Clay Renner's. "He was looking straight at me when he hit me."

Primal rage hit Reid like the leading edge of a storm. He locked his jaw so tight, he feared his molars might crack. He wanted in the worst way to go after the son of a bitch himself. But he knew he couldn't, for a lot of reasons. And the determination and cold anger he saw on Clay Renner's face reassured him.

"Then I'll get on with it," Renner said harshly and left without another word.

Reid sat down again, allowing the silence to build. He half expected Caleb would fall asleep again, but instead he turned his head on the pillow to look at Reid, his expression tormented.

"Paula and Roger… Are they in trouble? God, if only we hadn't gone out! Or if I could have gotten out of the way—"

"Then the truck would have hit Diego harder than it did. He might be dead right now."

Caleb's stricken expression didn't change.

"This isn't your fault, Caleb. None of it." Familiar theme, Reid thought. On a flicker of amusement, he wondered how many times Paula had given this same lecture. What had she said to him, not so long ago?

You have no *responsibility for your father's sins.*

In that microsecond, Reid let go of the belief that she was wrong. He only wished he'd have a chance to try to convince Anna that *she* bore no responsibility for her sister's death.

"I told you Dad wasn't in town," he said. "Paula and Roger didn't forbid you guys from going anywhere, did they? You had pretty girls in your sights. Why wouldn't you ride down to the county park? What is it, half a mile tops?"

Caleb's face relaxed some, although he remained troubled.

"Will they, like, go to *jail* or something?" he asked.

"I don't know," Reid had to admit. "I'll do my best to keep that from happening."

"And what about the other guys?" This was a cry. "What if they have to go back?"

This time Reid shook his head. "I'll fight to see that doesn't happen."

"You promise?" Caleb's eyes bored into his.

"Yeah." God. "I promise."

The tension left Caleb's thin body. "Okay." But then his eyes shot open even before he had let them close. "Dad? Does he know…?"

With so much else going on, Reid had forgotten to say this. "I got a restraining order, Caleb. He's not allowed to see you. There'll be a hearing as soon as you're well enough to attend. Unless you want me to look for your mother, I'm going for full custody."

Caleb searched his eyes. "You mean…I'd live with you?"

"Yeah." Reid reached for his hand again. Touching like this was starting to come more naturally. "You'll live with me. I'm sorry, Caleb. I thought I was doing the right thing, but I should have done this in the first place."

"'S'okay." Caleb's words slurred. "Took me away from Dad."

It seemed Reid's chest ached all the time now. "I wouldn't have left you, no matter what."

No response. Caleb had dropped off, maybe hadn't even heard him. Didn't matter, Reid realized. They'd said enough. *He trusts me.*

Doing nothing but watching his brother sleep, Reid stayed for another ten minutes before the lure of a shower got him to his feet.

As SHE DROVE, Anna kept an eye on Diego, who had pushed the passenger seat as far back as it would go to accommodate his cast. A pair of crutches lay on the back seat, but, given that he also had a cast on one arm, he wouldn't be making much use of them for a while.

They had sneaked him out of the hospital through the employee parking lot, and Anna was pretty confident they weren't being followed. Diego's body was rigid, though, and he kept glancing in the side mirror. The kid was scared to death that his father would find him.

"I picked these foster parents mostly because I thought you'd like them," Anna said. "But there was another reason, too."

Diego turned his stare on her.

"John is retired Marine Corps. Recently retired. From what his wife says, he was in a lot of firefights in Iraq and Afghanistan. He knows about your father. He'd be more than happy to take him on."

Tears appeared in Diego's eyes. He wiped at them, ducking his head. "I… Thank you."

She patted the cast on his arm, then put her hand back on the steering wheel.

"Did you get a chance to see Caleb again?" she asked after a minute. Diego had wanted to say goodbye. Proud that she'd kept her intense interest out of her voice, Anna waited anxiously. Reid had left her two messages this week, both updating her and ending each time by saying he wanted to talk to her. She wasn't ready.

"Yeah." Diego brightened. "Reid brought him to see me." Ironically, Caleb had left the hospital before Diego, whose injuries hadn't been life threatening. Partly, that was because Diego had the mobility issue, but also because finding him a home where he could be kept safe from his enraged father had been an issue.

"Good. You know, if you both stay here in Angel Butte, you'll go to school together."

"That'd be cool." From his downcast tone, she knew he didn't believe it would happen. "He has a hearing Monday. I mean, in court. He's pretty freaked."

"Tomorrow?" Her pulse picked up. "That was fast." Ridiculously fast. How had Reid pulled that off?

"Can you find out what happens? And let me know?" His puppy-dog brown eyes pleaded with her. "I mean, if he can't?"

"I will." She pulled into the driveway of Diego's new home and set the emergency brake. "Cross my heart."

He grinned, if weakly. Then looked alarmed as he gazed wide-eyed toward the house. "Is that *him?*"

Anna smiled. She'd had the same reaction the first time she met John Pannek. He was big, muscular and mean-looking—until he smiled. Walking down the driveway toward them, he wasn't smiling yet. "Yep. Think he can take on your dad?"

"Yeah!" Diego exclaimed.

Half an hour later, she was back in her car. Usually she took longer to settle a kid into a new foster home, but this time she'd been able to tell she wasn't needed. For all the abuse he'd suffered, Diego had stayed a nice, levelheaded boy. The Panneks had fostered for her before, and she had complete confidence in them. It was pure luck they'd decided they were ready for another child right now, ending her waffling about where she could safely place Diego. They'd taken to him instantly, and vice versa. If Hector went looking for him, it would appear that Diego had vanished. Unless they sent him in a wheelchair, Diego wouldn't be able to start school for at least another month. A former teacher, Beth was going to homeschool him until the custody issue was resolved.

Anna drove a few blocks, then pulled over.

Eight other boys still lived at the Hales'. Remained vulnerable the way she and Molly had been. Because *she* hadn't done what she should have done and reported the couple hiding kids from all legal authorities.

She'd been telling herself she wouldn't have to, that with the sheriff's department investigating, it would all come out anyway. She squeezed her eyes shut, feeling shame. Whatever her duty should be, whatever her conscience said, she didn't want to be the person Reid would blame for destroying the people he loved. She didn't know if that made her a coward or someone whose eyes had been opened to shades of gray.

Caleb's hearing was tomorrow. The most private of men, Reid would need to expose everything he'd suffered. He had already taken his brother home with him, even though he hadn't believed he had it in him to be a father figure.

Was he just doing what he thought he should do? she wondered. Or had he changed his mind? And if so—was it because he'd listened to her? Believed her?

With a moan, Anna bumped her forehead against

the steering wheel. She had to go tomorrow. Chances were good Reid would prefer she not be there; in fact, she suspected he'd like to have as few witnesses as possible. But…she had to be there anyway.

Because he might need me.

MOST OF THE seats in the small courtroom were empty. In contrast to criminal trials, custody hearings like this were closed to curiosity seekers, thank God. A couple of times the door in back had opened and closed. Except when he himself had testified, Reid hadn't looked to see who was coming and going.

This morning, he'd fielded several phone calls from people who knew about the hearing, including Roger and Paula. He'd told Phil Perez what was happening, and Phil had called to say he'd be thinking about him. Alec Raynor and Jane Renner had both stopped by Reid's office to say they'd be hoping there were no problems. *Problems.* Nice euphemism. That Caleb wasn't condemned to hell again was what they meant.

Caleb had declared he wanted to stay with Reid, but their attorney insisted on locating his mother. She had gotten hysterical at the idea of Caleb going to live with her. Dean would kill them both. She had agreed, if necessary, to relinquish her parental rights. Reid hadn't been able to tell how his brother felt about that. Caleb must have been hurt. On the other hand, his mother had left him a long time ago. This couldn't be a surprise.

Once finished with his own testimony, Reid could only sit and listen, unable to control the direction of the proceedings. The experience was frustrating enough when he was present for one of his own investigations. This was agony. Reid kept finding new levels of fear. Dante would have written eloquently about the one that gripped him when Caleb had testified.

Damn, Reid was proud of him. Despite his father's presence only feet away, Caleb held his head high as he talked about the abuse he'd suffered. A few times his voice shook, but he answered every question anyway. Only at the end did he look Dean in the eye, when he said, "I had to take off. It was getting worse. I thought he might kill me the next time."

The bailiff had had to forcibly insist Caleb's father resume his seat and shut his mouth until it was his turn to speak.

The only other cop Reid knew in the courtroom was Clay Renner, present because in the course of the investigation, he had looked seriously into the previous allegations regarding Caleb's treatment at the hands of his father. Renner had spoken to several former teachers, coaches and school counselors, and was prepared to testify as to what they'd said.

So far, the judge hadn't called him up. Reid didn't know if that was good or bad. He kept reminding himself that she'd seen most of Renner's testimony in written form.

Dean Sawyer was on the witness stand now. Already his face was mottled red with barely suppressed rage. It was probably the first time in his life every word he said wasn't accepted as gospel, Reid thought with cold satisfaction.

The judge, a woman who looked to be in her fifties, wore reading glasses on a thin chain around her neck. She had them perched on her nose as she studied a small mobile light box, which showed an X-ray. From where he sat, Reid couldn't see which one. It didn't matter.

"Your oldest son has an implant and two bridges to replace teeth knocked out while he was a boy," she remarked.

"He was an athlete. Basketball and football." Dean paused, his gaze briefly connecting with Reid's. "Took a beating sometimes."

Reid's muscles turned rock hard. His attorney laid a hand on his arm. He ignored it. He had no intention of visibly reacting to the taunt. The back of his neck prickled with an awareness that there were other people in the courtroom listening to this. *My life.*

The judge's eyebrows rose. "I see. And is there a reason why you took him to three separate dentists to have the work done? It appears you yourself continued to go to the same dentist for annual checkups and any needed work, but Reid rarely saw the same one twice."

"I had coverage through work. For my kids, it was whoever had an opening. The work was expensive on a cop's salary, so I tried to find the best deal."

"Yet Caleb seemingly *had* a regular dentist, until he needed work subsequent to having a tooth knocked out," she murmured. "At that point, you took him to an entirely new clinic when he needed a bridge." She made a production of flipping through papers on her desk. "Let's see. That was in November of this last year. Right after he alleges you gave him the last beating 'he was willing to take.'"

Reid rested his hand on his brother's arm. He used the action as an excuse to look over his shoulder. *Oh, hell,* was his first thought. Alec Raynor sat at the back. But then he saw who else was there, in the seat right beside the door. His gaze locked with Anna's, and he froze. His father was talking, but he didn't hear.

"Reid?" Caleb whispered urgently. "What are you doing? What's wrong?"

He gave his head a small shake and turned back around. "Nothing."

How had she known about the hearing? Why had she come? His heart was pounding as if he'd just brought down a suspect after a multiblock chase.

The judge was talking again.

And he needed to be listening. There'd be time for Anna later.

She's here. The knowledge sang in him. She had to care, or she wouldn't have come. Would she?

"Your oldest son was able to provide a number of X-rays showing broken bones, too," Judge Valdez remarked.

"He was clumsy."

"Children and teenagers are rather resilient, Mr. Sawyer. I'm told their bones don't break as easily as those of adults. It takes quite a lot of force to do the damage I see on these X-rays."

The judge carefully lifted the glasses from her nose and let them fall. Her gaze pinned the man on the witness chair. "You should know, Sergeant Sawyer, that I also requested your first wife's medical records from multiple clinics and hospitals in Spokane." She paused. "Since she, too, apparently felt she couldn't be seen more than once by any doctor given the rather suggestive nature of her injuries."

Reid gaped. *What?*

"Given the hurried nature of this hearing, not all arrived, but some did," she continued.

Dean half rose from his chair. "Those are completely irrelevant! You had no right!"

"I think I did." Her voice cooled. "I believe they are entirely relevant. If your second wife hadn't already left you, I would seek out her records, as well."

Face beet-red now, he stood up, shoving the chair back. "This is bullshit!"

"Please sit down, Sergeant Sawyer."

He glared at her for a moment long enough to have her exchanging a significant glance with the bailiff. Then he reluctantly resumed his seat, his movements angry.

Dean's attorney was on his feet, protesting the inclusion of records relating to an individual not properly part of the proceedings. One look from the judge sliced him off midword.

She eyed Dean again. "Have you anything you'd like to add, Mr. Sawyer?"

He did. He'd been shaken from his game, though, by her obvious skepticism and by the united front against him. This courtroom wasn't packed with his uniformed cronies giving their support. The judge wasn't one he'd appeared in front of a dozen times when he was on the right side of the law.

He talked about raising two boys and doing his best for them. About just wanting his youngest home again. About how there had been bitterness between him and Reid, and he blamed Reid for influencing Caleb to make up these lies.

"You check with anyone back home, ma'am. They'll speak highly of me. I'm a decorated law enforcement officer. I may have taken a hand to my boys a few times when they needed it, but nothing that was out of line. I love my boy. I don't even know how all this blew up." Did he look genuinely confused? "I just want to take him home."

"Is that all?"

He shot a look of vitriol at Reid. "My oldest son

is new in town here. You don't know him. People are taking him at his word, but they shouldn't be. He broke the law when he stole Caleb from me. He's been hiding a minor for months. You can't tell me that's right."

"Have you proof that in fact Captain Sawyer has had his brother with him?" she asked sharply.

His jaw muscles spasmed a few times. "He was too smart to have the boy at his house."

"In other words, no." She waited for a moment, then nodded. "Thank you, Sergeant Sawyer. You may step down now."

Looking less than happy, Dean scraped the chair back and lumbered to a seat next to his attorney.

"I believe I've seen enough." She looked at Reid's father. "You ought to know that I did take the precaution of speaking to two people in Captain Sawyer's previous department in California, his captain and an undersheriff. Both spoke extremely highly of him and were pleased to forward his records to me. Are you aware that in recent years he served on the Family Protection detail with a focus on domestic violence?"

His father said nothing.

Now her gaze touched briefly, unreadably on Reid before softening as she nodded slightly at Caleb. "I had intended this to be a preliminary hearing," she said. "However, the evidence overwhelmingly supports the allegations of child abuse brought against Sergeant Dean Sawyer. It's apparent that Caleb's mother is not in a position to take him into her home. Therefore, without hesitation I remand custody of the minor child, Caleb Sawyer, to his brother, Reid Sawyer. I see no reason to revisit this decision." She lifted a gavel and brought it down with a sharp rap.

Caleb's body lurched in a wracking sob. Reid wrapped his arms around his brother, stunned to discover his own cheeks were wet. He squeezed his eyes shut, choosing not to see the scuffle taking place on the other side of the courtroom as his father bellowed invectives.

"We're done with him," he murmured to Caleb. "The son of a bitch is out of our lives."

Caleb cried in enormous gulps that shook his whole body. Reid turned his head enough to see the back of the courtroom, hoping Anna would be walking down the aisle to them. He'd never needed her more. Instead, all he saw was her back as she slipped out the door.

The emptiness inside him expanded, the pressure feeling like a giant, dark vacuum.

He had Caleb. At least he had Caleb. Thank God.

Reid laid his cheek on his brother's head and closed his eyes.

CHAPTER FIFTEEN

LEANING AGAINST HER kitchen counter, Anna was waiting for the microwave to beep when the doorbell rang. She stiffened, her heart leaping and then hesitating before resuming a seminormal rhythm.

Reid? Or Hector Ramirez, deciding now was the moment to confront her?

Would Hector ring the doorbell to announce himself?

It had been two days since the hearing. She'd half expected Reid to show up, but he hadn't. No calls, either. She'd told herself she was relieved, even as she knew she wasn't. She had this awful fear that he had given up on her. She couldn't blame him if he had. Why was she being so stubborn in refusing even to listen to him?

All she knew was that a terrible conflict still raged inside her. When she slept, her dreams were of her little sister. Cuddling close and whispering, tremulous, "I'm scared, Anna. Are you scared?"

Yes. Yes!

Waking and sleeping, Anna saw Molly's dead face. The terrible angle of her neck.

Yes. Yes! I'm scared.

I'm still scared, she admitted to herself. Afraid to trust. Unable to forgive. No promise should ever be broken.

He didn't break one. Look what he has *done for his brother.*

She was being unjust, and she knew it. Unforgiving. Unreasonable. She knew all that, too. Listening to the horror Reid and his brother had suffered, she had felt something completely unexpected: fierce gratitude to the Hales for doing what no one else would. Sitting there in the back of that courtroom, Anna would have given anything to go back in time and protect the boy Reid had been.

Stung by shock, she asked herself: Did that mean she'd do anything for him now? Including aiding and abetting him in shielding a shelter that violated *her* bone-deep principles?

Or…had her principles begun to quake and crumble?

The microwave dinged, making her jump. The garlic chicken on rice smelled good, but she stayed rigid, listening hard. If it were Hector, would he circle the house looking in windows? What if he appeared in the kitchen window?

Anna made herself draw some deep breaths and tiptoed to the front room. No peephole in her door, so she sidled up to the window and lifted a slat of the blinds enough to peek through. Reid's SUV was parked at the curb, and he stood beside it, looking back at the house, not moving. An air of resignation and maybe sadness surrounded him. For a moment, it seemed as if he were staring right at her, as if he knew she were there, huddled inside, watching him.

He shook his head and got into his Expedition. A moment later, he drove away. By that time, she felt sick. The freshly warmed leftovers didn't smell as good anymore.

REID DIDN'T LIKE knowing that Ramirez was lurking in town and had followed Anna a few times, but so far they hadn't been able to do anything about it. Ramirez hadn't confronted her and was keeping his distance. Nobody had figured out how he'd discovered it was her who'd been responsible for placing Diego in a home. He had a right to stay in Angel Butte if he chose, considering the hearing he needed to attend was next week. Until then, they were in a state of limbo.

Jane talked regularly to Anna, who was very sensibly staying away from Diego. They were all waiting Hector out. Jane was also keeping Anna informed about the manhunt for Randal Haveman, which frustratingly had failed to locate him. He had to have guessed that he'd been identified, even though Renner had managed thus far to keep his name from the press.

Haveman's wife—TJ's mother—had become hysterical when her husband failed to come home from his last business trip. His personal vehicle, a white Yukon Denali, was located at a Dodge dealership in Bend, which had reported a black Dodge Ram pickup with canopy stolen. Everyone knew the bastard was still around. Unfortunately, the weather had taken a turn for spring, which meant he could be camping out—and in this country, the options were almost limitless. Alternatively, this in-between season offered him a whole hell of a lot of choices of vacant homes and cabins if he wanted to break into one.

Nobody thought it was safe to leave TJ with the Hales. Reid would have taken him home, but he'd been too visible visiting Caleb in the hospital. To Reid's surprise, Clay Renner offered his home with his wife's blessing.

His wife, who the day after Caleb's court hearing had let Reid know she was indeed pregnant and intended to keep working as long as possible. She was due around the first of October. She wanted to come back to work after a maternity leave, but possibly part-time. Not willing to lose her, Reid had promised to make that happen, although he didn't yet know how.

Promised, he thought wryly, with a last scan of Anna's town house before he drove away. He'd been making a lot of those lately. If she'd give him a chance, he was ready to make the kind of promises to her he'd never believed he could or would. Pretty clearly, though, she wasn't going to give him the chance.

Living with that constant ache of emptiness, he

tried to convince himself he just had to give her time. He had unknowingly—no, God damn it, why lie to himself? *knowingly*—violated a tenet so essential to her, she'd fashioned her entire life around upholding it. No, he hadn't known about her sister, but he could have guessed something like that lay in her past. And he'd lied anyway.

What else could I do?

He still didn't know.

So far, both the sheriff's department and Angel Butte P.D. officers knew the Hales had been shielding a boy on the run. Renner hadn't yet come out with the whole story. Reid appreciated the fact he was trying to protect them, although Roger and Paula were resigned to letting all the boys go once it was safe to make plans. So far, there was no indication Anna had reported them, either. The fact she hadn't was extraordinary enough to give him hope, even if she was still refusing to talk to him.

Reid was pulling into his own driveway when his phone rang. Frowning, he saw that the number was the Hales'. Speak of the devil. He set the brake, turned off the engine and answered.

"Reid?" The strain in Roger's voice sent Reid into cop mode. Something was very wrong.

"Roger. What's up?"

"Haveman is here. He's demanding that someone bring TJ to him. He's holding us hostage until that happens."

Reid tried for calm. "Us?"

"Paula, me and three of the boys. Isaac, Damon and Truong." He paused. "Damon's hurt, Reid. He tried to take him on."

Jesus. "He asked you to call me specifically?"

"Yes. He apparently saw you out here. He… knows you placed Caleb here and have been protecting us."

Haveman had been off before, but still managed to function well enough to have an outwardly normal, financially successful life. Now he'd derailed completely. He couldn't possibly imagine he'd be able to return to that life. If he wanted TJ delivered to him, it was so he could kill him and then probably himself—and very likely the Hales, whom in his rage he would blame for "stealing" his son. A crazy like him would see no reason to spare the other boys, either, who in his eyes had sinned by running from their own fathers.

"Can you tell me what kind of weapons he has?"

"Guns." Roger's voice shook. "He's, uh, got one pressed to my head."

Reid kept the expletive he was thinking to himself. "Okay, Roger," he said calmly. "Ask him if he'll talk to me himself."

Roger's words became muffled.

"I want my son." The craziness seething in his voice raised Reid's hackles. "Bring him. One hour, or I'll kill someone. The scrawny kid." He sounded as if he was thinking it out. "Yeah, him." Decision made.

"I don't know where TJ is. I'll have to make some calls."

"Sure you don't. One hour." He was gone.

The shit had hit the fan. Struggling to maintain his usual cool-headedness, Reid called Clay Renner and told him what was happening.

"I'm on my way out there," he said. "I'll try to talk to him."

"I'll call out SWAT and get a negotiator." Renner hesitated. "No way in hell am I bringing his kid, even to tempt him out."

"Hell, no!"

"Do you know where the other boys are?" Renner asked. "The ones he doesn't have?"

"That's why I'm going there as fast as I can. We can't let him get his hands on any more of them, and if they don't know what's happening…"

"I've probably got a deputy closer."

"They'd hide from him. You know they would."

Renner swore. "Do you have tactical gear with you?"

"No."

"I'll bring it."

Dead air told him Renner was gone.

Caleb had been looking out the front window, probably wondering why he was sitting out here talking on the phone instead of coming in. Reid had no choice but to tell him.

He moved swiftly. The moment he was inside, he said, "TJ's father is at the lodge. He wants his son."

He hesitated. "He's holding Roger and Paula and some of the boys at gunpoint. I have to go out there."

With his good hand, Caleb gripped the arm that was cradled in the sling. "Can I come? If I stay in the car? Please?"

"You know you can't." His voice grew rough. "I'm not risking you. Stay inside with the doors locked. I'll check in when I can."

"He'll kill them, won't he?"

"Yeah." Reid caught his brother in a quick, hard hug, one that was careful of his damaged shoulder. "We won't let him."

Caleb only nodded, although stark fear filled his eyes. "You'll be careful?"

"I'm always careful."

Reid paused on the doorstep long enough to hear the dead bolt slide home, then ran for his Expedition.

He backed out, turned on his flashers and pushed every speed limit. "Careful" wasn't something he'd often thought about before, but he hadn't had much to lose before, either. No one to leave behind. That had changed. He wanted to call Anna and say, *Take care of Caleb for me if something goes wrong,* but he knew she wouldn't answer. Knew she'd do it without him asking anyway.

He desperately wanted to hear her voice, but the distraction would be dangerous for him.

Focus on what you're going to do and how you're going to do it.

ANNA HAD JUST scraped most of the garlic chicken into the garbage and was pretending her kitchen needed cleaning when her phone rang. The caller wasn't in her address book and she didn't recognize the number. *Not a crisis in a foster home, please.* Right this minute, she was running on empty.

"Ms. Grant?" It was a man's voice that cracked halfway into a boy's. Scared. "This is Caleb Sawyer."

Her adrenaline surged. "Caleb. What's wrong?"

"It's not me. It's Reid."

She thought her heart might stop. "He's hurt?"

"Not yet. But I think he might, like, I don't know, *trade* himself or something."

"What are you talking about?" she said sharply.

So he told her. TJ Haveman's father was holding hostages at the lodge, including both foster parents and some of the boys. Reid was on his way out there to get the other boys to safety and then to talk to Haveman.

"Did you know TJ's not there anymore? One of the cops took him home to stay."

She had known, although that placement, too, was unofficial.

"Reid says he wants TJ," Caleb continued, "but they can't let him have him."

Of course they couldn't. Dear God, that poor boy. If other people died in his place—

"Reid's not going out there alone, is he?"

"He says they've called out the SWAT team. But

I'm scared. Paula and Roger are like Reid's parents. And he feels responsible. I think he'll do anything to save them and the other guys, too."

Yes. He would. Because that was the kind of man he was, one who'd spent his entire career trying to save the battered women like his mother and the hurt kids like he and his brother had been.

The man she loved.

"Where are you?" she asked, even as she tugged on a down vest and grabbed her handbag and keys.

"Home. I mean, his house. He made me stay here. I wish he'd let me go so I'd know what was happening," he exclaimed in frustration.

"No, he was right. But I'll drive out there, Caleb. I'll…I'll try to keep him from doing anything too risky. Okay?"

"Will you call me?"

"I will," she promised, running across the backyard to the detached garage behind her town house. "As soon as I know anything." Behind the wheel, she had a thought. "How did you know to call me?"

There was a momentary silence. "He told me about you. I mean, a while back. He said he'd met a woman. I could tell… You know. And, well, he talks about you sometimes."

If she weren't sitting, she might have crumpled from the agony. He'd told his brother about her, as if—

As if he loved her.

She had to talk to him.

She backed out of the garage and shot through the alley with reckless speed.

REID HAD BEEN involved in a hundred situations like this before, and he always felt a sense of incredulity at how the official response mushroomed so ludicrously. Official vehicles now lined the Hales' driveway: several SUVs, his own being one of many, squad cars with flashing lights, fire truck, aid cars. Police radios crackled. Dusk was approaching, after which it would all look even more surreal, surrounded by woods as they were.

Reid stood in a conclave with Renner; Lieutenant Vince Brown, who was Renner's immediate superior in the sheriff's department; the head of the combined city/county SWAT, whose name Reid knew but couldn't remember at the moment; and Alec Raynor, who was here because Reid was. He'd heard somebody say Sheriff McAllister was on his way.

A new voice made them all turn. "Haveman answered this time, but says Captain Sawyer is the only person he'll talk to. He reminded me that your hour is about up."

The negotiator. Renner had assured Reid that the guy was good. He'd been trying, first by phone then with a bullhorn, to talk to Haveman.

Renner's lieutenant nodded unhappily, his eyes meeting Reid's. "You know what to say?"

"Delay him."

"Then do it."

Reid lifted his phone to his ear. Two rings, and Haveman said, "Where's my boy?"

"He's not here yet. We'd placed him in a foster home. We had trouble reaching them."

The negotiator, holding Reid's gaze, nodded his approval.

"Is he on his way here or not?" the guy screamed.

Reid unclenched his jaw. "Yes, but you have to be patient. And—you know we can't send him in. Best I can do is give you a chance to talk to him."

"We'll talk about that when he's here." Haveman was eerily calm again.

"If you hurt anyone, you won't have that chance," Reid said in a hard voice. "Get Roger or Paula on the line for me. I need verification everyone is all right."

"This is the last time until you show me my son." There was a pause.

"Reid?" It was Roger. "We're holding on. Except for Damon. He's puking up blood." Urgency infused his voice.

A couple of the men surrounding Reid swore softly. He closed his eyes for a moment. "Okay, Roger. Let me talk to him again."

Haveman came back on. "Bring me my boy."

"Let the kid who's hurt go. If you want to see TJ, you need to demonstrate some good will. If you've already killed a kid, there's no way we can let you get in touching distance of your son."

Silence. The negotiator looked alarmed. Usually able to maintain dispassion dealing with the worst of scum, Reid knew he'd sounded coldly angry. Less than conciliatory.

They all waited. Reid wasn't breathing, and he doubted anyone else was, either. Eyes were glued to the phone held to his ear.

"Him only," Haveman said abruptly. "If he can walk. If anyone tries to rush the door, I start shooting. You come to meet him. No one else."

"All right. Me alone."

The call ended.

"You haven't put a vest on yet," Renner said, turning to rummage in the back of his Jeep, behind which they stood.

Reid shrugged out of his shirt and pulled on the tactical vest, realized his dress shirt wouldn't button over it and accepted a T-shirt from Renner. On top of that, he donned a black windbreaker with *POLICE* across the back.

With a nod of thanks, he started toward the porch. Behind him, he heard someone say, "Sharpshooters in place?" and crackling confirmation as one by one they responded.

The front door of the lodge opened and a body tumbled out.

As she ran up the driveway past a dozen or more emergency vehicles, Anna didn't know how she'd find Reid among the crowd. Then she passed the bulk of a fire truck and saw ahead to an old lodge with a gently sagging porch roof. Somebody had just fallen out the door, which immediately slammed close.

She stopped, staring, and pressed her fingers to her mouth in horror. Oh God, oh God. Was it a *body?* Had TJ's father just murdered someone and tossed him out? *Please, not one of the boys.*

But then the body—not a body—pushed up and crawled forward to the top of the stairs. And that was the moment when Anna saw the man who ran forward, mounting the stairs two at a time, and bent to lift the boy onto his shoulder in a fireman's carry.

Reid. Of course it was Reid.

Terrified, she waited for gunfire, for him to go down.

Instead, he came down the steps more carefully than he'd gone up and then crossed the yard in long strides. Moments later, he was engulfed by others, and the boy was lifted from his shoulder and laid on a waiting gurney.

Anna's legs trembled, weakened. She flattened a hand on the cold metal of an SUV, not sure if she'd stay up without the support. What determination she'd had leached out. She'd never imagined this kind of circus, with him one of the ringmasters. A private conversation would be impossible. Did she even want to pull his focus from doing his job?

But this wasn't only a job for him, she thought with a shudder of fear. He had the training, the experience—but this time his emotions were involved.

He shouldn't *be* on the front line, not when it was his family inside. Suddenly, she was raging. Why him?

I promised Caleb.

Her laugh had an edge of hysteria. Wonderful. She'd promised to march up to Reid in the midst of a bunch of other cops and say, *You can't risk yourself.*

Great time to realize she couldn't say that. She would be asking him to be…less than himself. To not give everything he had to the people he loved. She suddenly wasn't sure she had the courage to seek him out at all.

I have to break a promise.

Medics carrying the gurney rushed straight at her. Anna flattened herself on the SUV to let them pass. Intent on their patient, they didn't seem to see her. She saw the boy's face covered by an oxygen mask—and the blood spatter on the inside of the mask.

She moved tentatively forward, passing unseen. In the short time since she'd left her town house, the sky had deepened to purple. It was getting harder to make out even the trunks of the pines to each side of the narrow driveway. Her eyes were dazzled by emergency lights left blinking on some of the vehicles, who knew why. Even as she became aware of how fast dark was descending, a floodlight blinked on, a brilliant white illuminating the front porch. In contrast, other shadows grew deeper.

Anna passed an older-style Jeep Cherokee. Ahead of it was an SUV she thought was Reid's. By the front bumper stood a group of men. She stopped maybe ten feet away when she recognized Reid as part of the group, although he had his back to her. And…wasn't that Angel Butte police chief Alec Raynor? What was he doing here? Oh, and Sergeant Renner—she'd talked to him a couple of times now.

Reid had his phone to his ear. Everybody in his group stood silent. After a minute, he shook his head and pocketed the phone. They started to talk, voices low and urgent. A few words made it to where she lurked in the near dark.

"…back."

"Window?"

"…need distraction. If he thinks his kid is here…"

Then, louder, "…shouldn't have turned the damn floodlight on. Now he'll be suspicious if we turn it off."

And, in a lull, Reid's voice: "…might have to do it."

Anna would have sworn she hadn't made a sound, but Clay Renner's head turned suddenly and he saw her. Something in his expression changed. Everyone in the group turned to see what he was looking at, Reid last. His gaze locked on her, unblinking.

Her face heated. She shouldn't have come. All her presence would do was embarrass him.

He tilted his head and murmured something to Clay, then walked toward her.

"Anna." His voice was low, husky. It sounded the

same way it did when he wanted to kiss her. Half expression of intent, half plea.

"Caleb asked me to come," she defended herself.

Apparently unconscious of the watching men, Reid wrapped a hand around her nape and tugged her forward, until she leaned against him and he could encircle her with his arms. "Anna," he murmured again.

"I'm sorry," she whispered.

He shook his head. "No. I'm sorry. I never should have lied to you."

She pulled back enough to look up at his shadowed face. "I shouldn't have sulked for so long. I was just…all mixed up. I missed you so much, Reid."

"I saw you at the hearing."

"I was so proud of you."

Both kept their voices low, the intimacy unconscious.

"Did you see Caleb testify?" Reid murmured. "That took guts."

"I loved the judge. I wanted to cheer. I hope Diego gets as lucky."

"Yeah." His voice died.

They looked at each other, trying to distinguish more than could be seen in the gathering darkness.

"The other boys," she said tentatively. "Are they all in there?"

"No, most were in their cabins. Jane Renner came to get them. Haveman only has three. Had. Did

you see that he released one? Damon's not looking good."

"No, I saw." She shivered at the memory and his
arms tightened.

"Why did Caleb send you?" he asked.

"He's afraid you'll offer to trade yourself for some
of the hostages." She wasn't surprised by the shift
of expression on his face. "Oh, no," she whispered.
"You're planning to, aren't you?"

"That's...not standard law enforcement practice,
Anna. We don't put ourselves in that position." He
hesitated. "In this case, if he offers the chance, I
may need to take it. He's filled with rage, and we
assume he's suicidal. The only reason he's holding
off now is that he still thinks we may deliver TJ
to him." Her eyes widened and he shook his head.
"We won't. And his patience is short-lived. Having
someone inside to distract him while the assault
team gets in place could be huge. If he hears something and guns down the kids and the Hales..." His
throat worked.

Hot tears burned the back of her eyelids. She
willed them not to fall. "Why does it have to be
you?"

"He's fixated on me. So far, I'm the only person
he'll talk to."

She nodded, wanting to be numb. "I knew Caleb
was right."

"And you came to talk me out of it?"

"Could I?"

He grimaced. "Maybe. I'd rather you didn't try."

Oh, God. He was telling her he would do anything for her, even compromise his sense of integrity. The knowledge gave her the strength to say what she had to.

"I won't." Anna tried to smile, knowing it was a flop. "I just wanted to tell you how important it is that you stay safe. Caleb needs you, and—" she closed her eyes "—I do, too."

"Anna." There it was again, the gravel and the yearning. He rubbed his cheek against her head. When she lifted her face, his mouth moved softly over the bridge of her nose, her jaw, her lower lip. Not settling, just…touching.

"I love you," she whispered. "Maybe you don't want that, but I had to say it."

He groaned, low and deep. "Anna."

"Reid?" The voice came from behind him, polite but unmistakably an imperative.

His muscles went taut under her hands. Then he made a near-soundless sigh. "Okay, we'll finish this later," he murmured to her before planting a quick, hard kiss on her mouth.

And then he turned and strode back to the huddle of high-ranking law enforcement officers who were apparently, as a group, willing to sacrifice him for the hostages inside.

As he was willing to sacrifice himself.

A burning ball of fear swelled in her chest as

she slipped through the trees to an out-of-the-way vantage point where she'd be able to watch without distracting Reid.

"WHICH KID SHALL I kill first? Haveman snarled. "Or shall I make it the woman?"

Reid's fingers tightened on the phone. "TJ is still half an hour or more away." This time, Reid managed to keep his voice calm, even soothing. "You've got to give us more time. If you kill someone in the meantime, there's no deal. You understand that?"

"I understand you're playing me."

Rage had corroded Haveman's vocal cords. That didn't worry Reid as much as his unpredictably shifting mood, from black fury to slyness to the pleasure he felt every time he threatened to hurt someone. Reid remembered telling someone that of all the abusive parents he'd been investigating, Randal Haveman stood out for not being wired right. *I never spoke truer words,* he thought.

"So what's the solution?" he asked. "I can't produce your boy out of thin air. All I'm asking is for patience." And time to get his troops into place.

"I want to talk to you face-to-face. You say no, I kill one of the kids."

"I've told you, if anyone dies, you'll never see TJ again."

"Then here's the deal. You put yourself in my

hands, and instead of killing one of these punks, I'll let him go to show my *good will*." He leaned on Reid's earlier words in clear mockery. "Your choice." And then he chuckled, the geniality another startling shift of mood. "A conundrum. How will you choose?"

"Both of them. You don't need so many hostages. Especially if you have me in there. The more people you need to keep an eye on, the greater the risk to you."

"No. The young are so much more...compelling. Decide."

Shit. He didn't know either of the remaining boys that well. Except...Isaac was the good kid, the one who would be eighteen in a matter of months. The math genius who tutored the others.

Did that make him worthier?

Truong was physically smaller, more vulnerable. *So, what, I flip a coin?*

"Can't do it, can you?" Haveman gloated. "Too bad I don't have your brother here. I'd have you by the short hairs then, wouldn't I?"

Reid's simmer became a raging boil. He clamped a ruthless lid on it even before he saw the negotiator's frantic head shake. "It's lucky for you that you don't," he said coolly. "Truong."

"What?"

"You'll let Truong walk out. He's my choice."

"The scrawny kid."

"That's right."

Haveman laughed. "I'm looking forward to talking to you."

Reid pocketed his phone and stared at the front door. "He didn't agree to extend his deadline."

"I noticed." Clay Renner stood beside him. He shook his head. "Does he really believe we'll just hand over his son?"

"Hard to say. It's difficult to figure out what a real crazy is thinking."

"You've dealt with one before?"

"Couple of times." The memories were no comfort at the moment, given the finales in both cases. "We ready?"

"Let me check." Renner spoke quietly into a handheld radio. Voices murmured back. Reid didn't listen. A man who had unfailingly liked to be in charge and on top of every detail, he had discovered in himself the ability to let go. Clay Renner was good at his job and a good man. He was trustworthy.

A hand clasped Reid's shoulder and he turned his head. His boss looked steadily at him. "For the record, I want you to know I'm opposed to this. It's not smart to put yourself in his hands."

Reid smiled crookedly. "You wouldn't do the same for any of those kids?"

Raynor scowled at him. "I didn't say I don't understand. I said it's not smart."

"Maybe not, but I think it's our best bet."

"Then take the son of a bitch out fast." He nodded and stepped away, leaving Reid waiting.

"It's a go," Renner said. "You be careful in there."

Reid actually laughed. "Careful is my middle name."

Clay grinned at him. "Sure it is."

Reid hesitated only for one moment, when he did a quick scan of the onlookers for Anna and failed to find her. But she wouldn't have left, and the sight of her distress might have shaken him. It was best this way.

He started across the yard toward the front porch.

CHAPTER SIXTEEN

DREAD GRIPPED ANNA as Reid crossed the brightly lit open ground to the lodge, his stride long and confident. Who had he bargained his life for? she wondered miserably. One of the boys? Paula Hale, whom Caleb believed Reid saw as his mother? How would that person live with the price if Reid died tonight?

How will I live? She couldn't imagine.

She had seen heavily armed men in tactical gear melting into the darkness to surround the lodge. If they were trying to break into the old building, it had been silently. No shattering glass or thud of an ax. The boys who hadn't been captured likely had keys. To the back door? But TJ's father would be expecting that. He'd have blocked the door somehow, surely.

Reid mounted the steps, never pausing. He had reached the top when the door opened and a boy slipped out. From here, she couldn't make out his face. She saw Reid briefly clasp his shoulder and bend his head to say something. The boy sidled sideways and ran to the end of the porch. He clambered over the railing and dropped to the ground just as Reid went inside the lodge and the door shut again.

Anna pressed a hand to her mouth to hold in a sob.

THE BARREL OF a handgun jammed against Reid's neck the second he stepped inside. He hadn't even gotten a good look at Haveman. "Don't move," the slug snapped, and Reid obeyed, waiting while he closed and double-locked the door. "All right," he said, "walk. Slowly."

Reid had already seen Paula, Roger and Isaac sitting stiffly in a row on one of the scroungy sofas arranged in front of the fireplace. Roger, in the middle, had one arm around Paula and the other around Isaac, the skinny kid with the beaky nose. All three fastened their gazes on Reid as if looking for a miracle. No, he thought in dismay, what he saw in their eyes was unnerving trust. He wanted to say, *This may not work,* but knew it was just as well he couldn't.

"You. The woman. Come here." When Paula froze, Haveman said, *"Now."*

Reid gave Paula a slight smile and the suggestion of a nod. Roger's eyes filled with fear, but he lifted his arm from her shoulders. She stood and came toward Haveman and Reid. The pressure of the barrel eased and then disappeared as Haveman backed off.

"Pat around his hips. I'll know if you find a weapon, and I won't hesitate to shoot you."

"It's okay," Reid said softly.

He'd come in with his holster empty, his Glock locked in his glove compartment. No point in giving it to Haveman.

"Now crouch down. Lift his pant legs."

She gingerly removed the snub-nosed Colt he wore on a holster there, and Reid gave a mental shrug. There'd been a chance Haveman would be careless enough not to check for a backup weapon. Paula followed orders and laid the gun on the floor. Haveman kicked it away.

"Other leg."

There was nothing there.

"Take off the jacket. Very slowly."

Reid peeled it off, exposing the T-shirt stretched over the Kevlar vest.

"Think I wouldn't notice you were wearing one?" their captor mocked.

"No, it's obvious," Reid said mildly. What he hoped like hell wasn't obvious was the way he had his belly sucked in—to prevent Jane Renner's small Ruger from creating a bulge.

"You." Haveman waved the gun in his hand at Paula. "Go sit back down."

She obeyed.

"*Captain* Sawyer." In another of those lightning changes in mood, Haveman went from angry and commanding to pleased. "Over by the wall."

Having a gun held on him from behind made Reid's skin crawl. He was damned if he'd give this nutcase the pleasure of seeing any reaction from him, though—unless that became good tactics. Without a word, Reid followed instructions.

"Turn around."

At last, he could see TJ's father. He'd already noted the strong familial resemblance from the driver's license photo. Reid knew exactly what kind of torment that was for the poor kid. Randal was considerably stockier than his son, not quite fat but heading that way. Shorter than his kid, which he probably hadn't liked. Haveman senior was probably five foot nine or ten. Reid outsized him by four inches or more— but the advantage was outweighed by the National Guard Armory of weapons Haveman had brought along.

Reid couldn't be sure, but the nine-millimeter in his hand looked like a SIG Sauer. A police- or military-style tactical holster suspended from his belt and strapped to his thigh held another big handgun. At least two extra magazines in cases hung from his belt, too. Against the far wall rested a semiautomatic rifle. That one gave Reid a momentary twitch. The watchers outside needed to move back. Did Haveman intend to spray them with bullets? Before he shot everyone in the lodge...or after?

"So what's the plan?" he said. "Are we all going to hang out until TJ gets here? If so, how about a cup of coffee? I don't know about everybody else, but it's been a long day."

Haveman's face darkened in anger. No sense of

humor. "You're going to admit you've been lying. TJ isn't on his way, is he? An officer of the law, you're denying me my son."

Not a question he wanted to answer. "You won't leave here unless you're in handcuffs," Reid observed. In a body bag was a likelier outcome. "You know that, right?"

"Thanks to you. I came to get my kid. That's all." The pistol pointed at Reid never wavered.

Reid looked him in the eye. "Bullshit."

Haveman pulled the trigger. The bullet slammed into a log inches from Reid. There was a sharp sting of splinters on Reid's arm, bare below the sleeve of the T-shirt. Isaac lurched in panic, Paula screamed and Roger swore. Reid couldn't help flinching, but with an effort of will he kept his expression implacable. *That's it,* he thought. *Make noise. Lots of noise.*

His eyebrows climbed. "Shooting when you didn't mean it wasn't smart. You're lucky an assault team didn't crash through the door. You know they're itching to." He'd raised his voice in case the team was now in hearing distance. They'd talked about wiring him, but decided not to take the time. What was said in here didn't count; taking Randal Haveman out before he could kill anyone was the goal.

Hatred burned in Haveman's eyes. "By the time they get in here, you'll all be dead." Suddenly, he yelled, "Hear that? I'll kill him if anyone makes a move. I'll kill them all!"

"Just here to pick up your son, were you?"

Roger was looking at Reid incredulously, and Reid sympathized. Taunting a madman wasn't usually recommended. But Reid wanted to keep him talking, focus his attention right where it was so he didn't have a chance to pace and listen for other sounds—or decide to get a start on his killing spree. Reid wanted to shake him up.

Roger no longer had his arms around Paula and Isaac. His body was tense, coiled for action. Reid couldn't do anything as obvious as shake his head, but he tried with a glance to communicate a message.

Wait.

"That's why you ran my brother down," he said coldly. "Or was he just collateral damage? Because you never intended to take TJ home, did you? Your little terror campaign was designed to punish him for rejecting you, wasn't it?"

"All he's ever done is defy me!" Spittle flew, and a vein in Haveman's forehead throbbed. He leaned forward, lips drawn back from his teeth. "For the last time, *is he coming?*"

WHEN A SINGLE gunshot rang out, Anna's whole body jerked. She grabbed on to the tree beside her, her fingers digging into the rough bark. The tree was all that held her upright.

Oh, dear God. He could be dead, just like that.

Consternation spread through the watchers. Taut, urgent voices rose in what might be an argument. Her gaze swung between the unrevealing front of the old lodge with its blank, curtained windows, and the group of commanders who didn't look happy, but weren't doing anything except talking.

Her phone vibrated in her pocket, and she took it out with a shaking hand. The number was the same one Caleb had called from earlier. She desperately didn't want to answer, but knew how scared he must be.

Nowhere near as scared as I am.

On the fourth ring, she closed her eyes and answered. "Caleb?"

"Is he…?" His voice faltered. "Did you talk to him?"

"Yes." She wanted to lie, to say, *He can't talk right now, but he's okay.* Only…Caleb would find out. Especially if Reid *wasn't* okay. "Reid's the only person Mr. Haveman will talk to," she said. "He… A few minutes ago, he insisted that Reid go in."

"I knew it! I knew he was going to do that." Tears thickened Caleb's voice.

"He…" Her throat tried to close. "He traded himself for one of the boys. Um, I think someone said Truong."

"Truong came out? He's safe?"

"Yes. Reid talked Mr. Haveman into letting Damon go, too. Damon was injured, I don't know how, but he's been taken to the hospital. I think there's only one boy left in there, along with the Hales."

"And Reid," he whispered.

"Yes."

"Are they planning an assault?"

"I think so," Anna said. "I've seen guys in SWAT gear sneaking around back, but then nothing has happened." Except a gunshot. She couldn't make herself say that.

"Will you call me?"

"Of course I will."

"I'm scared."

"Me, too," she admitted.

She heard a distinct sniff, then, "Okay." And he was gone.

"THE DECISION TO bring TJ out here or not isn't mine," Reid said, trying for a reasonable, let's-keep-talking-about-this tone. "We're outside the city limits here."

Haveman's eyes narrowed. "Then why am I wasting my time with you?"

"You asked for me, not the other way around."

"Because you took your brother from his father." His voice lowered, became guttural, then rose to a roar. "You helped my son hide!"

The flicker of movement in the kitchen doorway came at a really good moment. Haveman was losing it. Reid hadn't had to say, *No, you'll never set eyes on your son again.* The guy knew. As the knowledge sank in, his rage escalated. There was no longer any reason for him to delay taking the revenge he'd planned from the beginning.

God damn, Reid thought. If Haveman turned his head an inch, he'd see the first man sliding through the doorway, followed by a second.

But they couldn't see the intention forming in this crazy son of a bitch's eyes. As he stared at Reid, his pupils shrank, then suddenly dilated.

Now, Reid thought, and yelled, "Down!"

As he threw himself sideways, he saw Roger shoving the others forward off the coach. Time seemed to slow into microseconds, snapshots taking less than the blink of an eye. The terror on Isaac's face. Roger's mouth open in a bellow as he threw himself forward. A black-garbed figure with gun held in firing position. A chaos of yelling voices.

Reid's ears rang with the crack of shots. Something slammed into his chest. As he crashed against a chair and to the floor, he lost sight of Haveman. His nostrils filled with the acrid odor of gunpowder. And God damn, did he hurt.

Bang, bang, bang.

Inside, a gun battle had erupted. Or—please, no—Randal Haveman was executing all his hostages.

Her breath shuddering in and out, Anna felt as if an electrical current ran through her body.

A window shattered.

Cops charged toward the lodge, converging on

the porch. A silence fell, as terrifying in its own way as the barrage that had preceded it. Within seconds, they yanked the door open and lunged inside with weapons in firing position. A key, she realized; they hadn't had to break down the door.

Being able to do nothing but wait was terrible. Becoming light-headed, she thought, *Breathe*. Then, as her eyes burned, *Blink*. Automatic functions had ceased.

Please, please, please, let him be safe. She wouldn't ask for anything else. Even if he could never love her, let him be safe.

The first figures appeared in the doorway. She recognized Sergeant Renner half supporting a tall, skinny boy. Renner was turning his head, looking for someone. She was moving before she had consciously known she intended to. Before his eye lighted on her and he nodded.

This is what I do.

She met them at the same time as a pair of EMTs, one of whom said, "Come on, son, let us check you over."

A couple was walking out now, too. The bearded man Anna recognized. The woman had a long braid, mostly gray. She was leaning heavily, shock robbing her face of normal expression. The Hales.

If Reid was *able* to love, it was because of these two people. The teenage boy seemed to be in good hands, so Anna veered to meet the Hales. The whole time, her attention was riveted on the door. Cops were coming out, some in SWAT black, some who'd just gone in the front. None were Reid. They hadn't called for a paramedic, which meant he didn't need one.

He either wasn't hurt...or he was dead.

No, don't even think it.

She reached the Hales. "Let me walk you to an aid car."

Roger shook his head. "We're not hurt. Maybe some bruises."

"Someone should look at your wife," Anna said gently.

He looked down at her, blinked a couple of times, then nodded. Anna led them toward a second aid car.

Terrified to ask, she had to. "Reid?"

His brown eyes were bleak. "He was shot. I don't know—"

Her teeth chattered.

"He was surrounded, and they wanted us out."

Trying desperately to hold herself together, Anna nodded.

Please, please, please.

An EMT helped Paula Hale into the back of the vehicle. As he listened to her heart and her husband watched helplessly, Anna went back to staring at the front of the lodge.

And then two men appeared. Police Chief Alec Raynor, supporting Reid, who moved with obvious pain, but was on his feet and walking. He wore the windbreaker but the bulk of the vest beneath appeared to be missing.

Anna's feet seemed to be rooted.

His head was turning. He was looking for something, someone. Maybe the Hales. But then he saw her and never looked away. As Raynor helped him down the steps, Anna started to walk, then to run. His eyes never left her.

He held out an arm, but she stopped, quivering, before she could throw herself at him.

"You're hurt."

"You're crying." His tone was strange. Wondering.

Anna put a hand up and discovered her cheeks were wet. "I was so scared."

"He's okay," Chief Raynor said kindly. "He needs to get an X-ray, though."

"Anna," Reid said, in that way he had of imbuing her name with such rich emotion. "Come here."

Raynor stepped away as she walked the last small distance and let Reid's arm close around her. She put her arms around him but didn't lean. Just let herself feel his warmth, breathe him in. He'd survived. She was having trouble believing that.

"I love you," he said in a low, gravelly voice. "I should have said that before I went in. I'm sorry I didn't."

"It doesn't matter." God, she was totally pathetic. Tears streamed down her face. Probably snot, too.

"Will you forgive me?"

"If you'll forgive me for being a…a *prig*."

His chest vibrated with what she realized in astonishment was a laugh. "A *what?*"

Anna wiped hopelessly at her face and looked up. "I was so…self-righteous. I don't know how you *can* forgive me." The last was a wail.

"No. You were…wounded. I understood that. I wish I'd known earlier. I'd like to think I'd have done things differently."

She was about to protest when she caught herself. He'd just been shot. This was hardly the moment for her to be confessing her sins of self-absorption.

"Come on." She moved to his side and slipped one arm around his back. "I'll walk you to the ambulance."

He grunted. "I don't need an ambulance. Or the hospital."

"Typical man." Face still soggy, and she was teasing.

He might deny being injured, but he was leaning heavily on her. They'd taken ten or fifteen steps when he abruptly stopped. "Oh, hell. Are those TV cameras?"

They were, and she hadn't noticed them.

"Caleb," he said.

"Oh!" Anna fumbled for her phone. "I'll call him." She went to recent calls, touched Send and handed her phone to Reid.

After a pause, he said gruffly, "No, this is Reid. Hey. I'm okay. We got everybody out."

Anna couldn't make out Caleb's response.

"He's dead," Reid said, even in his bluntness sounding…something. Anna couldn't quite decide what, but the next instant knew. *Any man's death diminishes me.* John Donne.

Caleb spoke again.

"They're insisting I go by the hospital. I wore a vest, but I took a couple of bullets to the torso. Chances are good I have broken ribs." His tone became dry. "Not for the first time."

He was talking about his childhood, not his job. She hadn't been able to see the X-rays or medical records he'd submitted to the court, but she'd heard enough to suspect how horrific they'd been.

Caleb's, too.

And I thought it was wrong for him to help Caleb escape however he could.

Reid had ended the call while she brooded, and he handed the phone back to her. They resumed their slow walk across the yard. Reid exchanged a few words here and there with other cops. When he saw Sergeant Renner, he asked, "Isaac okay?"

"Kid's mostly worried about Damon."

"Yeah, Caleb is, too, and I kind of gather Damon wasn't well liked."

"But he's one of them," Renner said simply, and Reid nodded.

Reid looked at Anna. "Will you help us figure out how to protect the rest of the boys?"

"Of course I will." She smiled shakily first at Reid, then at Renner. "And the Hales, too."

The sergeant smiled back at her, his approval obvious. "Good." He eyed Reid. "I'll get somebody to drive your vehicle to town. You're in no shape to do it. I'll deal with things here, too. If the doctors release you, go home. Tomorrow's soon enough to give a statement."

Reid nodded.

Stubborn man that he was, he adamantly refused to ride in an ambulance. He said, "No," and kept saying it. He insisted on walking the full length of the driveway to Anna's RAV4, parked out on the road. Once in, he groaned as he leaned back. She started the engine and cranked the heat as high as it would go, remembering when he'd done the same after they'd skied. She waited while an aid car and two police cars emerged from the driveway and started toward town. Even then, she didn't shift into gear. Headlights kept glancing off them, but somehow leaving them alone, as if they were in a cocoon. Safe.

"Does everyone know now what the Hales were doing?" she asked, almost at random.

"I'm not sure." There was a hint of caution in Reid's voice. "Clay has done his best to keep the full story from getting out."

She turned her head to stare at him. "You mean, he knew, too?"

"Uh…yeah. I guess there was an incident out here

last year that brought them onto his radar. From what I can gather, Jane was abused as a kid. She made him promise to keep his mouth shut."

Anna didn't say anything for a minute. Then, feeling a familiar ache, she murmured, "So many kids being hurt."

"You're not responsible for saving them all."

The weight of his gaze was tangible even though she wasn't looking at him and, with only lights from the dashboard, wouldn't be able to see him well if she did. "Trying isn't such a bad thing."

"No. As we've already agreed, we both carry our memories into our jobs."

She sniffed, then said, "Excuse me," and reached to open the glove compartment, where she kept a box of tissues. Reid watched as she blew her nose firmly and wiped her cheeks.

Then, having gotten herself together, at least temporarily, she finally pulled onto the road and drove toward town. Reid must hurt, and she was the one on the verge of falling apart. Not what he needed.

"Did you mean it?" he said suddenly.

"Mean it?" She frowned at him. "Mean what?"

"That you love me."

She swallowed hard. "Yes." Damn it, her eyes were watering again. "It happened so fast. I never have before, you know."

"I didn't know I could." His voice was impossibly tender. "Do you know what I thought the first time I saw you?"

Wordless, she shook her head.

"I saw ghosts in your eyes." With one finger, he touched her face beside her eye.

She tilted her head just a little, enough to savor the warmth and security of even this slight touch.

"Your ghosts scared me," he said, when she stayed silent. "But...I was drawn to you, too."

"You saw a reflection of your own pain."

"Maybe." He seemed to be thinking it through. "Partly. I don't think I could trust someone who didn't understand."

"No." Naturally, he was right. "No," she repeated, lowering her high beams, then turning them back up when the oncoming car passed.

"You know Caleb's mine now."

"Of course he is." Puzzled, she waited to find out his point.

"He called you."

"Yes. He said, um, that you'd told him about me."

"Yeah." Reid made a sound. "Probably not very coherently. I think he was glad that I'd found some-body."

In self-defense, Anna went into social-work mode. "It would be healthy for him to see that you can build a trusting, mature relationship."

"Don't make me laugh. It hurts."

"I wasn't trying—"

"I know. I'm trying to work my way around to something here."

The lights from one of the area's fanciest resorts

glinted on the dark water of Arrow Lake to their right. They'd be in town in less than five minutes.

Heart thumping, Anna stole a sidelong look at Reid's profile. "What?"

"I don't think we need to wait for Caleb to get on board with the idea of us being together." Reid's usual ease had deserted him. He sounded awkward. "I know my timing probably stinks, and probably this is too soon, but I need to say this. I want you there when I go home after work. I want to wake up with you in the morning." He stopped, then started again. "You *are* home for me. I've never had one before."

The hot rush of fresh tears took her by surprise. "Damn it," she muttered.

"I shouldn't have said anything yet—" He sounded chagrined. Or maybe hurt.

"No." She reached out a hand blindly, finding the hard muscle of his forearm. "I just— You keep making me cry."

"Pull over."

Laughing and crying both, she did. They had reached the outskirts of town, with curbs and sidewalks and streetlights. Unfortunately, he'd be able to see her. Reid opened the glove compartment again and handed her another tissue, waiting patiently while she blew and mopped. *Wouldn't you think I'd have run dry by now?*

Anna crumpled the tissue in her hand and looked at him through puffy eyes.

His were so dark, she couldn't have guessed at color if she hadn't known. "I love you," he said again. "Will you marry me?"

Her heart seemed to have swollen to fill her entire chest cavity. *Her* ribs hurt, and she wasn't the one who'd been shot.

"Yes," she whispered. Then, louder, "Of course, yes! And I want to throw myself at you, but I know I can't."

He was grinning, looking as foolish as she probably did. "But you could kiss me if you're really careful."

"Reid." She leaned toward him and their lips met. Softly. He nibbled at her mouth and she savored his. It was the sweetest kiss of her life, even as desire simmered beneath. He wanted to go to bed with her every night. Wake up with her every morning.

She was his home.

"I can't believe this."

He gently nipped her lower lip. "What can't you believe?"

She laid a hand on his chest, feeling the hard beat of his heart. "That I would ever feel safe enough with anyone—"

She didn't have to finish.

"I won't let you down, Anna. I won't hurt you." He rubbed his cheek against hers, then said the words that meant everything to her. "I promise."

Her vision blurred, but still she pulled back just

far enough to be able to see him. "I won't hurt you, either. I won't let you down." Her smile shook. "I promise."

"I love you."

She echoed him, unwadded the tissue to do another minor cleanup, then pulled back into traffic and drove him to the hospital.

SHE STAYED WITH him as if there was no question whether she should. Reid was almost sorry nobody challenged her. He'd have liked to have an excuse to say, *She's my fiancée.* Words that should have scared the shit out of him, but didn't. Not yet, at least. No, he thought he'd moved through the fear, the doubt, and come out on the other side.

They had exchanged the most sacred of promises.

The first thing he'd done on arriving at the hospital was ask about Damon's condition. The boy was in surgery, but the report was optimistic. It would be hours before they'd know any more.

Reid and Anna were left alone in a tiny waiting room while the technician checked to be sure that the X-rays were clear and didn't need to be retaken. Reid doubted he looked his best in a too-small hospital gown, his legs bare except for the socks he'd left on because the vinyl floors were cold. Getting *un*dressed had been painful, though. Damned if he was going to put his pants on and then find out he had to take them off again.

After sitting in silence for a minute, Reid realized

something she'd said was clinging like a burr in his mind.

"You don't feel like you should report the Hales?"

Anna's shock was obvious. "Of course not!"

"Wouldn't you, if a couple of months ago you'd learned what they were doing?"

"You mean, before I met you." Tiny lines puckered her forehead. "Probably. Yes."

"I don't want you—" he had to think how to put this "—violating your conscience for me."

"No." She gripped his hand. "It's not like that. I still think there are horrendous dangers to what they're doing. But I also think they saved a lot of kids who would otherwise have been lost." Her fingers tightened. "And you're one of them. For that, I'll be eternally grateful."

"Okay," he managed, past the lump in his throat. He kissed her temple, such a vulnerable spot, the skin so silky. Her fine hair tickled his nose.

"In fact, I was, well, thinking. If we can keep their role secret. Will they go back to doing what they have been?"

"I don't think so. It's gotten so too many people know about their operation. After this, there's no way they'd stay under the radar. I suspect they've begun to have doubts, too. Having Caleb and Diego injured like that and not being able to stand at their sides, that hurt."

Anna nodded, her expression earnest, the gray of her eyes soft. "Do you think they'd be interested in fostering for Angel's Haven? I could really use another group home for teenagers who don't fit well into the average foster home. If all goes well, some of the boys they have now could stay with them."

He hadn't thought he could love her more, but he was wrong. "Yeah," he said hoarsely. "I'm betting they'd love to do that. They really are good people, Anna."

"I know they are." A smile wobbled on her lips. "If they weren't, you wouldn't be such a good man."

"Let's get married soon," he said, urgency adding roughness to his voice. "Call me old-fashioned, but I've got a kid now. That makes sleepovers tough to have."

His Anna smiled for real. "I agree. Although, it might be nice if you don't have broken ribs on our wedding night."

"I heal fast," he said huskily, and they just looked at each, the air charged.

Right now, he couldn't see her ghosts at all. Along with the lust, an unfamiliar emotion filled him: peace. He kind of thought she might be feeling the same.

His optimism was new, too. But he found he really believed that with a little luck, some work and a determination to keep their promises, they could hold on to this hard-won peace.

The curtain was swished aside and the radiation tech appeared, beaming at him. "You can get dressed now. We're all set."

Yeah, Reid thought, shaking off any last disbelief, they were. He stood, kissed Anna and said, "Give me a minute. Doc said he'd get me in quick when we were done down here." The last thing he said was the best: "Then we can go home."

EPILOGUE

CALEB WAS THE last person out of Reid's SUV, and he hung back momentarily when Anna and Reid walked ahead carrying food—a totally gigantic potato salad and a crock of baked beans. His job was to haul the cooler with drinks.

Anna's voice drifted back. "Oh, the Renners are already here." She sounded pleased.

Had she been hit by the weirdness of them all being here at the Bear Creek Resort for a Labor Day potluck and reunion, or was it just him?

The front yard was swarming with people. Foster parents of the boys who had stayed in Angel Butte but no longer lived at the resort, some new boys Anna had sent to the Hales and, strangest of all, cops and their spouses. Caleb remembered the way he and the other guys had all sort of faded out of sight if anyone unexpected showed up here. *Especially* if a cop showed. And now look. He'd never seen big tables set up on the lawn, either, and the horseshoe pit was new.

He bet Roger and Paula still made their boys do chores, though.

It would be kind of cool seeing all the guys,

though. Only a few wouldn't be here. Apollo's sister had taken him in, TJ had gone back to live with his mother now that his father was dead, and Isaac had left a week ago for college. He had been so close to eighteen, the judge had just sort of dragged her feet until his birthday came. Given his special circumstances—that was the way Anna described it—he'd been accepted to the University of Oregon even though his application was way late, but he'd told everyone he was going to apply to transfer to MIT for his sophomore year. Caleb bet he'd get in, too.

Diego and Trevor were in the same foster home. Their foster dad was a scary dude who could stand up to Diego's father and Trevor's uncle, both of whom Reid, at least, thought were still potential threats.

The one Caleb didn't get was TJ. Had he *wanted* to live with his mother? Caleb guessed he sort of loved his own mother still, but he knew he'd never be able to trust her. How could TJ feel any different about his? But nobody had said—maybe he hadn't had any choice. The judge might have decided that was best for him, no matter what he wanted. Parental rights—slam dunk. Even though Caleb felt sort of sorry for him, he was just as glad TJ wasn't here today. Yeah, he'd had bad shit happen to him, but that didn't mean he wasn't an asshole.

"Caleb?" It was Reid who had stopped and looked over his shoulder. "Aren't you coming?"

"Uh…yeah." He got his feet moving.

Diego spotted him and jogged over. "Hey, dude." He grabbed one side of the cooler and helped carry it to the shady spot in front of the porch where the food was being laid out on long plank tables. Caleb opened the cooler and they both took soft drinks. He almost bumped into Anna when he straightened.

She smiled at him and went on tiptoe to kiss his cheek. "Thank you."

He turned away, knowing his cheeks were hot. He wasn't used to being hugged and kissed. He wasn't the only one. Sometimes he could tell Reid was still startled when she went up and put her arms around him or kissed him in passing for no reason, but he obviously liked it. Caleb was getting so he didn't mind so much, but, jeez, in public?

Diego and Caleb walked toward the horseshoe pit, where a match between Colin McAllister—the sheriff of the whole county—and Sergeant Clay Renner was happening. The audience hooted when the sheriff's horseshoe clanged off the stake and slid several feet away. As he shook his head in disgust, Sergeant Renner grinned and wrapped his next throw around the stake, pretty as you please.

"Your sister-in-law's cool," Diego said.

"I guess I'm lucky," Caleb said awkwardly. "But I like your foster parents, too." He spent quite a bit of time at the Panneks', since he and Diego had stayed friends. That meant Trevor was mostly around, too, but that was okay.

He hadn't seen the other guys since school let out in June, and not that much of some of them even then. Jose and Palmer had been freshmen, so they hadn't been in any of Caleb's classes. Damon, Caleb mostly avoided.

He wandered over now, too, though, looking... less tense, maybe, than Caleb mostly remembered him. Maybe near-death experiences had changed both of them.

"You didn't go out for football," he said to Caleb who shook his head. He knew practice had started a couple of weeks ago.

"I might have, except it overlaps basketball. That's my sport."

Diego wasn't big enough to play either sport. He'd said he had wrestled his freshman year at his old high school, though, and he thought he'd try out for the team in Angel Butte. He was strong and wiry, if short. Since wrestling had different weight classes, he might be good.

"So Reid married the social worker." Damon wasn't watching the horseshoe contest; he had his eyes on Anna. "I can see it. She's kind of hot."

Once in a while, Caleb noticed she was, too, but that was really too weird for him, so he didn't dwell. Anyway, he had sort of, almost a girlfriend now. They hadn't called it that, but he'd hung out a lot with Hannah this summer. She was kind of shy still, so although he'd kissed her he hadn't pushed for sex yet. One thing he liked about her was that she lived in a foster home. She hadn't exactly said why she couldn't stay with her own parents, but Caleb figured she'd tell him eventually. He just hoped it wasn't anything really terrible. And especially not something sexual terrible. Because, man, he *really* wanted to have sex, and it would be a serious bummer to find out she *really* didn't.

And he knew that was selfish even to think.

Just a few weeks ago, he'd been helping Reid build a small deck on the back of the house he and Anna had bought, and when they paused to drink some lemonade, Reid had asked about Hannah.

One corner of his mouth had quirked up in an I-can't-believe-I'm-saying-this way, before he said it anyway. "This is a safe-sex talk."

"Anna put you up to it."

He'd laughed in a comfortable way. "Yeah, but I'd have worked my way around to it on my own."

"I know about condoms."

"Yeah, but do you have any? Do you carry one, in case an, er, opportunity arises?"

Knowing his face was blazing, Caleb had mumbled, "Uh…yeah. I've started to." Like a few days before.

"Good. You don't have to answer this, but have you used one yet?"

"You want me to *talk* about it?"

"Strictly optional." Reid set down his glass and

reached for the hammer again. "Here, can you hold this?"

They were working on a railing now.

"It's... I haven't asked," Caleb heard himself confess. "She's said things that make me afraid—"

Reid had turned a sharp look on him. "That she's been molested?"

"Yeah. I mean, I don't know, but—" He sucked in a big breath. "What if she has?" Wow. Anna probably *knew*. That hadn't occurred to him before. If he asked, would she tell him—

Not a chance.

Lines formed on his brother's face. "If she has... then you're either really patient, or you call her a friend and move on."

"I feel like such a creep," Caleb had confessed miserably. "Even thinking that's, like, a deal breaker. You know?"

"I do know." Reid had gripped his shoulder hard for a minute. Under Anna's influence, he was getting better at the touching thing. "But you're a kid. Give yourself a break. If it turns out Hannah needs fixing, the job may be more than you can take on. You are still a kid, you know."

Caleb had been thinking about that ever since. He wasn't so sure he'd ever exactly been a "kid." More weirdness: he felt more like one now than he could ever remember. Not having to freak if he got into trouble at school, living with his brother, who had claimed to be too damaged to take him in, bu was now changing, too… Sometimes Caleb woke up in the morning and lay there wondering why he wasn't all tied up in knots and dreading getting up. And then he'd remember. Life was good.

Day after tomorrow, he would start his junior year in high school. And…he really liked Hannah. If it turned out he had to be patient for her sake, he thought he could do it. Reid would have waited for Anna if he'd had to. Anything big brother could do, he could do. That was Caleb's resolve.

Followed by Roger, Reid had just sauntered over to slap Colin McAllister's back in mock sympathy. Still grinning, he spotted Caleb. His eyebrows rose.

"What do you say, Caleb? Think you can take me on?"

Caleb studied him suspiciously "Have you ever played before?"

"Never thrown a horseshoe in my life."

"Then you're on." How hard could it be? He felt a belated burst of caution. "If we can take some practice throws first," he tacked on.

Reid slung a casual arm over his shoulder and squeezed. "Deal."

Sheriff McAllister chuckled evilly. "Oh, this is going to be fun."

On his opening toss once they officially began, Caleb threw a ringer.

First time he'd ever done anything *better* than his big brother.

"Well, damn." Reid's grin held a challenge, but something else, too. Pride.

Sometimes seeing that expression choked Caleb up.

But not so much he didn't laugh when Reid threw a clanger—and then his own next throw hooked the stake again, spun and clanked down right on top of his last horseshoe. He pumped a fist. "Man, I'm good."

And, damn, he really was.

* * * * *

Look for the next book by Janice Kay Johnson!
Coming in November 2014 from
Harlequin Superromance.

LARGER-PRINT BOOKS!
GET 2 FREE LARGER-PRINT NOVELS PLUS
2 FREE GIFTS!

HARLEQUIN®

Romance

From the Heart, For the Heart

YES! Please send me 2 FREE LARGER-PRINT Harlequin® Romance novels and my 2 FREE gifts (gifts are worth about $10). After receiving them, if I don't wish to receive any more books, I can return the shipping statement marked "cancel." If I don't cancel, I will receive 4 brand-new novels every month and be billed just $4.84 per book in the U.S. or $5.24 per book in Canada. That's a savings of at least 19% off the cover price! It's quite a bargain! Shipping and handling is just 50¢ per book in the U.S. and 75¢ per book in Canada.* I understand that accepting the 2 free books and gifts places me under no obligation to buy anything. I can always return a shipment and cancel at any time. Even if I never buy another book, the two free books and gifts are mine to keep forever.

119/319 HDN F43Y

Name	(PLEASE PRINT)

Address	Apt. #

City	State/Prov.	Zip/Postal Code

Signature (if under 18, a parent or guardian must sign)

Mail to the **Harlequin® Reader Service:**
IN U.S.A.: P.O. Box 1867, Buffalo, NY 14240-1867
IN CANADA: P.O. Box 609, Fort Erie, Ontario L2A 5X3

Want to try two free books from another line?
Call 1-800-873-8635 or visit www.ReaderService.com.

* Terms and prices subject to change without notice. Prices do not include applicable taxes. Sales tax applicable in N.Y. Canadian residents will be charged applicable taxes. Offer not valid in Quebec. This offer is limited to one order per household. Not valid for current subscribers to Harlequin Romance Larger-Print books. All orders subject to credit approval. Credit or debit balances in a customer's account(s) may be offset by any other outstanding balance owed by or to the customer. Please allow 4 to 6 weeks for delivery. Offer available while quantities last.

Your Privacy—The Harlequin® Reader Service is committed to protecting your privacy. Our Privacy Policy is available online at www.ReaderService.com or upon request from the Harlequin Reader Service.

We make a portion of our mailing list available to reputable third parties that offer products we believe may interest you. If you prefer that we not exchange your name with third parties, or if you wish to clarify or modify your communication preferences, please visit us at www.ReaderService.com/consumerschoice or write to us at Harlequin Reader Service Preference Service, P.O. Box 9062, Buffalo, NY 14269. Include your complete name and address.

HRLP13R